NOTHING
SACRED

THE MANY LIVES AND BETRAYALS
OF ALBERT WALKER

Alan Cairns

Seal Books

NOTHING SACRED/An Original Seal Book

For information address: Seal Books, 105 Bond Street, Toronto,
Ontario M5B 1Y3

ISBN 0-7704-2766-9

Seal Books are published by McClelland-Bantam, Inc. Its trademark,
consisting of the words "Seal Books" and the portrayal of a seal, is
the property of McClelland-Bantam, Inc., 105 Bond Street, Toronto,
Ontario M5B 1Y3, Canada. This trademark has been duly registered
in the Trademark Office of Canada. The trademark consisting of the
words "Bantam Books" and the portrayal of a rooster is the property
of and is used with the consent of Bantam Books, 1540 Broadway,
New York, New York 10036. This trademark has been duly registered
in the Trademark Office of Canada and elsewhere.

Cover design by Jim Plumeri
Text and insert design by Heidy Lawrance Associates
Printed and bound in Canada

UNI   10   9   8   7   6   5   4   3   2   1

To the honest people.

CONTENTS

ACKNOWLEDGEMENTS

Researching and writing this book was an enormous and onerous task that I could not possibly have accomplished without the assistance and understanding of many people.

I would first like to thank my very special buddy, Jennifer Beale, for providing me with the support and inspiration I needed to both enter and finish this project. Your love, support and encouragement were invaluable. To Jennifer's family — John and Ruby, Susan, Barbara and Pamela. To Keith and Vera Jackson and Dave Holahan. Your support, acceptance and friendship are appreciated.

Special appreciation to my *Toronto Sun* colleague and friend Joe Warmington, one of the most hard-working and dedicated reporters I have ever met. When the story of Albert Walker's arrest broke in December 1996 it was Joe who rushed to England the night of his own birthday and for two weeks chased around Essex and Devon getting a handle on this most complex case. Joe passed on the story (and probably this book) to me when he left the *Sun* to become a columnist at the *Calgary Sun*. Joe, I benefited greatly from your hard work and the goodwill you instilled in the many people you met.

I wish to salute professional therapist Isabel Rogers, an intelligent, principled and forthright woman who had little to gain from speaking with me at all, other than to help me get the facts straight. Isabel, you showed tremendous strength, courage and trust in coming forward to share your story with me and my readers. Through all of our discussions, your primary concerns were to ensure that a true picture emerged so that people could understand this incredible story, that the partners at Solutions in Therapy were portrayed in an objective light and that any therapist-client relationships involved were kept strictly confidential. Isabel, I hope I have not let you down. The therapy profession is lucky to have someone as dedicated as yourself. Good luck to you and Neil!

To Ed and Marion Jones, I appreciate the friendship and trust and the principles you upheld at all times. I wholly respect your refusal to betray confidences. The golf game was great!

To Audrey Mossman and Frank Johnson, thank you for welcoming me into your home, into your private lives and to your dinner table.

From the streets and churches of Ontario, to the dirt roads of Woodham Walter, to the quays and pubs of Brixham, there are so many others who assisted me during this project. To them all goes my sincere appreciation. Unlike Albert Walker, all of them are "real" people. Some I have named, others I cannot name. Some could not come forward in person because of unnecessary protectiveness and outright suppression. Some were ordered and coerced not to talk because other people had their own agendas! Others with knowledge refused to talk. All had their own reasons, whether personal, emotional or financial. To some people, it seems, greed is a way of life.

Thanks too, to the editors at the *Toronto Sun*,

especially assistant managing editor Gord Walsh and Metro editor Bob McConachie, for their unflagging support of this story and for granting the time off I needed to write this book. Special thanks to executive editor Peter O'Sullivan for helping with the cost of photographs and for his encouragement for the book. A warm thank you to all the great *Toronto Sun* photographers whose fine work appears in this book, to Stuart Clarke of London and to the Apex agency. Salutations to all the great guys and gals at the *Sun*, who are just too many to name.

To my literary agent, Helen Heller: you are unstoppable. May we work together again.

To my publisher, John Pearce, and all the staff at Seal Books: your warm encouragement was most uplifting. You can have the boardroom back!

To my editor, Beverley Sotolov: your commitment to this project was probably stronger than my own. Your ideas, suggestions and changes were right on.

To Scott Burnside, sports columnist at the *Windsor Star*, formerly my reporting colleague at the *Windsor Star* and *Toronto Sun* and fellow author of *Deadly Innocence*: I give thanks for all the effort and talent that you put into our first book. Without that experience, this book would never have been. I miss working with you.

To Christie Blatchford: every day your columns were an inspiration. I miss you too.

To Ted, Tula and Steve at High Seas restaurant in Etobicoke and to Fab and Christina at the Far Side Café in Toronto — thanks for putting up with my notepads and binders and keeping the food and drink coming!

To Drew McAnulty and family and Grant and Liz Cameron, a huge thank you for all the years of great friendship.

Special thanks to my father, Ivan Cairns, and brother, David Cairns.

Last, but never, ever least, thanks to, and for, Robbie Cairns. A wonderful son and a great buddy!

I also wish to acknowledge the following books:

Agatha Christie: An Autobiography. London: HarperCollins, 1993.

A Village History: Woodham Walter, by Patricia M. Ryan. Essex: The Plume Press, 1989.

Exploring Agatha Christie Country, by David Gerrard. Leyburn, North Yorkshire: Trail Publishing, 1996.

The Life and Crimes of Agatha Christie, by Charles Osborne. London: Collins. 1982.

Without Conscience: The Disturbing World of the Psychopaths Among Us. by Dr. Robert Hare, New York: Pocket Books, 1993.

Chapter titles in this book are from works by Agatha Christie.

One

DEATH IN
THE AIR

SWARTHY JOHN COPIK turned away from the handful of junk fish in the belly of the trawl net and looked at his son.

"Hey, Bat, this is your fault. You're a real Jonah!" John accused.

John and Craig, nicknamed Bat by his father because he liked to party all night long, had netted nothing of worth in two coastal trawls from their trusty trawler fishing boat *Malkerry* on July 28, 1996, but they had decided to try it once more before heading into historic Brixham port and home. John returned to the cramped wheelhouse and set the *Malkerry* chugging south as Craig again dropped the trawl nets into the English Channel.

It was an almost cloudless day and the calm blue waters shimmered in the sunlight. Onshore, perhaps five or six miles to the west, the rugged red-soil cliffs and rounded hilltops of the Devon coastline were accented with the picturesque towns that had spread from the estuaries of their birth centuries ago and were now as much a part of the panorama as the terrain itself. Earlier, after setting out from Brixham on a northeast course up the coast, the Copiks had passed the resort towns of Torquay, Paignton and Babbacombe; now they were directly off the postcard-perfect town of Teignmouth, with its famous wooden pier, ochre, white, beige and pink waterfront hotels and jaunty hillside houses bathing in the bright sun. Out to sea, a handful of yachts played in the gentle swells.

They were trawling a rocky patch aptly named the Roughs. John Copik, with more than two decades of commercial fishing under his ample belt, had a sense — perhaps it was just wishful thinking — that schools of bass might be hanging around the rocks. A good catch was worth a fortune: the tasty species netted £8 a kilo at the boathead, compared with 15 pence a kilo for whiting. Once, albeit a different time of year and a different place, he had hauled in £15,000 worth of bass. It had been like winning the football pools. Blessed days like those, however, were few and far between.

To allow operations in the Roughs, Copik had rigged the *Malkerry*'s trawl net with a rock hopper — a line of rubber discs fastened to the net bottom. When the net reaches rocks or other obstacles, the discs act like wheels and hop over them, preventing the net from entangling and ripping apart. The net had two other ingenious features invented by wily fishermen over the generations: chains attached to the front to startle fish into the net, and a bridle attached to the bottom to kick up a wall of sand that keeps them there. Fish, the theory goes, are too stupid to see the net coming, and once in it too dumb to get out.

There was nary a breath of wind as they held their southerly course for another two and a half hours. At about 12:30 p.m., John wheeled the boat tightly and Craig once again winched the net to the side to check out the catch. As the net surfaced, the elder Copik was elated at the number of silvery bass that appeared, but he strained his eyes to make sense of something large and white amid the bounty. At first he thought it might be a dead porpoise. He had seen them in the nets years ago while fishing off Iceland. Abrasion wears away their sleek dark skin, leaving a smooth white underskin. As Craig hauled the catch closer, father and son realized it was no skinned sea creature. Resisting the urge to throw up, both men pondered the dead man before them.

They hoisted the net in and dropped it onto the wooden catch board, then peered at the haul. Thousands of frantic bass flipped and flapped their last breaths underneath the body. It was a good catch of fish, with a value of £1,000 or more. Too bad they would have to dump it once ashore; because of the body, it would be declared contaminated. The corpse lay in a cramped fetal position. John figured the arms and legs must have been forced together when the body was squashed into the belly of the net. At first the body appeared to have no wounds, but when they examined it they saw the red liquid oozing from a gash in the back of the head. Looking at the lifeless face, Copik concluded that the head had been bashed in. The eyes, though, were still in place, which suggested the body hadn't been in the water long. Copik wondered aloud if it could be the eighteen year-old man who only a week earlier had stolen a paddle boat from the Teignmouth pier for a lark and was last heard crying for help as the tiny craft was swept out into the darkened sea. But the dead man before them was a lot older than a kid; besides, it didn't make sense that the kid would be so far offshore.

The corpse wore a blue checked shirt and forest-green Levi's cords, from under which a pair of Calvin Klein boxer shorts peeked through. Brown loafers were still on the feet. He had a gold necklace around his neck and a Rolex watch on his right wrist. Both Copiks noticed the peculiar tattoo on the right hand, shaped like a star or a blue emblem of some kind. John noted that the pants pockets had been turned out. He thought perhaps it was a foreign seaman. Maybe the guy had fallen overboard. Maybe somebody had robbed him and thrown him over the side. Maybe he threw himself over the side. Or maybe another boat had found the body and, after liberating the contents of the pockets, had flung the corpse back into the water.

For a few moments, they said nothing, just stared at the corpse. Then the elder Copik considered the practical problem now facing him. First, if they took in the body they would lose the catch. Second, the law of the sea decrees that whoever finds a body is responsible for its burial. In short, the corpse was an expensive catch for a fisherman of modest means.

"We can do one of two things, Craig. Forget we ever seen him and lose the catch, or swing him on board and go home." Copik ran his hand through his hair in deliberation. "But we've got to realize, he could have been one of us."

"Right," said Craig, nodding.

"He belongs to someone. We've got to bring him in," John declared.

It was the right thing to do, the honest thing. Even if they were unfairly stuck with the costs of burying a man they had never met, even if they lost their catch, at least they would have a clear conscience.

As the Copiks reeled in the trawl net onto its drum, they noticed a small plough anchor caught up in the nylon. John mused over this unusual catch. It was rare considering they'd been using a rock hopper. John had lifted many admiralty-style anchors — the kind with hooks at each side — but never a plough anchor, named because it is cast in a plough shape so it can dig into a sand bottom. To get into the net, he reasoned, the anchor must have been attached to something . . . but this thought faded into obscurity as he instructed Craig to prepare for the trip home.

The wind picked up as Copik entered the wheelhouse, raised the Brixham coast guard on the VHF marine radio and reported their find. Off Berry Head, a sturdy coast guard inflatable hove alongside the

Malkerry in the now-choppy waters, and two of its three occupants boarded the lurching fishing boat. An officer explained that they would put the corpse in a body bag and turn it over to police at the coast guard dock.

At Brixham harbour, police had taped off a section of the King's Quay wharf to facilitate examination of the corpse. John scanned the wharf as they approached. A sizeable crowd had gathered, perhaps expecting to see the latest drug bust, perhaps with nothing better to do on a Sunday afternoon in the summertime.

Before the inquisitive crowd, John Copik answered cursory police questions and waited. After what seemed like forever, a police doctor boarded the *Malkerry* and set about inspecting the corpse. Two and a half hours later the initial investigation began to wind down. Trying to be helpful, Craig caught the surgeon's attention and pointed out the Rolex watch on the corpse's wrist.

"Hey, have a look on the back and see if his name's on it."

The suggestion didn't go over well with a uniformed officer. "You've been watching too many detective movies, sonny," the officer rebuked, then bent over the body to check the watch. "It's a fake," he announced with the utmost confidence. "It's not a Rolex, 'cause it's not going. If it were a Rolex it would still be working!"

At last, before the gawking townsfolk, fishermen and tourists, the body bag was whisked off to the

Torquay morgue. The plough anchor caught John's eye again and he mentioned it to another of the police officers, but there wasn't much interest. As the hubbub died away, John Copik steered the *Malkerry* around a dividing wharf and into the fishing boat pens at the north side of the harbour. While he was tying his boat to the dock, his friend Derek Meredith came alongside. The two were exchanging the usual pleasantries when Meredith spotted the anchor in the fishing net.

"What are you going to do with that?" he asked.

"Dunno," said John.

"I'd like it for my speed boat."

"It's all yours." The cops didn't seem to worry about it, thought John, so why should he?

So Meredith scooped up the anchor, a 10-pound Sewester, almost brand new.

As the long day drew to a close, Copik was ordered to dump his catch. What a shame — it was the best one he'd had in a while. Oh well, he'd done the right thing.

Later that night a police officer came to John's home and took a statement on his macabre find. The interview hadn't been completed before the officer was ordered elsewhere on a major call. John never got around to mentioning the anomalous anchor.

Two

THE CLOCKS

THE FIRST QUESTIONS police ask themselves when investigating an unusual death are, who is the victim, how did he or she die and where? If they can answer even two of those three questions, finding out the story behind the corpse becomes so much easier. A death can be ruled an accident, a suicide or a murder. The possibility of murder is always in a detective's mind. Most murders are domestic — a husband and a wife, a boyfriend and a girlfriend — or else related to a feud. In most cases police have a body, a crime scene and direct evidence such as a weapon to go on. Making headway is tougher, however, when the death you're probing is what veteran homicide detectives call a dump — a corpse dumped away from the crime scene, with no obvious clues. It's even tougher if you don't know who the person was or where he or she was from. And when a body is dumped in water, vital evidence such as fingerprints, fibres and body fluids are often washed away.

With ten years on the Devon and Cornwall Constabulary under his belt, Det. Ian Clenahan had proved himself a seasoned investigator. The affable twenty-eight-year-old Liverpudlian had served with the force in Plymouth and the north of Devon but had arrived at Torquay-area Criminal Investigation Division (Paignton CID) only four days earlier. A gangly fellow with a big grin, sense of humour and a chirpy Scouse accent, Clenahan had become an instant hit with the rank and file at CID. It was hard not to like such a congenial bloke.

As the official investigating officer on the case, Clenahan knew his first task was to find the identity of the corpse and determine a cause of death. Maybe then, by trying to trace the man's last movements, he might come up with clues to the how, when and why of the man's demise.

The corpse lay untouched in the Torbay Hospital morgue until Monday, July 30, 1996, when a police surgeon's physical examination failed to show a cause of death. However, police coroner Dr. Robin Little concluded that because the body showed only signs of early decomposition it could have been in the sea no more than about seven days, most likely four or five. After noting the gash in the head and bruising on the left hip, Little took a dental impression. If a potential match turned up, he reasoned, he could compare it with past dental records and make a formal identification. Little estimated the man's age at about thirty-five to forty-five, which automatically ruled out the eighteen-year-old thrill seeker from Teignmouth.

As Little surveyed the corpse, common sense, not

medical know-how, told him the man wasn't a sailor who had fallen overboard. He didn't have the telltale "sailor's tan." In fact, his arms and legs weren't tanned at all. Suicide, although a possibility, was also improbable, thought Little. There was no evidence or reason to believe it was a murder. But how did the body end up on the sea bed six miles offshore? Typically, the bodies of accident and suicide victims are found floating, not dragged from the bottom of the sea in a fisherman's net.

Little turned his attention to the watch on the man's right wrist. It was a self-winding Rolex Oyster Perpetual Chronometer. He shook the watch and it began ticking. After being advised by an assistant that each Rolex was stamped with a serial number, Little removed the rear case and found an engraved number. He would contact the Rolex company to see whether they could trace an owner.

While awaiting results from Dr. Little's query to Rolex, Clenahan, his immediate boss, Det. Sgt. Bill MacDonald, and their colleagues at CID pored over missing persons reports from across the British Isles. No match turned up. Clenahan released information on the mystery corpse to the Torquay newspaper, complete with photographs of the unusual tattoo and the Rolex. In all probability, he and his team reasoned, the man was from Devon or Cornwall or had spent his last days in the area. Maybe someone would recognize him. The photographs stirred much interest among the dogged reporters who were somewhat attuned to weird crimes, given that murder mystery queen Agatha Christie had been raised in Torquay and had lived most of her later life in Greenaway mansion, at the foot of Greenaway Quay, only a few miles up the River Dart from Brixham. Sensing that a real-life whodunit was developing in their own backyard, the local press put the story on the front pages and, in Christie style, dubbed the unknown corpse "the Rolex Man." The story piqued the interest of natives, who wondered, as police did, why a man with such an exclusive and expensive watch would die in such an unexplained, perhaps violent way. Before Clenahan arrived at whodunit, however, he had to find out who-was-it.

On Tuesday, July 31, Dr. Gyan Fernando, a forensic pathologist appointed as a consultant to the Devon and Cornwall police by Britain's Home Office, performed an official autopsy on the corpse. The twenty-five-year medical veteran and university lecturer determined the man was at least forty years old, thin, with dark hair, five feet nine inches and about 139 pounds. There was nothing unusual in the scratches over the entire body, ruled Fernando; these were to be expected from the fish scales and sand that would abrade the body as it washed along the sea bed. Fernando noted the usual indications of early decay on the face, chest and abdomen. The hands and feet showed signs of what his profession had for decades dubbed washerwoman's chains, a puckering of the skin that occurs on bodies submerged in water for some time. Fernando also noted, as others had, the odd-looking blue tattoo on the back of the right hand. He suggested it depicted a maple leaf.

He paid particular attention to the laceration on the back of the head. It was nearly impossible to tell, he concluded, whether the cut had come before or after death, or what had caused it. It could have come from an attack with an axe or a steel bar while the victim was alive, but it could just as easily have come from the propeller of a passing boat after the victim drowned. If from a blow, however, Fernando doubted the blow had killed the man. There wasn't sufficient damage to the brain to cause death, although the blow had likely been severe enough to cause unconsciousness. The fact that blood was oozing from the wound when the Copiks picked the body out of the water didn't mean much, either, he told Clenahan; blood oozes long after death because it cannot clot in an inert body. After noting a 2-inch bruise on the left hip but not reading anything special into it — bruises like those could be caused either three hours before or thirty minutes after death — Fernando moved on to the surgical part of the autopsy.

The heart and the rest of the cardiovascular system were normal, except for the expected putrefaction. The upper respiratory system was also normal, but when Fernando checked the lungs he found both organs waterlogged and bloated. This could mean only one thing: the man had died from drowning. There was no other possible cause. If death had occurred before the man entered the water, the lungs would not have filled to such an extent. Taking into consideration the head wound, Fernando felt the man had been unconscious when he entered the water, and then drowned. Perhaps he had drowned a week or two ago.

At the end of the day, Clenahan didn't know much: he had a drowning victim with a head injury that might have happened before or after death. Whether the case was an accident, a suicide, or a murder, it was too early to tell. Still, finding the body so far out at sea continued to niggle at everyone involved.

Dr. Little's Rolex investigation, however, bore fruit. Henry Hudson, general manager of the Rolex watch company in Bexley, Kent, told Little that the watch had been made in Geneva in 1967 and had twice been serviced in the 1980s — for a Mr. Platt of Harrogate, North Yorkshire in 1982, and in an apparent misspelling, for a Mr. Patt of the same city, in 1986. Following up various addresses, Clenahan learned that the watch found on the mysterious Rolex Man had belonged to Ronald Joseph Platt, whom he subsequently traced to an apartment in Chelmsford, the Essex County seat of government, about twenty miles northeast of London. It appeared from the frequency Platt had changed addresses that he was a bit of a drifter. This was why, Clenahan concluded, if Platt was indeed the Rolex Man his disappearance and demise might not have raised any alarms.

With other matters pressing for his attention, Clenahan couldn't see himself driving three or four hours to Chelmsford on what was a routine fishing expedition, not to mention the time spent on research, plus the return trip. As is regular practice in cross-jurisdiction matters, Clenahan notified his Chelmsford counterparts and asked for assistance.

Three

THE SECRET ADVERSARY

DET. SGT. PETER Redman was up to his eyeballs in work at the Essex County Constabulary's CID office in Chelmsford in early August of 1996 when he received Ian Clenahan's request for help. Redman, a stocky man whose pleasing face, gentle mannerisms and soft gentleman's voice belie an astute detective's mind, had to take care of a few priority items first but within a few days assigned uniformed officers to inquire at 100 Beardsley Drive about a man named Ronald Platt. The officers duly reported that Platt no longer lived at that address. But Redman, a fifteen-year veteran who had learned never to leave a stone unturned, wasn't finished yet.

First, he checked the local council tax records, hoping to find a clue to Platt's whereabouts. The tax department told Redman that Platt had written on his termination notice: "I'm moving to France and I am no longer liable for paying property tax." Next, Redman contacted the local post office to see if Platt had given a forwarding address. Sure enough, the man had requested that mail be directed to the Little London Farmhouse in the nearby hamlet of Woodham Walter. Before following up that lead, Redman contacted Platt's former landlord, Stephen Powl, to jog his memory for additional information. Powl recalled that Platt had been given a reference by a friend, David Davis, and he passed on the telephone number Davis had left.

No stranger to the delicate matters of death, Redman prepared himself before calling Davis on August 20, 1996. Aware that he would be telling Davis that his friend might be dead, he wanted to talk to Davis in person when he delivered the bad news. Redman dialled the number for what he knew was a mobile phone.

"May I speak with Mr. David Davis, please?" he said.

"Speaking."

Redman introduced himself. "Is it possible we could meet? I have some news to impart to you."

"Yes, what is it?" Davis asked impatiently, in a deep, soft voice with a hint of an American accent.

Redman didn't want to say on the phone, but he felt he couldn't hold back. "We think Devon and Cornwall police have recovered the body of a friend of yours. Could we meet?" When Davis paused, Redman continued, "I'd much sooner do this in person. You live in Woodham Walter, don't you?"

"Yes."

"I'll come see you," offered Redman.

"No, I'll come see you . . . it's easier," Davis replied. "I know Chelmsford. It's no problem."

They arranged to meet at the Chelmsford police station on August 22, 1996, at 4:30 p.m. It was almost spot on when Redman took a call from the front desk that Mr. Davis had arrived. Redman walked out through the CID unit and into the reception area. Before him stood a tall, upright man, immaculately groomed and razor-sharp in brown casual clothes. He gave off the aura of a distinguished man of impeccable habit, taste and character. Redman led Davis back into the anteroom he used for interviews and meetings. He offered a cup of coffee. When Davis declined, Redman got right to the point.

"The police have found a body in Devon," he reiterated. "They think it's Ron Platt."

A gnawing look appeared on Davis's face, but he kept his composure.

Redman went on. "You're the only person we've been able to find who knew him."

Davis nodded and told Redman that he hadn't seen Platt for some time, since June. He asked Redman if they were sure it was Ron.

"Inquiries into the Rolex watch worn on the body have linked it to Mr. Platt," said Redman, adding that Devon police were still trying to make a formal identification.

Davis remarked that Platt had once served in the British Army and perhaps his service records would

help police with their investigation. He added that he
and Platt had been friends for a couple of years. In
fact, he said, Ron had been his best friend. They had
sort of a "kindred spirit" because Ron had dual
British and Canadian nationality, just as he himself
did, and they both liked boats. Platt loved to watch
the large boats, recalled Davis, especially the British
navy fighting ships that moved in and out of
Portsmouth.

Redman asked if Davis would mind speaking
directly to the investigating officer.

"Not at all," Davis replied.

Redman phoned CID Paignton and after a brief
discussion with Clenahan turned the phone over.
Davis repeated his story. Clenahan, hoping to bolster
Platt's identity beyond just the Rolex, asked him
about the tattoo on the right hand. Davis couldn't
recall a tattoo of any kind on Platt's hand, only some
form of ink art on an arm. Yes, he did remember an
"old" Rolex that Platt had bought many years ago
while in the army. Davis added that he had last seen
Platt in June, when Platt set out for France to start
up a business. He'd even loaned Platt £3,000 to help
him out. Davis had no address or phone number for
Platt, but he believed he had gone to La Rochelle
area. Davis lamented that he had expected to hear
from his friend after a week or so in France but Platt
hadn't contacted him. He certainly hadn't expected
to hear about his death from the police. Davis confirmed to Clenahan that he lived at the Little London

Farmhouse in Woodham Walter and, yes, Ron Platt had redirected his mail there. Responding to Clenahan's questions, Davis said he wasn't aware of any reason Ron would be in Devon and added, "No, Ron didn't have a boat."

As Davis talked, Clenahan scribbled notes as accurately as he could. Notes, he knew, were important, given that defence lawyers routinely subpoenaed them if a case went to trial. Anxious to contact Platt's relatives, Clenahan asked whether Davis had any connections.

"No," said Davis. "I know his mother is still alive. She lives in High Wycombe. He has two brothers somewhere, but I don't know their names."

After Davis hung up with Clenahan, Redman asked whether he had any photographs of Platt.

"I'm pretty certain I have one," responded Davis, and said he would track it down.

Four days later a small, out-of-focus photograph of Ron Platt arrived in an envelope devoid of any sender's name or return address, and without even a note. The photo showed Platt under an umbrella with a horse. Redman was pleased. Obviously the photo had come from David Davis. How nice of him to help out. Redman had the photo enlarged and sent it to Clenahan in Devon, expecting to hear nothing further about the case.

Four

THE PALE HORSE

AS AUGUST PASSED into September, Clenahan and his fellow officers made further efforts to delve into Platt's movements after he had left Chelmsford, but to no avail.

Despite the slow pace and some scepticism that they would never know what happened, the detectives hadn't given up. As a matter of policy, they had to exhaust all leads before they could shelve an investigation. In the last few weeks of September, British Army officials dug out Ronald Platt's military service records at Clenahan's request and delivered copies to Devon police. Included were dental charts, which Clenahan had Dr. Robin Little compare with the dental impression he had taken from the body in the Torbay Hospital morgue. The dead man was Platt, all right, Little said, with a 90 per cent certainty. The records also listed Platt's next-of-kin as Brian Platt, a commercial cartoonist living in Hay-on-Wye, Shropshire. Det. Sgt. Bill MacDonald accompanied Clenahan on the trip to see Brian Platt. The pair were anxious to close the case on the Rolex Man, one way or another. The need to conclude the investigation was deemed all the more urgent by the arrival of a new head at Paignton CID, Det. Chief Insp. Phil Sincock, a highly reputed boss who, despite his knack for administrative duties, hadn't lost touch with the streets and with the subtle mix of encouragement, coaxing and logistical support his officers need to work them. Sincock, born and bred in neighbouring Cornwall, had enjoyed a meteoric rise from sergeant to his current position after some notable detective work during his posting in Exeter in the late 1980s and early '90s. As field boss of detectives, he was responsible for all detective matters in Paignton and the flanking communities of Brixham and Torquay.

Brian Platt was, of course, stunned to hear that his younger brother Ronnie, who at fifty-one was some nine years his junior, had drowned off the Devon coast. Yes, he told Clenahan and MacDonald, Ron had a Rolex of some kind, but he couldn't remember much about it. He had a tattoo on the right hand as well, a tattoo depicting the maple leaf, the national symbol of Canada. Ronnie, as Brian Platt called his brother, had maintained a love of and fascination with Canada ever since the family immigrated there in 1955. Brian hadn't gone because at the time he was serving in the Royal Air Force. While Ronnie and his other brother, Jeff, had spent their teen years in Canada, Brian had lost touch with them in an emotional sense. Brian related that their father,

Eric, had worked as a schoolteacher in the small prairie town of Pense, Saskatchewan, but when Ronnie reached sixteen he returned to the United Kingdom and soon after that joined the army. Brian described Ron as a loner and said he really hadn't seen much of him in the past ten years. It wasn't that there was anything wrong with Ron, mind you; he just liked keeping to himself. For instance, said Brian, he'd last seen Ronnie six months earlier, when he brought their ageing mother to Hay-on-Wye on a social visit.

Ronnie, Brian continued, had married in 1965, and in 1967 he had a son, Malcolm, but after he and his wife divorced in the 1970s he had seen his son only once or twice. Although Ronnie's family life had fallen apart, his work life held great prospects. He came out of the army in 1973 with skills in electronics and television engineering. For years he worked as a TV repairman for DER Ltd. and later repaired televisions and video machines on a contract basis.

Canada, recalled Brian, had always been on the tip of Ronnie's tongue. He never lost his passion for the country, acquired during his formative years.

In the 1970s, Brian noted, Ron had met a woman named Elaine Boyes, and the pair were close for many years. Elaine, he said, still lived in Harrogate. Although she and Ronnie had split up in 1993, she could likely tell the police an awful lot more than he could. Elaine and Ronnie had gone to Canada in 1993, Brian said, but that summer Elaine had returned to

England and stayed. Ronnie returned in 1995, his dream shattered.

Could Ron swim?

"I'm not sure," said Brian. He suggested that Elaine might know.

Clenahan shared with Brian Platt that he had talked to a David Davis, who told them that Ron had apparently set off for France two or three months earlier. Police had no known address for Ron and no sign of his belongings. All they had was the Rolex and the clothes found on his body.

Brian recalled Ronnie telling him at their last meeting that the American Davis had been really good to him. Brian had asked his brother why: "What does he get out of it?" Typically, Ronnie had just pushed the question aside. He had always been reluctant to discuss his private affairs. Brian had the feeling that Ron, being such an introvert, was simply flattered by Davis's interest in him.

As MacDonald and Clenahan were about to leave, Brian Platt asked if they would put David Davis in contact with him. Ronnie had had possession of some family furniture that Brian would like to inherit. Besides, he would like to know more about Ronnie's last days and what had been going on in his life.

Five

ONE, TWO, BUCKLE MY SHOE

DET. SGT. PETER Redman was at his desk, preparing the next day's trip to a Suffolk prison in a spanking-new rental car, when his phone rang around midday on October 14, 1996. On the line was Det. Ian Clenahan, whom he hadn't spoken to for a couple of months. Clenahan advised Redman that the body was indeed that of Ron Platt. But Clenahan acknowledged that wasn't why he was calling. Platt's eldest brother wanted to ask David Davis about some furniture and other items of his brother's that had sentimental value and that Davis might know about.

"Problem is," said Clenahan, "I've mislaid Davis's cell phone number. It's not urgent," he added, "but when you get a moment, maybe you could pop around and see him at the Little London Farmhouse.

Redman got off the phone and considered Clenahan's request. The sun was shining and in the parking lot sat a brand-new car, a Vauxhall Victor — much nicer than the beat-up universal cars the detectives normally used. It was just too tempting. Redman looked up Woodham Walter on a large wall map. It wasn't far away. He went outside and got into the Vauxhall.

Woodham Walter is a hamlet of about seven hundred people some six miles due east of Chelmsford. Beyond the village of Danbury, Redman took a fork to the north at Runsell Green. From there a winding country road, boxed in by tall hedgerows, led him into the tiny heart of Woodham Walter.

The isolated hamlet is actually three or four ancient settlements, now considered one. Its roots go back to Saxon times. *Woodham* is Saxon for "the settlement in the wood." *Walter* comes from Fitzwalter, the name of the family handed the lands after the Norman occupation. The lands were divided among farmers after the breakdown of feudal England, and with the decline of agriculture in the late nineteenth century, they were further divided into smaller plots, many of them bought up by the emerging business elite. Now the town is host to the likes of soft-handed doctors, velvet-tongued lawyers and salesmen and affluent retirees and is chiefly known for its quaint, colourful pubs. It is one of those lovely little places to visit on a Sunday afternoon.

Redman drove along the main street, past historic St. Michael's Church, then the Bell, a charming inn dating back to the sixteenth century. No sooner had he ridden by a few old stone homes, the Queen Victoria Pub and a tiny post office than he was in the country again. A couple of hundred yards out of town he turned left onto West Bowers Road. Just beyond a tidy bungalow, Redman made a sharp right onto a little dirt road, Raven Hall Lane, where he expected to find the Little London Farmhouse and, presumably, David Davis. A tall hedgerow partially hid his view, but across a farm field and around a bend in the road, Redman spotted a two-storey white stucco house and beyond that another white-sided building. Driving slowly by the neat but nondescript house, he laid eyes on its quaint neighbour, an ancient cottage, its white-washed walls and red roof a perfect foil for the tiny black-framed windows. The front garden was resplendent with rose bushes and hollyhocks. Apart from a neglected house farther up the lane and stately Raven Hall, the old manor house from which the lane took its name, those were the only two homes in sight. There were no signs or numbers on the houses, but the pretty cottage before Redman befit the name Little London Farmhouse. Still, he wasn't sure. He left the Vauxhall running on the secluded dirt road, its door open, as he went to knock and find out.

A matronly woman of about sixty or seventy, the laugh lines on her face suggesting she'd had a happy life, gave him an infectious smile as she pulled the heavy door ajar. Redman could hear a number of ladies chattering away. He had obviously interrupted a social occasion. A tall, proud man in his seventies, perhaps older, came up behind her.

"Sorry to bother you. Is this the Little London Farmhouse?" asked Redman.

"That one next door," the woman offered. "Who are you looking for?"

"Uh, David Davis," responded Redman, somewhat embarrassed upon realizing that he had knocked on the wrong door.

The older fellow piped up knowingly, "Oh, no, Ron Platt and Noël live there. They're not home right now."

Redman tried to digest what he'd just heard. Shit, what the hell's going on here? he thought. Ron Platt, who is dead, is living in the same home as David Davis, who helped identify the dead man as Ron Platt?

Much to the bemusement of the elderly couple, Peter Redman quietly introduced himself and asked if he could have a word with them.

"Certainly," offered the elderly chap. "Come in."

Redman excused himself momentarily and returned to the Vauxhall. He switched off the engine and left the car in the middle of the lane. No need to worry about traffic — he wasn't exactly on the M1!

When he got back, the man introduced himself as Frank Johnson and his lady friend as Audrey Mossman. Frank explained that they weren't married and it was best to tell everyone that fact up front. Audrey offered Redman a cup of tea, but Redman declined. As traditionally English as Audrey and Frank seemed and as Redman himself was, this matter was suddenly far too serious for discussion over a tea pot.

Redman followed Frank Johnson through the entryway of the beautiful old cottage into a cosy study with a splendid view of the backyard. Redman didn't want to say too much — it was clearly a time to just sit back and listen, and then contemplate the next move. Redman asked discreetly about the neighbours.

The Platts, Ron and Noël, were up in York, or was it Scotland, Frank said. He and Audrey were looking after the house for them. That was the way it was in Little London, he said, neighbours looking out for neighbours. He went on to tell Redman that Ron Platt was an older chap, perhaps in his late forties, while his wife, Noël, was much younger, in her early or mid-twenties. They had a baby and a toddler. Ron was an American, as was his wife.

Redman couldn't resist scratching his head. So that was it! David Davis was masquerading as Ronald Platt! It must be so. How many more Americans could be living at the Little London Farmhouse under the noses of friendly neighbours like Frank and Audrey?

One thing puzzled Frank, however. "I don't think they're married. There's something they're keeping from us."

Redman had learned all he needed to know. Although Frank and Audrey asked what on earth was going on, Redman said he could not tell them. He asked that they keep his visit a secret. It was most important to do so.

Back in his car, he drove by the white stucco house he now knew was the home of David Davis, or was it Ronald Platt? It was pointless for him to knock on the door. One, the "Platts" were not home. Two, police strategy and common sense told him he should not do anything until he'd discussed his find with Clenahan.

On the way back to Chelmsford police station, Redman was oblivious to the nice car and the beautiful scenery. He remained deep in thought about his meeting with Davis and over what had just transpired with Frank Johnson. It was in the late afternoon when he sat down at his desk, collected his thoughts and called Ian Clenahan.

"Are you sitting down?" he asked.

"Sitting down? Why?" Clenahan wanted to know, his mind a million miles away from Ronald Platt's death at sea. Understandably, Paignton CID was on high alert after the reported abduction of a ten-year-old girl by someone who lived in her building. Sincock, fearing the worst, had told all the detectives on duty that they were to stay until the incident was resolved. At the moment Redman phoned, Clenahan was in his third-floor office awaiting a briefing. Sincock and MacDonald were in Sincock's office on the second floor, discussing available personnel and strategy.

"It's that fella David Davis, Ronald Platt's best friend . . ."

"Yeah?" asked Clenahan, alerted by Redman's tone.

"The man I met here in the station is holding himself out to be Ronald Platt. There is a woman there, too, who calls herself Noël Platt." Redman recounted what the neighbours had told him. And the Ron Platt they described fit his own recollection of David Davis. The possibility of murder was so obvious that Redman didn't even say the word.

After a long pause, Clenahan spoke, his voice revealing his sudden excitement. "I'm going to find the boss! I'll phone you back."

Nothing more was said. There was no room to voice their incredulity, since each man knew that one day any discussions between them could be in issue at court.

Clenahan raced down to the second floor. He knocked on Sincock's door and burst in on the meeting of Sincock, and MacDonald and others. "Sir, have you got a couple of minutes?" he asked.

An impatient frown crossed Sincock's face and the lines creased on his balding forehead. Clearly, he was under a lot of stress.

"No, not now," he responded.

"Sir, it's important," said Clenahan.

"No, not now," said Sincock. "I've got this abduction on. Can it wait?"

"It's important!" said Clenahan. He left it there.

"Give me a couple of minutes," said Sincock, grasping the urgency in Clenahan's voice.

Clenahan retreated to his office. A couple of minutes later Bill MacDonald showed up and asked

"Scouse" what was going on. Clenahan recounted Redman's visit to the Little London Farmhouse. MacDonald was incredulous, as was Sincock when the two told him the story. Sincock kept the rest of the detective shift on the abduction but assigned Clenahan to find out as much as he could about the Little London Farmhouse and this fellow Davis. He later assigned a team of four officers — MacDonald, Clenahan, Chris Amey and Michelle Lewis-Clarke — to the investigation. The team would work out of Paignton under MacDonald's command. They would pull together any public information they could: electric bills, tax records, birth records, health records, anything they could legally get their hands on. As well, Sincock instructed, Clenahan should use his police authority to obtain phone records. The investigative team should also run Davis's name past American police. Was he wanted in the States? French authorities, too, should be called. Did Platt ever make it to France?

Redman was at his desk when Clenahan called back.

"The boss is sitting in a darkened room trying to get his head around this," said Clenahan. He told Redman that Phil Sincock and Bill MacDonald would visit Essex in the next few days for a full briefing.

On October 16, 1996, Redman met with the two Devon officers in Chelmsford and reviewed the facts with them. The little girl had been returned unharmed the previous day. Now Paignton CID could devote all their time and energy to the Rolex Man.

Satisfied that the case would prosper with MacDonald and Redman on it as a team, Sincock returned to Devon. Over the next few days Redman and MacDonald gathered all the information they could. In short order they pulled up two copies of Ron Platt's signature that bore no resemblance to each other. One was signed R. Platt, while the other was R. J. Platt, and the handwriting differed.

Meanwhile in Devon, Clenahan called Davis's mobile phone number on Thursday, October 17, to see what kind of response he would get. A young woman with an American accent answered. She introduced herself as Noël Davis and told Clenahan that David wasn't available. She took the policeman's name and number and said she'd relay the message. Davis returned Clenahan's call at 4:15 the next afternoon. He called from a pay phone, explaining that he was on the road, in Birmingham, and he apologized for not returning Clenahan's call any sooner. Davis quickly asked Clenahan if he was certain that the dead man was his friend Ron Platt.

"We're sure it's Ron Platt's body," said Clenahan, opting to play Davis's game. He asked Davis why he wanted to know. Davis replied that he'd like to send flowers or a card to Platt's mother. He also told Clenahan he had forgotten to mention that in the days before his last sighting of Platt, his friend had stayed at a hotel in Essex and that at their last meeting over coffee Platt had told him he intended to visit the Tait Gallery in St. Ives, Cornwall, before he left for France.

"Mr. Davis," said Clenahan, "I would like to arrange a meeting in Essex. We would like to go over a few things with you."

Davis replied that he couldn't make any commitment because he didn't have his diary with him to check his engagements. He said he would get back to Clenahan the next day, Saturday. They arranged that he would call between six and seven in the evening.

Working the evening shift Saturday night, Clenahan sat by his phone from 5:30 until 8:30. No calls came. When he left the office on another task he put his answering machine on, but when he returned there was no message from Davis. By the end of the next week, Clenahan still had not heard from Davis, but suddenly there was light at the end of the tunnel — detectives had tracked down Elaine Boyes. She was living in Harrogate. At this point, the Devon team had no idea what exactly was going on. For all they knew, Boyes might be part of it. They would tell her only a few details, while at the same time elicit as much as they could about her ex-boyfriend.

On Wednesday, October 23, Bill MacDonald called Boyes's home. Her mother, Joan, answered, and when MacDonald wouldn't reveal the nature of his call she pressed for more information. MacDonald said that Elaine's friend Ron Platt had been found off the coast of Devon a few months ago

and they would like help identifying some of his
belongings. Joan Boyes replied that Elaine was at
work; she would have her daughter call back, but only
after she herself had told Elaine about Ron. Elaine,
she said, was a very sensitive girl.

Boyes phoned Clenahan the same night and they
arranged a meeting in Harrogate.

Six

A POCKET FULL OF RYE

ON MONDAY, OCTOBER 28, 1996, Detectives Ian Clenahan and Michelle Lewis-Clarke drove north to the North Yorkshire town of Harrogate, a quaint spa and university town built up by money from the wool and cloth-weaving trades and today filled with picturesque common land, trendy boutiques, cosy tea shops and exquisite homes. Situated thirteen miles north of Leeds, it is a far cry from the grimy working towns that remain a legacy of the Industrial Revolution. Because of its beauty, seclusion and wealth, some refer to Harrogate as Britain's "Little Switzerland." It is now a favoured home to the intelligentsia, musicians, not-so-starving artisans and well-to-do retirees.

Over coffee at McCoy's, Clenahan and Lewis-Clarke gauged Elaine Boyes as a naive, trusting, gentle person. The short, brown hair around a strong, square bespectacled face gave her a homely appearance. Elaine was also a talkative type, but she didn't tell her police interviewers that first meeting how she had voiced her suspicions about Davis's involvement in Ron's death to her mother only seconds after Joan had told her about it.

"He did it, didn't he! He killed Ronald!"

"Elaine, calm down," Joan and other family told her. "You can't just go around accusing people of murder."

Elaine had been so distraught over the weekend that she had even visited a psychic. "Tell me that it wasn't murder," Elaine said to the diviner.

"Elaine, you're right . . ." came her answer.

Now, as Elaine sipped coffee and spoke to police about Ronald, she didn't let her feelings overwhelm her. She had resolved to play it cool.

But when Clenahan began by confirming with Boyes that the Rolex and the tattoo were both Ronald's, she became emotional. "The Rolex was on him all the time. It was his pride and joy." Then he gave her the facts surrounding the death and noted that Ron's best friend, David Davis, had said Ron was on his way to France. Davis said he last saw Platt in June. Elaine gave a startled look. David Davis had known since August that Ronald was dead? She had called Davis not two weeks ago and he never mentioned anything. How strange! She also called Davis in late September or early October. He wasn't at home, but she left a message saying that her mother was having legal problems over the ownership of her house and she needed to speak with someone knowledgeable like Davis.

A few days later Davis had returned her call. After they talked about the house, Elaine asked if he had recently seen Ron; she hadn't spoken with him in over a year. Davis told her Ron had left for France in June to start a business. Elaine recalled to her riveted listeners how flabbergasted she was at this news. Why would Ronald have gone to France. He didn't speak a word of French and hadn't really liked France. And why would he have left England without even contacting her or her family? Even though they were no longer linked romantically they still shared an affectionate bond. The move seemed so out of character.

"There's something funny going on, isn't there," Elaine quizzed.

"Don't be daft, Elaine," Clenahan quickly said. He couldn't allow her to be suspicious. Not at this crucial stage.

Realizing the importance of Elaine's information, Clenahan and Lewis-Clarke wanted a formal account of her story. They whisked Elaine off to a Trust House Forte Hotel and took down a full statement. In that meeting and subsequent interviews, Elaine told the detectives all they needed to know about Ronald Platt — and almost everything they wanted to know about the mysterious David Davis.

Elaine recalled that she met Ronald at a party back in 1980 and liked him almost immediately. She was only twenty-one then, and still living with her mom in Harrogate. She'd never had a steady boyfriend to speak of. Ron was an attractive man, about thirty-five. "He was very mild mannered, very nonaggressive. A very nice person. He didn't really mix easily. He had one or two good friends, but he was very quiet and shy. You had to make the conversation first. It was not easy for him to communicate with people."

Within six months Ron and Elaine were living together in a flat on the King's Road in Harrogate. From the start, Ronald talked of his younger years in Canada, his continued affection for that country and his dream of returning there — the sooner, the better. He saw life in Canada, it seemed to Elaine, through the rose-coloured glasses of childhood. Still, she found herself fascinated with his descriptions of the great outdoors, the wide-open prairies.

During the 1980s Ron twice went to Canada, while Elaine stayed at home. She had encouraged him to go and had planned to join him if everything worked out. His first attempt to settle failed after only a few weeks because he had not gotten a visa and work permit and soon found himself broke. A second attempt in 1987 failed because he was lonely and missed Elaine. He returned just as Elaine was about to take a nanny position in Italy that would give her job experience. Elaine went to Italy anyway and enjoyed her time there. Ronald was working as a technician at Harrogate College when she returned, but his love affair with Canada still ran in his blood.

In 1989 Elaine began working for Harry Spencer

auctioneers in Harrogate. By this time Ron had left the college and was subcontracting repairs for various television companies. It wasn't that lucrative, and Ron worked only a day or two in any given week.

In February or March of 1991, she remembered, a tall, distinguished man with an American accent came into Spencer's and inquired about a painting. It was a quiet time of year, so she didn't mind spending time with the handsome, seemingly well-to-do man. They talked for two hours — they talked about their love of art, the man's love of Scotland, her love of photography, their love of travel. He introduced himself as David Davis, from Vermont, in the States. He had run a financial business and had recently worked as a private banker. He had been very successful — a success he attributed to never losing: "I always make the right decisions." He was currently living in London, after just moving from Geneva, and was looking for a house in Harrogate. Elaine found him "really nice, charming."

Out of the blue, Davis asked Elaine to come to work for him as his personal secretary.

"I said, 'What do you mean? What kind of work?'"

"Anything, really," Davis replied. He hinted at extensive European travel. "We could start an antique business."

As Elaine dreamed in words about what kind of business she would like, Davis reassured her that they could do anything. She reiterated her interest in photography, and Davis told her he was planning to publish a coffee table book featuring the fountains of Geneva.

"I've worked in Geneva and the number of fountains there is amazing."

Elaine was awed. There was no limit to his dreams.

"It really doesn't matter what we do," he told her. "I know how to make money!"

It was as if Prince Charming had swooped in and promised an end to her humdrum life.

Despite her excitement, Elaine was suspicious, "He was so kind, charming, and he smiled a lot. I was hoping that he didn't feel 'Gosh, this is a nice young lady . . .' so I made it clear I had a boyfriend." She told Davis not only about Ronald but that he dreamed of returning to Canada and they would likely go in a few years. All they needed was the money.

"I know Canada well," said Davis. "If you work for me, in a year or so you'll have enough money saved to move to Canada. Canada is a beautiful country. You'll love it!"

Elaine was thrilled but tried to keep her feet on the ground. "I felt, 'Elaine, don't be silly. This can't be real.' "

The conversation continued. Elaine, though, was getting nervous; the visitor had overstayed his welcome. But he wouldn't leave, and the phone didn't ring. Elaine felt powerless to just excuse herself. Finally, she told the American, "Look, I don't know you from Adam. Give me your business card. I'll talk to my boyfriend. We'll see what happens."

Davis handed her his card and said he'd ring her in a couple of weeks. He gave a charming smile and left. Elaine forgot about the offer — he couldn't possibly be serious.

But two or three weeks later the phone rang. It was the mild-mannered man with the American accent. "I'm coming up to Harrogate to look at more properties," Davis told her. "Is it possible to meet?"

They met at the auctioneer's, then had lunch at a nearby bistro. Davis asked many questions about Ron and what he and Elaine wanted out of life.

"I think it would be a good idea if I met Ron," he ventured.

Elaine agreed and arranged to meet Davis at an Italian restaurant with Ron.

The two hit it off from the start. Ron, of course, talked about Canada. Davis did, too, and even knew some of the places Ron mentioned. At some point during dinner Davis looked Elaine in the eye and said bluntly, "So, I've met you — you've met me. Will you come to work for me?" She was making only £9,000 a year, he pointed out, then offered her £12,000.

Elaine turned to Ron. "What do you think?"

Ron just shrugged and said, "Why not?"

Elaine had already decided; she was merely seeking Ron's approval. In her mind, she had nothing to lose.

Elaine left Spencer auctioneers on May 10, 1991.

She would work for Davis and his new company, Cavendish Corporation, which he told her he had bought "off the shelf" from a company that sold old company names. Davis appointed Elaine and Ron directors. The bank accounts would be under her name and Ron's, but only Elaine could sign the cheques.

"You're never to write a cheque to me, Elaine. Is that clear?" Davis ordered.

Elaine thought this was all for tax reasons, or because of what Davis had told her and Ron about his wife: she was in Canada and had begun legal proceedings against him for alimony and child support.

As they opened bank accounts in the Cavendish name in Harrogate, Elaine had her eyes opened to her new boss.

"How much are you talking about?" one bank manager asked Davis.

"Millions," he replied.

Elaine recalled thinking, Oh, my God, and wondered how much money this breezy American really had.

Once they had opened a company account it was Davis who controlled it. Boyes said she just did what Davis asked of her; he was so much smarter in business than she. Her only business education had been a couple of night-school courses.

Initially, Boyes accompanied Davis to auctions, where they bought paintings and antiques. They would hang on to them, he said, and over time the investment would grow. Every five or six weeks she would travel to the Continent, where she would look at properties, photograph them and prepare a report for Davis. Whenever she took one of these trips, always flying by the Gatwick Express, Davis would give her Swiss currency to convert into pounds at the Bureau de Change. Davis paid all her expenses in cash. Ron, meanwhile, laboured as a television repairman. Although his name was associated with Cavendish, he was only a silent partner.

In these first heady months, Elaine also opened bank accounts in Switzerland, France and Italy. Often, Davis would take Ron and her to London for the weekend, and thought nothing of paying £200 for dinner at an exclusive restaurant. There were always great quantities of food and wine, and Davis would entertain the pair with stories. He bragged of flying on the Concorde, having champagne with Rod Stewart, meeting Ronald Reagan and moving in the influential circles of the world's business elite. He dropped names as readily as a child drops pennies into a wishing well.

But sometimes he came off his happy-go-lucky roller coaster and talked about his family. He introduced Elaine and Ron to Noël, his teenage daughter, who was living in England with him, and said he had two more daughters in the United States. The youngest, Heather, would be coming to Britain in two or three years. The eldest, Jillian, in her late teens, was living with her boyfriend in New York. He missed the other daughters terribly.

Elaine travelled to Europe through the summer and fall of 1991, but in early 1992 Ron's work began to peter out. Davis helped him open up a television and radio repair shop, which Ron and Elaine named Rutland Radio because of its location on Rutland Road. With Davis's help, Elaine bought a flat. He told her that with the profit from the flat and the savings from Rutland Radio they would compile enough cash to get to Canada.

But Rutland didn't go well. "It was not in a good area of Harrogate. It wasn't right. We should never have started it, really," Elaine said.

Ron didn't have the knack of dealing with people the way he did with inanimate objects such as televisions. If the customer was happy, he was happy. If the customer was unhappy, Ron just didn't know what to do.

But good fortune appeared to shine on Ron Platt Christmas Day 1992. Davis invited Ron and Elaine for Christmas dinner at the Harrogate house he'd bought. His daughter Noël joined them.

"This reminds me of the family life, having all of us together," he said cheerfully.

At that dinner, Davis gave Ron and Elaine Christmas presents. Each received a book, inside which was an envelope containing a card, with a promise that Davis would buy two air tickets to Canada. But there was a caveat — his offer had to be redeemed by the end of February 1993.

Ron was shocked at Davis's generosity, but his excitement overrode any reservations he may have felt. Elaine, on the other hand, was nervous. A strange land with strange people. It seemed so frightening. Still, she loved Ron, and this had been his dream for the twelve years she had known him; she must go with him. However, she told Ron and Davis she would need a two-way ticket so she could attend her sister's wedding in July; she was in the wedding party and could not let her sister down. Ron didn't want a return ticket. To Ron, this was it: free air tickets and a promise from Davis that if he found a business in Canada, Davis would help him finance it.

On February 22, 1993, Ron and Elaine flew to Calgary, Alberta. The cold winds chilled Elaine to the bone almost as soon as she stepped off the plane. She and Ron had landed in the midst of a frigid Canadian winter. It was −35 Fahrenheit and the infamous western winds whipped the freezing cold at them for another three months until spring came. They lived in a small detached house to the northwest of the city. Elaine found her English jackets and sweaters inadequate for the deep freeze. In the first few days, she had to buy a cheap padded coat just so she could walk outside without freezing to death. Despite the warmth from the odd uplifting Chinook, Elaine's mood was as cold as the weather. The arrival of spring failed to buoy her. "By then I was desperately depressed, as I had no job and neither did Ron."

Ron and Elaine called Davis one day and told

him of their despair. He suggested they drive to
Vancouver, on the West Coast, and check out all the
little towns on the way. Maybe they would find a place
they liked. They took his advice, but they ended up
back in Calgary.

On July 20, 1993, Elaine returned to England for
her sister's wedding. Davis couldn't meet her at the
airport, but he met her at her mother's in Harrogate.
He was alone; Noël, he said, was in Scotland. Elaine
wanted to talk about the Canada situation, but Davis
suggested she get her feet on the ground first and
they'd discuss it in a few days.

Elaine broke into tears. "I don't want to go back
there!"

"So what are we going to do, then?" Davis asked.
"Come on, Elaine, give Ron a second chance. Every
man deserves a second chance — go back! I'm hoping you'll go back to him."

"No, I'm not going back. I'm so unhappy."

Davis tried to persuade her to move away from
Harrogate, if not to Canada, then to Italy. After all,
she had enjoyed her time there.

Within a week of her sister's wedding, Davis himself moved away, telling Elaine that he was first going
to Scotland, then to France. He didn't leave her a
phone number, just a postal box number in London.

"I was very depressed, living in my mom's house.
Just plodding, really. Looking at jobs I couldn't get."
She was on prescription drugs for her depression and
under the care of a psychologist and a psychiatrist.
Davis phoned every ten days or so, to ask how she was.

In April 1994, she did go to Italy, to teach English to a family, but after three months she returned to Harrogate.

In 1995 Ron wrote to tell her in a letter that he was on his way back to England. Canada had failed. He had lost his job and there was nothing in sight. Besides, he too couldn't stand the long Canadian winters. He called Elaine in June 1995. He was living with his mom. Davis called her, too, voicing his exasperation that Ron had returned. Within a few weeks, however, Davis called her again, rejoicing.

"Ron's got a job! A week back in England and he got a job. I can't believe it." But just a few weeks before Christmas of 1995, Davis rang up once more. "You won't believe it — Ron's lost his job!"

She had last talked with Ronald in May 1996. He was trying to find work in Reading. "He seemed okay. He seemed positive. . ."

Clenahan and Lewis-Clarke left Elaine that afternoon unaware that while they were talking to her Davis had called Clenahan at Paignton CID. Det. Sgt. Bill MacDonald, who picked up the phone, explained that Clenahan was in Harrogate but added quickly that it wasn't on the Platt matter. Davis asked MacDonald to mention to Clenahan that he had phoned. Clearly, the man called Davis was getting a little anxious. MacDonald told Davis that detectives would like to speak with him, just to tie up a few loose ends. Could he meet them in Chelmsford three days from now, on Thursday, October 31, at 4:30 p.m.? Davis agreed.

Seven

TOWARDS ZERO

AFTER DAYS OF sleuthing, Detective Sergeants Redman and MacDonald finally hit pay dirt on Wednesday, October 30, 1996. They had secured a birth registration certificate showing the January 14, 1996, birth of Lillian Clare Platt. The document showed the parents as Ronald Platt, born in Merseyside, and Noël Platt, also known as Elaine Boyes. After meeting with the registrar in Southminster, Essex, Redman and MacDonald discussed arresting the phoney Platt for lying under oath, a modern-day equivalent of the FBI's arrest of Al Capone for tax evasion. At least the fraudulent-oath charge would get them into the Little London Farmhouse, and who knows what else they would find there!

Redman and MacDonald were in the middle of the Essex countryside, returning to Chelmsford, when MacDonald answered his pager. It was Elaine Boyes. She pleaded with MacDonald to call her urgently at work. Redman found a phone booth and MacDonald called. Elaine was scared out of her wits.

Davis was on his way to see her right now. She had told him she knew about Ron's death and he coerced her into meeting him for lunch.

MacDonald calmed her down, then advised her to have lunch with Davis in a public place. She reassured MacDonald that she would take Davis to her workplace coffee shop — lots of people there. Help, MacDonald promised, would be on the way. Then he warned, "Don't give away too much, Elaine. And don't ask any questions." MacDonald jumped into the unmarked police car and told Redman to hit Chelmsford fast. They would call police in Yorkshire and ask them to protect Elaine.

Elaine waited nervously at work for Davis to arrive. She told all her friends there what was going on. She'd been surprised by the call. It had happened so fast.

"Hi, it's me. How are you?" the familiar American voice had asked.

Elaine hesitated, pretended she didn't know who it was.

"It's David!" the voice reminded her. "How are you?"

Elaine didn't have it in her to lie. "I'm not that well, actually," she said. Then she couldn't help herself. The words were out before she could stop them. "Have you heard about Ron?"

"Yes," Davis responded. "It's very sad."

He explained he was calling because he wanted to contact Ron's mother and offer his condolences.

Elaine said she couldn't help him because she didn't have a phone number.

She had been so inquisitive. "Where did Ron go in France?"

"A little place near Bordeaux."

"And how much money did you give him?"

"Two thousand pounds." There was a pause. "What are you doing for lunch?" Davis asked. "Can I come see you?"

Elaine was so frightened of this man. He could be a killer. "Where are you?"

"At the station in Leeds."

"I'm sorry," said Elaine. "I can't stop for lunch. I don't really have breaks."

"Come on, Elaine," he persisted. "They've got to give you tea breaks. It will only take you twenty minutes."

And that was it. She couldn't say no.

Davis arrived in about thirty minutes. Elaine was shaking when she led him into the cafeteria. As if to break the ice, Davis chatted innocently about the coffee shop and how nice it was. But then the talk turned to Ron. Down to business, for both of them.

"How sad," offered Davis. "I shed a tear for him on the train."

"I've been saying prayers at night for him."

Elaine couldn't help being "naughty." There was too much emotion within not to ask the questions. Davis said he'd seen Ron a few times and he had been down and out, just walking the streets.

Elaine was incredulous. This wasn't the meticulous man she had known for thirteen years. She wanted to tell Davis that, but he asked the next question.

"They don't know what happened to Ron. Do they?"

Elaine nervously replied that she didn't know. They hadn't told her much about it. She was about to end the odd meeting and get back to work when he wanted to know, "What do I do about Ron's possessions?"

The answer was obvious to Elaine. "Take them to the police . . ." Then she spoke a bewildered thought. "They don't know where Ron's possessions are?"

Davis didn't respond. It was time to go. He kissed and hugged her and said he'd be back in a couple of weeks.

Shortly after Davis left Elaine, Bill MacDonald was on the phone to her. It was too late for protection, but at least Elaine hadn't come to any harm. Almost simultaneously, Ian Clenahan called MacDonald. The previous day he had secured copies of Davis's mobile phone records, and after cross-referencing them, he found that in June and July of 1996, in the weeks before Ronald Platt's presumed death, Davis had made numerous calls from his mobile phone to the 863 numbers in the South Devon area, but Clenahan dialed the numbers Davis himself had called. The owner of an inn confirmed that a Ronald and David Platt had stayed there for several days in July. A ferrymaster confirmed that the man he knew as Ronald Platt, a tall American or Canadian, owned a sailboat on the River Dart.

MacDonald and Redman, after discussing this latest information, concurred that they should arrest Davis that night on suspicion of murder. They had enough evidence now. Besides, they couldn't risk another incident like the one with Elaine Boyes.

Anticipating that Davis would be returning to Chelmsford by train that night, the pair stood at the end of the platform through the late afternoon and early evening. Redman strained to catch sight of the man he had laid eyes on only once, two months ago. Davis didn't appear, however, and there was no sign of his car, not in the parking lot and not outside the Little London Farmhouse. MacDonald called Sincock. The boss gave the go-ahead to arrest Davis the next morning. They couldn't wait for the afternoon appointment set up by MacDonald three days ago. Besides, Davis might not even show. Surely he was anxious after his meeting with Elaine Boyes.

Later, Redman, with MacDonald at his side, again knocked on the door of the pretty little cottage he had once mistaken for the Little London Farmhouse. The two detectives filled Frank and Audrey in: tomorrow they would arrest the Platts upon suspicion of murder.

At the detective's request, Audrey led them to the second floor. They wanted to see if they could use Audrey and Frank's place to put surveillance on the Little London Farmhouse. There was no view, however, from any of the windows. Undeterred, MacDonald and Redman came up with a plan to arrest Davis the following morning, October 31.

Eight

PARTNERS IN CRIME

BACK ON OCTOBER 14, 1996, Audrey Mossman and Frank Johnson had no idea that their brief encounter with the man who knocked on the wrong door shifted a police murder probe into high gear. Even though unannounced visitors were few and far between in Woodham Walter, especially on secluded Raven Hall Lane, Audrey hadn't given the policeman a second thought. She was so engrossed in other things that she didn't even think of mentioning it to her next-door neighbours, Ron and Noël Platt, when they returned in late October from a trip to Devon. Besides, the Platts were far more interesting than anyone who visited them. She was intrigued and amused by the odd couple and often found herself thinking back to the first meeting with them, when they moved into the Little London Farmhouse in September 1994.

A mix of genuine warmth, curiosity and rural practicality prompted Audrey and Frank to introduce themselves to the newcomers as they unloaded a rental van. It was so exciting for them that someone was moving into the Little London Farmhouse again; it had been left uninhabited and in disrepair since an elderly couple moved out in the late 1970s. Audrey and Frank adored their dreamy old cottage on Raven Hall Lane, they loved being tucked away in such a hidden corner of Woodham Walter. They also loved each other's company. But like many isolated country people, Audrey and Frank found that without others around life could get boring, lonely, even depressing. Now that the landlord had brought the Little London Farmhouse back to liveability and people were moving in, Frank and Audrey hoped they could form a cordial friendship with the new arrivals.

Summer's warmth was fading fast and the autumnal dampness would soon be at hand, but the sun was out and it was a near-perfect day as Audrey and Frank walked the three score yards up the lane to where the moving van was parked. Frank, who had lost any shyness through his war years in Palestine as an engineer with the British Eighth Army and for decades after as a large fruit crop grower, gave the man, likely in his late forties or early fifties, and the woman, about seventeen or eighteen, a hearty welcome and introduced himself and his "friend," Audrey.

"We're not married, you see . . . but we've lived together for twenty years," Frank stated bluntly, explaining why he hadn't introduced Audrey as his wife. It was always best to tell the truth, he believed. That way you didn't get caught up in any lies.

When the man dismissed Frank's concern, Frank and Audrey heard an American accent. With a firm shake of the hand, he told them his name was Ron Platt, then introduced the young woman as Noël, his wife, and the little girl Noël held as their daughter, Emily. Given that the woman was wife and mother, Frank decided she must be a young-looking twenty-five. That still made for a large age gap, but it was not uncommon for an older man and a younger woman to live together these days, especially not in modern Essex, where it had become almost predictable for middle-aged men in a second marriage. As they spoke, Frank noted that the young woman was nervous; she paced back and forth, clutching her child to her chest. He also noted that the couple had brought very little furniture with them.

"We've been around here a long time," Audrey said. "Anything we can do, anything you want to know, just ask."

The newcomers didn't seem to need any help at that moment, so with this short welcome, purposefully kept brief so they would not be a nuisance on what was obviously a busy day, Audrey and Frank bade their new neighbours good day and returned home.

Raven Hall Lane had once served the farming settlement of Little London. Still with the same red-dirt surface it must have had all through the centuries, the lane lies atop a ridge that slopes gently down a few hundred yards of grain fields to become the south bank of the Chelmer River. Four homes stand in what once was Little London. The first on the lane is the plain white stucco Little London Farmhouse; immediately next door, to the west, is Frank and Audrey's quaint Little London House. Around a slight zig-zag, a dilapidated wood house sits abandoned; at the end of the lane is the impressive Ravens.

The front windows of the Little London House and the Little London Farmhouse offer a splendid pastoral view. The sloping farm fields and meandering Chelmer were visible from the couch where Frank and Audrey sat when they first entertained the Platts. It was a week or so after Christmas and the festive spirit was still alive; Frank and Audrey had invited the Platts over for holiday drinks. The ancient living room's log fire crackled warmth as Emily played contentedly on the floor with building bricks and a Noah's Ark toy. Ron Platt sat on a chair by the fire telling his hosts about his past life in big finance, how he used to run back and forth between Switzerland and the United States doing various deals. While her husband did all the talking, Noël lay on the floor, opting to stay out of the adult conversation; she obviously preferred having fun with her daughter.

Audrey, a mother and a grandmother herself, surveyed the room with satisfaction. The lunch had gone over just fine. When the topic switched briefly from finances to Emily, Audrey saw her chance to bring Noël into the gathering.

"So, will you be having any more children?" she asked Ron Platt, but directed her look at Noël.

"Oh, we want four," Platt answered quickly, beaming.

Audrey chuckled. "Well, jolly good," she said, at the same time thinking what an unbearable workload four children would be.

Noël didn't even look up. She continued to play with Emily as if she herself were an infant friend.

"So you switched from finance to counselling?" asked Frank, picking up his earlier conversation with Platt.

"I took over the setup of a counselling business in Brentwood. I'm in control and I'm looking after the premises," Platt responded, a glass of his favourite port in hand. "The partners are delighted with how it's working out. At the end of the year they had quite a share-out and I was paid lots of money."

His main job, he went on, was to meet representatives from local councils and health authorities and negotiate terms for how his lecturers and counsellors got paid. Workshops had already been held in Aberdeen, Harrogate and the Orkney Islands. He pointed out that he not only took care of business affairs but also did counselling himself, for he was a registered psychotherapist.

"But what a change," Audrey chipped in.

"I want to help people," Platt explained. After all those years in finance he had concluded that it was soulless. He didn't get any joy out of helping people make money any more, but he enjoyed resolving their emotional troubles.

In the late afternoon, after several more ports and cups of tea, Ron, Noël and Emily Platt went home, leaving behind a good impression. Although Frank had some reservations about Platt, he felt he was trustworthy. Audrey saw he was a good dresser, carried himself well and was very charming. He had a knack of knowing what to say and when to say it. She, too, judged him to be sincere. Audrey and Frank chatted briefly about the age gap, and how Noël was so quiet and didn't appear to have much fun with the adults, but they quickly dropped the topic as they busied themselves with tidying up.

In the ensuing weeks, Audrey became aware of the early goings and late comings of Ron Platt. He was out of the house before nine and seldom returned until eight or nine at night. It was apparent that Noël could not drive and was essentially trapped at home with a youngster the whole day long. All she did was look after the house and go for daily walks with Emily. Audrey was puzzled that nobody ever visited; it was just Ron, Noël, Emily and the family cat. She felt sorry for Noël, who seemed so lacking in the verve and vitality women in their early twenties usually have.

As winter of 1994 turned into spring, Audrey tried her motherly best to bond with Noël and offer her friendship. Whenever she saw the young woman in the yard she would make a point of talking with her, perhaps offer a cup of tea. She always fussed over Emily, who was forever in the tightly hugging arms of her mother. But Noël didn't return the kindness. She would answer questions with a curt yes or no. She gave the impression she was self-sufficient and wasn't interested in stepping outside her small world. Once Audrey chatted with her for six hours and barely learned anything except that Noël came from New York. After a few doses of the near-silent treatment, Audrey began to think she might be poking her nose where it wasn't wanted. She tried to stop being so concerned. Perhaps the gut feeling she had about Noël and solitude was all in her head. Maybe she should just butt out. Maybe Noël wasn't too young for her, but she was too old for Noël.

Frank's attempts to make contact with Noël also fell on rocky ground. Although she obviously loved her child and gave her much affection, her soul seemed deeply buried. Frank found himself turned off. "Every time I speak with her," he told Audrey, "I have to keep the conversation going. It's not like a normal talk people can enjoy." Frank noted that Emily was very quiet, just like her mother. He wondered aloud to Audrey one day whether something might be wrong with the child, "You know . . . slow." Audrey scolded him and reminded him that all children were different. At some point Emily would come out of her shell.

The budding relationship with Platt, however, didn't falter. In contrast to his wife, Platt could talk your ear off. He was a decent neighbour too. Once, when Audrey's car was stuck in a snowdrift, Platt helped her push it out. When Frank asked Platt to trim the hedge between the two properties, he took care of it instantly and with gusto.

In mid-April, Platt, Noël and Emily were around at their neighbours' again, eating and drinking wine. Platt talked of money and of how money could make more money. This struck a chord with Frank. Although he had ensured his son's future by handing over his fruit crop business, he had yet to arrange his monetary investments so his two daughters would also benefit from his estate. Frank concluded that Platt, the self-professed financial wizard, could help him, so he asked Platt if he could invest money on his behalf and get him the kind of returns Platt had spoken about in the winter. Sure, Platt said, indicating that with a bit of good luck Frank could expect to make about 15 per cent all told. With this simple assurance, Frank signed a personal cheque for £200,000 and turned it over to his new neighbour. Platt then signed a receipt indicating he would retain the money for three years; it would all be returned in April 1998.

"The whole time the principal will be earning interest, Frank, so if you need money I could get the interest out for you. Now, you let me know."

Twelve months later, Frank needed some money. Sure enough, Platt gave him a £20,000 cheque, written on a personal account in Harrogate. Platt had made him 10 per cent in only one year. Sometime afterward Platt turned over another £5,000 — more reason for Frank to trust his neighbour.

But one day Frank left a sealed envelope with Noël, and in it a note to Platt about financial matters. As Frank was driving home down Raven Hall Lane that evening he saw Noël walking with Emily. He stopped and asked if she had given Ron the letter. Noël's answer made it clear that not only had Platt seen the letter but she, too, had read it. Frank was shocked at the breach in confidence. When he confronted Platt later, the American acknowledged that telling Noël had been a mistake and he promised it would never happen again.

That spring and summer, Audrey and Frank took up their passion for gardening, as they did every year. Audrey felt great pride in tending the flowers that turned their yard into a palette of colour. White and purple heather, red camellias, white and red rose bushes lit up the front garden. Purple, orange and yellow wallflowers bedecked the house's rear walls, while bright green ivy cascaded over the six-foot backyard fence. There were wild cherry, pear, greengage plum and walnut trees as well. At one time Audrey and Frank had grown their own vegetables, but that had become too much work at their age. The Platts, in contrast, made no attempt to beautify the Little London Farmhouse, apart from a few window boxes that didn't add much to the property. Much of Noël's time and effort that summer seemed to be spent on household chores, Emily and cutting the 75- by 50-yard patch of open lawn at the rear and side of the house. Platt had bought a mower, but it was Noël who cut the lawn every few days. Frank and Audrey would hear the mower's drone for hours as Noël struggled to get the job done. Frank was puzzled about why Platt hadn't done as he had and paid someone £40 a month to cut the grass.

To the east of the Little London houses stands Orchard Bungalow, owned by social worker Marion Jones and her husband, Ed, a telecommunications specialist. The Joneses, too, were perplexed by the goings-on at the Platt house. Initially, the couple had been delighted to meet the Platts. Americans! How novel, thought Marion, especially in a backwater like Woodham Walter. She had always adored Americans because they were so outgoing and energetic, so modern. And baby Emily was so beautiful, with her chubby face and those big brown eyes just like her mother's. Ed and Marion were not nosy people, but they didn't have to be to learn all about the Platts' affairs. Ron told them almost everything about himself within one or two meetings: he was from Liverpool but his parents had emigrated to Canada when he was ten; he had moved from Devon to Essex to take a counselling job in Brentwood; he was once in financial investing and his work had taken him across Europe, but he was now retired. When Platt had first moved into the Little London Farmhouse, he had spoken with glee about his new rural surroundings and gushed about the visit he and Noël had had with Martin and Vicky Emmett at the Ravens and about the massive fireplace in their home. Marion took from Platt's comments on the Emmett house that he was most impressionable. Noël, on the other hand, struck her as a bit of a wallflower.

Marion frequently saw Noël and Emily taking walks along the public right-of-way and into the apple orchard at the rear of their home. One day Marion invited them into her garden. From that moment on they became friends, albeit in an arm's-length way.

The more Marion got to know Noël, the more she became as concerned as Audrey about their American neighbour. She sensed that perhaps Noël was so quiet and introspective because she was having a terrible time adapting to British rural life. They spent many hours together, but Marion could not call Noël a friend, only an acquaintance. Still, she wanted to respond to this young woman, whom she felt needed human contact. Noël intrigued her. She could not understand how a young American woman could not drive a car, how a young American woman could be so passive.

"Why don't you drive?" Marion once asked her.

"One day I will, hopefully soon," Noël replied. As it was, she said, Ron took her shopping in nearby Chelmsford every Thursday night.

And that was the end of the conversation. There was no point pressing any further. If Noël was satisfied to be left at home all day and to be chauffeured around at her husband's whim, what more was there to say?

Trying to bring Noël out of her shell, Marion would focus on Emily, who charmed her no end. They would talk about Emily walking, Emily talking, Emily eating. Every chat, it seemed, was oriented to the child. Noël didn't reveal much about herself, except that her parents were from New York and she had grown up there. She said in her nasal twang that she and Ron and Emily had met her parents in Scotland the year before. Marion noted that when Noël talked about Ron she wasn't very animated. Still, years of experience working as a social services counsellor had taught her to listen and give support, not invade where she might not be wanted. If Noël didn't want to divulge anything more, she thought, then that was fine.

Marion made many attempts to integrate the Platts into the community. In the summer of 1995 she offered to take them to the yacht club at Blackwater, knowing Platt had a yacht in Devon that he wanted to bring to Essex. Unfortunately, Platt pulled out of the day's events because he had a counselling workshop, but she took Noël and Emily anyway. Noël seemed excited about all the family activities at the yacht club, but Platt never followed up. That summer, the constant whirring of the gas mower drifted across the field and into Marion's kitchen. Marion and Ed felt that at least mowing the lawn gave her something to do. Noël also stacked the logs for the fire. Whenever the Joneses socialized with the Platts they sensed an element of servitude that kept the young woman under her older husband's control. Marion went over Noël's situation again and again, but she could not single out one instance that would cause alarm. Some things, however, were clear: Noël was home all day; she never had any money or control of any cash. Despite her solitude, despite the possibility of depression, Marion noted, Noël neither drank nor smoked.

Marion introduced the Platts to the members of a small private tennis club in the nearby hamlet of Little Baddow. Platt was keen to play, and the tennis players were delighted at the prospect of a new member and paid Platt close attention at the club's first summer picnic. Committee members Paul and Philippa Hibbert tried to make Platt and his young wife feel welcome. Hearing that Noël was a mother, Philippa tried to break the ice, by asking who babysat for her and whether her daughter was well behaved. Noël's answers were terse, and instead of answering directly, she would look at her husband as if to get his approval to speak. When Platt told Philippa he was a psychologist she was intrigued. She loved the subject and began barraging him with questions. He seemed uncomfortable.

"It's fascinating," she said to Platt, "what happens to the mind. There is so much we don't understand about ourselves and why we do things."

But Platt didn't take the conversation much

further. She noted the absence of the usual knowledge, even the jargon.

Marion learned that an American artist friend of
hers was in Britain on a summer vacation and would
visit her. She saw a possible friend for Noël, since
Ron had told her he met Noël, the daughter of a best
friend, while she was in Britain attending Chelsea Art
College. Ron said his friend had asked him to keep
an eye on his daughter, but after they met, he said,
romance had flourished. When Marion and her friend
visited, however, they found Noël looking awfully pale.
She appeared tense as the artist inquired whether she
missed New York and where she had lived, and broke
off the conversation by asking if they wanted refresh-
ments. Back at Orchard Bungalow, Marion's friend
said, "She's not from New York! No way! She's with
the CIA or something." The woman badgered Marion
to tell her more about Platt and his wife. Something
didn't add up, she said.

Marion knew instinctively she was right, but
couldn't put her finger on what.

In various talks with Noël, Marion learned that
she would frequently stay up until two in the morning
ironing Ron's shirts until they were perfect. While
Noël dressed in jeans and T-shirts and looked per-
petually worn out, Ron was always smartly turned out.
He told his neighbours he shopped at Fortnum and
Mason in Piccadilly and Harrods in Knightsbridge.

One day, Marion and Audrey got together and
joked about how on earth Noël could stay with Ron.

"How does she put up with all this? What does she get out of it?" Marion asked Audrey, not out of spite but amazement. Such a beautiful young woman could have young men tripping all over her and treating her like gold.

Audrey was beginning to distrust Platt. She disliked his arrogance. Whenever she and Frank were alone and Platt's name came up, she referred to him as Mr. Know It All.

Ed Jones felt that Ron Platt tried hard to impress, in the way he dressed, acted and talked. It was all just too much. Ed, perhaps because of his own modesty, found it especially difficult to comprehend why Platt would boast so openly about his prowess on the stock market. As far as Ed was concerned, people who did well in life usually didn't brag. Ed and Marion had felt sorry for Platt when he told them he had to leave international finance because the stress was killing him, but were put off by how he stretched points to show how knowledgeable he was about money. He led you to believe he was well versed in other areas, too, but when you pressed him for detail, his knowledge was actually limited. He would talk about fine wines, for example, but when a discussion ensued it became obvious he knew only the brand he liked. He talked about plants, but when Marion, with her expertise, questioned him further, he could not answer her. He presented himself as a man of intelligence and refinement, but if you spent some time speaking with him and an inexpert bore emerged. Clearly, he was immature, with a great need to have people around and to be liked.

One night, Ed and Platt went to the quaint and cosy Cats Pub, about a mile's walk away down a winding country road. After downing a pint, they were returning home in the dark when Platt brought Ed's attention to the glow in the sky from the lights on the ground. He then droned on and on about light pollution and viciously attacked human development. Platt's intensity struck Ed as very odd. Still, he had enjoyed the drink with his neighbour, and a month or so later he phoned Platt on a Friday night to see if he would like a beer at the Queen Victoria Pub. Platt hemmed and hawed but sounded amenable. Then Ed chipped in that as a former finance man Platt would enjoy meeting the publican, Allan Smith, a former Citibank employee. After all, Platt had mentioned that he worked for Citibank at one point.

All of a sudden Platt's tenor changed. "No, sorry. I can't go 'cause I have a meeting," he said.

When Ed hung up he wondered why Platt had so suddenly realized he had a meeting — a Friday night meeting, to boot. Was it something Ed had said? Did Platt find him boring? Or did he have some reason for not wanting to meet Allan Smith?

On August 9, 1995, Platt invited Ed and Marion to Little London Farmhouse for a meal. Platt had learned that this day was Marion's fiftieth birthday and he fêted the event with unrestrained gusto. After dinner he presented Marion with a framed photograph of Little London Farmhouse taken for him by his babysitter. Marion appreciated the attention he bestowed on her on such a milestone birthday, but she found it odd that his gift was something someone had given him. An odd fellow indeed.

That same summer of 1995, Frank Johnson was enjoying a splendid day in the garden when he heard a "Hi, Frank." Ron Platt, decked out in business wear, as usual approached him.

"Hello, Ron. How are you?"

"Fine."

"And how is Noël?"

"She's pregnant — she's pregnant," Platt announced, barely able to contain his excitement. "Isn't that good? We're having another baby."

After Platt made his way to his car, Frank told Audrey who wasn't in the least surprised. After all, hadn't Ron said he and Noël were having four children?

Platt wasn't long in telling Ed and Marion Jones about Noël's pregnancy. By this time, so many things had happened the Joneses put little credence in what the Platts said and did. It troubled Marion that Ron and Noël were all by themselves. In the past year or so there had been no visitors at the Little London Farmhouse, and Noël never talked about her mom and dad in New York. Nor did it appear that either Noël or Emily was getting mail or gifts from her family.

There was similar talk between Audrey and Frank. Audrey had became a grandmother in 1990 and she doted on her daughter's child. Where were Emily's grandparents?

"Will your parents come over to see Emily and the new baby?" Audrey asked Noël.

"Oh, yes," she answered, then in her usual way didn't elaborate.

"When will they come?" Audrey inquired.

"They're going to Scotland and we'll visit them there."

"That will be lovely . . . But if they're in Scotland, why don't they just come down to Essex and stay with you here? There's lots of room in the house."

Noël never got around to answering her.

Lillian Platt was born at tiny St. Peter's College Hospital in Maldon, in January 1996. Marion told Noël in the days leading up to the birth that if she needed any help she would be by her side. But before any of the neighbours knew it, Noël was in and out of hospital and back home with the baby. Marion found out Noël was home only when she phoned Ron to ask about the birth and if Noël was comfortable in the hospital.

"Everything was fine," Platt told her.

"Oh. Lovely! When did she give birth?"

"Yesterday."

"And she's home already? That was quick."

"Yes, Noël got up and walked right out of there after the birth. They told us she walked out quicker than anybody else ever had. She discharged herself very quickly."

Marion offered assistance, but Platt declined. He could manage. If things got tough, he would take the baby to work with him and look after her himself. He reminded Marion that he had fathered several kids and he knew what he was doing.

Just before Lily was born, the Platts took Emily to a local nursery school, where she attended two days a week. Pam Seear, operator of the Spring Elms Day Care Centre, enjoyed having Emily in her care. The little girl was well balanced and very nice, thought Seear. She mingled easily with her young friends. The Platts were no problem, either; they paid their fees promptly by cheque. After Lily was born, Noël asked Seear if she could bump up Emily's time because the little girl seemed to enjoy the day care so much. In the summer of 1996, a spot came open and Seear could accommodate the extra days. But now Noël procrastinated; she didn't want Emily to feel pushed out of the house to make way for her baby sister.

Seear was warmed by Ron Platt's apparent love for Emily. He would bring her in in the mornings, take off her coat and change her outdoor shoes for indoor play shoes. Typically, the little girl would ooze out some loving words for "Daddy." There was little doubt in Seear's mind that both parents loved Emily and Emily loved her parents.

Nine

UNFINISHED PORTRAIT

IT HAD TAKEN Isabel Rogers four years of arduous, sometimes tedious part-time study to finally gain a therapy diploma. Now, with her academic counselling training finished, she was eager to apply her skills. She had a genuine interest in helping people identify some of the deep-rooted issues that dragged them down, and help them on their way to a more fulfilling life. Her short-term sights were set on joining other professionals in a practice, but one day she wanted her own office. A final hurdle remained before she finished her training; she had to experience therapy from a client's perspective.

With this in mind, Isabel called Brentwood-based Solutions Focused Therapy — or Solutions In Therapy, as it was also called — thinking the seminar group's focus on "the now" would not only fill the technical requirements for her diploma but would also be interesting. Besides, Brentwood was only a few miles from her home. In the back of Isabel's mind was the slim possibility that the partnership might hire her in an intern capacity.

A Ron Platt returned her call and invited her to his office for the client-perspective session; Platt told Isabel he would give her three sessions, each fifty minutes. She would have to pay, of course. Although nervous, Isabel was looking forward to the session and was confident that she would do well if an interview ensued. An attractive, dark-haired woman in her early twenties, Isabel opted to wear a smart business outfit. If her therapist was a man, she reckoned, a hard-boiled business appearance might get her more respect and avoid any gender games. Above all else, Isabel wanted to be taken seriously and viewed as a professional therapist.

Following the directions Platt had given over the telephone, Isabel found herself outside a renovated two-storey building in a road just off the Brentwood high street. A bit off the beaten track, she thought, but perfect for the discretion and anonymity that therapists try to offer and clients typically demand. The unobtrusive sign at the front of the building would be noticed only by those who came looking for it.

Isabel was surprised to enter only a one-room office. It wasn't much to look at. A desk and a computer were on one side of the small room and a couch and chairs beside the only window on the other side. Clearly, the administrative and counselling functions could not be physically separated. Certainly it wasn't the best setup, but it would work.

There was, by contrast, nothing penurious in Ron Platt's demeanour as he greeted Isabel with a firm handshake and a warm voice and encouraged her to sit down and make herself comfortable. Despite wearing a conservative business suit, the tall, dark-haired man seemed relaxed, even casual, about their meeting. As he seated himself across from Isabel and opened the conversation, her ears immediately picked up an American accent. That was unusual in these rural parts. But her eyes found something even more striking: a white fringe just above Platt's ears and at the bottom of his sideburns. He dyed his hair! And it was such an awful job. She subdued a chuckle and forced herself to shift her focus.

This outgoing American came across as an impressive fellow as he told her of his passion for psychotherapy and his belief in what the group was doing, augmenting his words with gesticulating hands and sincere facial expressions. But when it came time for the therapy session and Platt began his spiel, Isabel immediately realized how little acquainted he was with his subject. She plucked up her courage and told this near stranger of all the problems in her life, from her upbringing at the hands of strict Baptists to the trauma and lasting effects of the teenage years to issues over relationships. Like her own future clients would, Isabel experienced total vulnerability. Once she had finished baring her soul and Platt's turn came, she concluded that she knew more about therapy theories than did her would-be mentor. The mod-

ule he used on Isabel was so brief, so basic. Platt's
method was prefaced by his belief that quick-fix therapy could work; Isabel had sought an in-depth psy-
chodynamic model that would delve into the issues
that create fundamental character. When Isabel
brought herself to ask Platt about his training, he
admitted he had taken only a six-month part-time
introductory course at the Iron Mill Centre in Devon
and a four-day session with the Solutions In Therapy
founders. He explained that his partners had brought
the therapy model from Milwaukee. Designed for
American soldiers returning from war, it was a brief,
solution-focused therapy that revolved around half a
dozen steps; there were so many soldiers and so few
therapists that a brief model had to be used. Her
instinct had been right. She was disappointed, yet she
did appreciate his honesty.

Platt shrugged off her obvious dismay. When the
therapy session had ended he continued to barrage
Isabel with questions, most of them personal, and it
became clear to her that Platt had a limited understanding of professional boundaries. In short order
he had elicited confirmation that she was single and
was pumping her for more details of her life. He
seemed anxious to keep her talking. When she had
mentioned her Baptist upbringing, Platt had seized
control and told her that he, too, had been a Baptist
and had at one time been torn over whether to
become a minister. He had abandoned that path,
however, because he didn't feel he should work on

Sundays. This didn't make sense to Isabel. How could such a small point interfere with a faith strong enough for him to entertain a lifetime commitment to the church?

About forty-five minutes into the meeting, Platt suddenly asked her what she wanted to do with her career.

"I want to join a practice," Isabel asserted.

"I'll get you in here, but I won't tell the other partners. You could work one day a week in the office to start. It won't be part of the practice, but you can help me with my job. Instead of the practice paying you, I'll pay you myself. That will be a start and it can grow from there."

Isabel was dumbfounded. This offer, part-time though it was, had come so fast, so unexpectedly.

Perhaps sensing her disbelief, Platt told her that attitude and outlook were more important to him than experience. He said he wanted to work with enthusiastic people. Why not leave it a couple of weeks, he suggested, then he would call her with a start date. The partners wouldn't want anybody to join on such short notice, he added, but she should leave it to him to introduce her into the business gradually and within six months she would be a full partner. He let slip that the partners were keeping him back, and he wanted to move on with fresh people and fresh ideas.

"You determine the wages," he finished nonchalantly.

Isabel left the office on cloud nine.

It took only a couple of days for Platt to call.

"When can you come in to work?" he asked.

"I'll start as soon as possible," Isabel said, excited at her good fortune.

"I'll get some keys cut within the week. Can you start in two weeks, one day each week?"

"I'll give it my consideration," she said.

Isabel saw that working with the firm, even if it was unofficial and under the wing of a barely qualified mentor, would add hands-on experience to her education. She also knew that the other partners were already working as full-time therapists, which likely meant they would not have time to do all the major work, and golden opportunities would come her way. She returned to the office to complete her therapy sessions. Again, she bared her soul to this man, presuming that everything she said would be held in confidence. That was the way it had to be in therapy; there was no room for negotiation. In the second and third sessions she was taken aback when Platt extended the session past the fifty minutes until he arbitrarily declared it over. To Isabel's surprise, he then billed her for the overtime. Still, this was such a terrific opportunity, and she told Platt she'd take the job.

Within a few weeks, he had introduced her to the partners, Ian Marsh, Ron Wilgosh and David Hawkes. The men worked for local health authorities and hospitals but as a side interest conducted seminars that taught that therapists were meant not just to listen to problems but perhaps to assist their clients in finding solutions. After a couple of meetings, she learned that Platt had been with the partners only a few months. He had approached them after reading an article about them in the *Daily Mail*. After going through a four-day course, he suggested that he be their business manager. He would also help them with financing to help them boost their little business, and they could pay him back if the business turned a profit. They had accepted. But before they could even blink he had moved from Devon to Essex. Now Platt arranged the seminars and the partners did the teaching. From Isabel's viewpoint, everything seemed to be working out well. And the partners seemed reasonably happy with the situation. After that, she didn't see much of the partners, who, as she had anticipated, were so busy with their day-to-day duties and so confident in Platt that they were unaware that he was remunerating her out of his own pocket. He confided to Isabel that at some point he intended to recoup from the partners the wages he'd paid her.

In those first few weeks in the office, Platt set Isabel to work on administrative tasks — returning telephone calls, mailing pamphlets and helping him set up seminars. She found him a very mysterious person; he hardly told her of his movements and yet she was under strict orders never to reveal his whereabouts to anyone. He demanded to be informed immediately of any telephone calls. It was most important, he stressed, to respond quickly to business calls. He backed up his decree by calling the office three or four times a day when he was away to pick up any messages.

Because there were two Rons in the company, Platt would tell his clients that if they wanted to speak to him when they telephoned, they should ask for "Ron the Voice." The confusion wasn't only with the clients, however. Sometimes Ron Wilgosh would get a telephone call at his day job and the familiar American voice would say, "May I speak with Ron Platt, please?" "But you're Ron Platt!" Wilgosh would respond. Platt would give profuse apologies and tell Wilgosh he had been daydreaming and in another world. The joke got around among the partners that Ron Platt sometimes tried to talk to himself.

Isabel soon learned that Platt liked to inject humour into his seminars. It was his way of trying to make people comfortable. Because of his height, his dyed black moustache and his erect posture, he bore some resemblance to John Cleese of Monty Python fame. And he would imitate Cleese's famous goose-step walk in Python's Ministry of Silly Walks skit. This went over well with students who were raised with British comedy.

Within a month, the one-day-a-week gig expanded to two days. Again Platt said, "You name your own wages." So Isabel did. And he paid her cash out of his own pocket.

In those early days, Platt kept his distance from

Isabel. He didn't reveal much about himself, save for telling her he had been born in Liverpool, had spent most of his years in Vermont and had worked for many years in international finance. He had returned to England only recently and turned his attention to psychology, a subject that had always fascinated him. He told her he had obtained a degree from the University of Edinburgh. The only personal details he shared with Isabel surrounded his second wife, Noël, who he said was much younger than he, and their two-year-old child, Emily. Noël seemed so devoted to her husband that she would call several times a day. Platt would greet her calls with "Hi, Sweetie" and would end them with "I love you." Isabel thought Noël seemed nice, though she wasn't much of a conversationalist. At first blush, Platt came across as a happy-go-lucky American whose dreams had all come true. He had a career, money galore, a beautiful young wife, a lovely kid and, according to him, a gorgeous old house in the country.

Often Platt would disappear, telling Isabel he was off to London for the day. Then he would telephone her from his office, sometimes as many as four times a day. He called so often that Isabel never had a reason to ask him for a number where she could reach him. Other times he would call in the morning and tell her he was staying home for the day. Yet later in the day, Noël would call, asking Isabel if he was in the office or if she had seen him.

"What are you doing?" she quizzed Platt one day, referring to his frequent London trips.

"I have clients and friends who are giving me money to invest. I invest it for them, along with my own money," he said, then told her about his company, Cavendish.

Isabel, who knew little of such matters, asked how it worked and how he got paid.

"You have to realize, Isabel," he replied in a lecturing tone, "people give you their money 'cause they don't know what they're doing. I tell them how much they are getting as a return — they don't tell me!"

His personal lectures to Isabel continued. He told her of his strategies that had brought him success in finance and how that business success had made his life. "Why," he offered, "you could enjoy the same if you really wanted it." One day he boasted about stacks of gold bars he had stashed away, because, he said, he was wary of English banks. He loved gold. It was liquid. It was safe. The banks, on the other hand, used people by using their money to enrich themselves. People thought they were getting good interest rates, he mocked, when in fact they were being used. Gold, he said, would back his plan to open a series of one-stop therapy outlets across Britain. He told her that when he lived in America he had established ten businesses while investing in the stock market. Perhaps she should become a partner with him. Noël, he said, would like that. By this point Isabel had become quite familiar with Noël; in her daily calls to Platt, she quoted what he said were the latest stock prices.

"If we leave the partners and go on our own, you would have an equal share of the business and an equal say in the decisions," Platt told Isabel. Noël, he said, had been pushing him to make Isabel the first female partner in his new company.

This plan was pretty far-fetched, Isabel decided. Platt was a great talker, but could he pull it off? She didn't think so.

Whenever he was in the office, Platt would tune the radio to London's Classic FM station. Often he would stop whatever he was doing, flop down onto one of the comfortable therapy chairs and gaze out the window. He would pontificate about life and the therapy profession while Isabel tried to work on the computer. Isabel began to realize that she was doing everything; Platt would mainly answer the telephone, fetch sandwiches for lunch and listen to classical music. Sometimes after lunch he would light up a cigarette, always a Marlboro. More than once during a day he would suddenly ask Isabel to cease her work.

"Let's just stop and listen to this music and how romantic it is."

Romance, Platt had her believe, was most important. When Isabel commented on his expressive personality, he told her that more than one woman had remarked that he should not be doing therapy but should teach men courses on how to be romantic, because he was one of the most romantic men these women had ever met. Isabel was surprised he would say this. While he was expressive, passionate even, he wouldn't log too high on the Renaissance-man scale. Sometimes tears would well in his eyes as they listened to music, and he would emotionally tell of his fondness for a certain movement. During one music appreciation session, as they were listening to Rachmaninoff's Second Piano Concerto, he spoke quietly of his love of the first movement, his love of his children, and then he turned around to Isabel with tears rolling down his cheeks and told her bluntly, "And I love you, too!" Isabel was so shocked that she just wheeled on her chair, stared into the computer screen and pretended nothing had happened.

Shortly after his not-too-subtle pass, Isabel confided to Platt that she had been dating a man, Neil, and she liked him so much she was contemplating a future with him. Good, Platt said, adding that everyone needed love in their life. "What does he do?" he inquired. He almost barked when she said that Neil was a police officer.

"You can't trust cops," he said in a vinegar tone. "They're all the same." He then interrogated her on her new beau, about his personality, his maturity. He was behaving like an overzealous father.

To her disbelief, Platt advised her to break off the relationship and find another man. He came up with all kinds of reasons why a relationship with a police officer was doomed to fail. Isabel was furious about his hostility; he had not so much as laid an eye on

Neil, who, thought Isabel, was a considerate, gentle and loving man. Even when she became engaged to Neil, still Platt urged her to dump him. She found his attitude outrageous and believed Platt was simply jealous. There was certainly reason for her to think that. Whenever Platt took her out for dinner he wined and dined her and showed her off in a way that would have onlookers think they were a couple. He even put his arm around her a few times but then withdrew it after a few seconds when he realized her discomfort. Whenever Isabel wore a close-cut suit or a skirt and jacket, he would comment on how he liked it; he would also compliment her perfume, her hair. She felt he was trying to flatter her, but at other times he openly confessed that it made him feel good that other men would see him with such a beautiful woman who dressed so well. And when he was with her he even pointed out other women whom he thought looked attractive because of their clothes.

But he seemed jaded about his own life.

"When you live with a woman a long time, she stops looking like that," he lamented.

It was frustrating for Isabel to have her boss notice only her looks and her clothes — or those of other women. She felt he saw women only as fantasy images, not as individual free-thinking people, real people. Although in 1996 he sent her a Valentine's card with the words "Love, Ron," to her relief he never made another pass like the one in the office.

Over time, Isabel became a little fed up with

Platt's boasting and exaggerating and fascination with the grandiose, but she quietly put up with it. In college she had studied male behaviour and was aware that some males acted in ways they thought would attract women to them; it was an unconscious thing. She knew that as long as she stuck it out at the partnership she would be okay. Isabel had her own ideas of what was important and could leave Platt at the drop of a hat.

At a professional level, she fought with Platt over boundaries. He was of the opinion that therapists and clients didn't have to meet in a sterile office for a session. Rather, they should meet over coffee in their own office, over tea in their house or over a beer in their favourite pub. He would passionately wave aside Isabel's arguments that therapists and clients needed to be protected from any form of social relationship.

Often she accompanied him for lunch at the Café Rouge, a chic restaurant in Brentwood. After downing a few wines, he would talk for hours. He was an unabashed anti-authoritarian. He made it clear that he was religious, but he argued a strict refusal to conform to societal rules, even the church's. He had his own code of life, he said, and only he would sort it out, nobody else. If people told him he couldn't do something, then he'd do it just to spite them. Whenever the subject of ethics came up, he would launch into a self-righteous tirade.

"Nobody demands anything of me," he challenged. "If they do, then all hell will break loose."

Isabel found his attitude hard to reconcile with his station in life as a therapist. What on earth was he teaching his clients?

After a few wines one day, Platt told Isabel that he had the power to manipulate people and engineer events to work in his favour. It was a question of strength of the mind, he explained with a wide grin. Excitedly, he told her of how he had taken advantage of people in business, of how he had convinced them they should trust him because he knew what he was doing. He told her he loved being a puppet master. If they were out with a potential business client, Platt would finish his spiel and then give Isabel a knowing glance that said the master had just pulled the string. It was as if Platt believed he had the power to do whatever he wanted, whenever he wanted and to whomever he wanted. And it was totally acceptable to him. If people trusted you, he offered, then it was their own fault if they got taken. Isabel realized that Platt was telling all these secrets simply to feed his own ego. Isabel now saw him as a con artist of sorts. This was a turning point in their relationship. From that point on, Platt was aware that whenever he said something out of the ordinary Isabel would analyze it for truthfulness.

Inevitably, discussions around therapy issues turned to the tricky matter of dealing with the survivors and perpetrators of sex crimes, such as incest and pedophilia. Isabel said that she had empathy for the victims and would readily conduct therapy for them, but she would have a great deal of difficulty working with an offender.

"These people have wrecked other people's lives. I don't like it and I don't like the people who do it, and that's the end of it. Ugh! I don't want to help these guys. Let somebody else deal with them."

"These things are never what they seem," Platt protested, to her chagrin. "Quite often the children are happy with the situation and it is only outsiders who cannot see this and want to bring the matter to a police level."

Isabel fought to control herself as Platt appeared to defend incest.

"If the father wants to be forgiven, everything should be forgiven immediately, and that's the end of it. As long as the child or young person doesn't appear damaged or in distress, then it is okay. It doesn't matter what age they are. A person has a free choice, and if they are not fighting it, then they are obviously liking it." No, therapists don't have to protect these kids. For the most part, their parents loved them and maybe that was good enough. Even if a client confessed to child sexual abuse in a therapy session, he would not report it to the authorities, even though he was bound to do so by Britain's Children's Act.

And this, Isabel thought, from the man who professed to be one of the most romantic, sophisticated and enlightened men on earth.

Platt revealed that as a young boy he had detested some things about his mother because she was such a "very hard woman." She demanded work from him that should never have been expected of a boy. She had made him scrub the kitchen floor, wash and tidy clothes and do things that normally women and girls did. He had five siblings, he said, most of them girls, and he lamented that his mother felt closer to the girls than she did to him. He recalled with anger that his mother had unreasonable expectations of him, expectations he could never hope to fulfil. It wasn't fair, he said, that he, the boy, should do all the house-work while his sisters did nothing. Yet at the same time he described his mother as "soft." In contrast, he remembered his father as a "wonderful man," but he was also angry with the man because through the years they never enjoyed a "proper" father-son rela-tionship. He seemed to deeply resent that he'd never been able to get close to his father. There was little joy in the family he depicted to Isabel. He told her that often in his boyhood he would wander off along the country roads and across the fields just to get away from his hated home.

Anger over his mother also turned his attention to another woman he hated. Isabel felt that Platt despised his ex-wife even more than his mother. Once, when he was in a good mood, he explained in what seemed like an objective manner that she was a doc-tor and had always been a busy woman. He acknowl-edged that despite her demanding work she had raised the children almost solely by herself, as he had to go off on business. For a while, he said, life had been good. His business had flourished. They'd had an old house with a pool in the backyard. They'd had huge parties. He drove a Jaguar and took his sailboat to Lake Erie and Lake Ontario. He lamented that when his wife gave birth to the four children and simultaneously followed a career she showed a great lack of devotion to him and the kids. He said it became difficult for him to gain intimacy with her and that no amount of attempts on his part could bridge the gap. But on another occasion, when his mood was less benign, he told her that his ex-wife had controlled him and he had begun to resent it. He stated matter-of-factly that he would never let any person control him ever again. In fact, he said, it was her controlling and domineering personality that had caused both the business and the family to come crashing down. There were always arguments and fights because he was never home. The pain and the stress had led to the bust-up of the marriage and the business. Ultimately, he had had a breakdown. That's when he decided to get out of international finance and seek a new life and a new wife.

There had been four kids — three girls and a boy. Platt said he frequently sent his ex-wife money to help take care of the kids. He missed his son but was in close contact with his oldest daughter. Before he left America he set her up with a car and an apartment in New York City so she could go to school. He sent her money regularly and had even gone to New York in the summer of 1995 to see her. His other daughter was most upset, he said, because he had never been around when she was growing up. If he was in a wine-induced ugly mood, Platt would recall that his ex-wife was simply not an attractive enough woman to be with a good-looking fellow like himself. She was not of his calibre. He recalled the times he would deliberately infuriate his wife by flirting with other women right before her eyes. On vacations, he would hang out around the open-air pools, at the beach, in the Jacuzzi or the spas or wherever women congregated, and would wait for a woman to approach him. It not only satisfied his ego that women wanted him but it gave him great pleasure that his wife was in pain.

"She is a stupid woman," he told Isabel, chuckling. "If that's what she was prepared to put up with, then that's what I was ready to hand out."

Before the marriage break-up, he said, they had gone to a marriage counsellor, but he never did intend it to work. It was just a ploy to stretch things out so that he could get his ducks in a row to leave. His mind was elsewhere.

"There were plenty more women around," he said.

The children were there to be teased as well. If his kids left their pocket money out on a table or chair, he picked it up. He liked teaching them that the world was a distrustful place and you should never trust anyone, not even your own family, not even your own father.

This tale rang a bell with Isabel one day when she was in the office with Platt and he paid her in cash for the week's work. She put the money down on a desk so she could to do some filing, but when she turned around it was gone. She glared at Platt, but he gave her a blank look.

"Come on, Ron. You obviously picked it up. Come on, hand it over!"

Platt didn't move, didn't bat an eyelid.

"Come on, I'm not your daughter. Don't you play that game with me!" Isabel held out her hand and motioned him to give back her wages.

He was clearly annoyed when he handed over the money. He ignored her outstretched hand and put the money on the desk. As she reached for her purse he blurted out, "You should protect your money. Now, put it away. I don't ever want to see money lying around again."

When she once asked him if he taught Emily how to spend money on sweets, he said Emily didn't have money and she wouldn't be getting any. Women shouldn't have money. They didn't need it.

The first time Isabel visited Platt's house came when he had locked his keys in the office. She offered to give him a ride home and then be at the office in the morning to open up. Platt acquiesced, but on the drive home he called Noël twice to tell her that he was on his way and added, "Isabel's coming and I'll be coming in." When they arrived, Noël was there with Emily. Platt had portrayed Noël as a self-possessed woman of the nineties who was an inspiration to him. But there, in the downstairs of the house, she seemed to cling, figuratively, to her husband as tightly as she clung, literally, to her child. Platt gave Isabel a quick tour of the gloomy downstairs rooms. She found the house smaller than what Platt had described to her; he had made it sound palatial and opulent. There were both antiques and modern furniture, but nothing she could single out as being truly tasteful. The antiques and art were his, of course, while the modern stuff had belonged to Noël before they were married. As the brief tour continued, Noël quietly followed her older husband, almost touching him. It was as if, Isabel thought, Noël were scared to leave Ron's side because she was afraid he would talk about her. Isabel sensed a friction between herself and Noël.

The young woman was an enigma to Isabel. Whenever Platt talked about his ex-wife he frequently put her down for her lack of interest in sex. He would compare her shortcomings with what he said he had found with Noël. He would often return to work on a Monday morning boasting of what a great weekend of sex he'd had with his wife.

"Getting married the second time around was great, and sex the second time around is great," he once said. "Noël will do anything for me. She will do everything for me that my ex-wife didn't. Whatever your imagination can dredge up, then that's what we get up to."

He seemed so proud of having such a young and beautiful wife. He placed so much emphasis on her sexuality — or at least on sexualizing her.

"But there is such a large age gap between the two of you. How did you ever get together?" Isabel asked, trying to turn the conversation away from what she thought was an intimate matter that he really shouldn't discuss with her.

So Platt related the tale of how she had been at Chelsea Art College and his good friend in America had asked him to keep an eye on her. And so it was that they went for dinner not once but twice, and on the way home that night they were walking by the river when they began kissing. Two weeks later he moved in with her and in a few more weeks they were married at a registry office with no family present. Isabel wondered whether Noël's parents had voiced any opposition. Despite their initial scepticism, Platt replied, they had been most supportive. He added that he had had his own concerns at first, but Noël had convinced him that she loved him and age didn't matter and everything would be okay.

And he said everything *was* okay. They had a beautiful child, with another on the way, and they were still deeply in love; he said he couldn't bear to be apart from Noël. But still, Isabel perceived, even this "love" revolved around sex. Once, while on an evening-long seminar, Isabel decided to stay overnight in a hotel, given the long drive back home. It was late. She suggested that her boss too, should get a room, for it would be dangerous to drive at such a late hour. He shook his head and smiled. "Do you think I can stay away from home when I have a twenty-two-year-old wife waiting for me? I can't stay away for one night!" It was all so over the top.

"It's quite a shame that Noël is stuck out at the farm with no ability to drive," Isabel remarked one day.

Platt shrugged it off. He said that his wife was happy there and that to break the monotony they got a babysitter and went out for dinner once a month.

"Noël puts her hair up and she puts make-up on. She looks just lovely. I feel great having her hang on my arm and having all the men look at me thinking what a lucky guy I am to have such a beautiful young woman by my side." They would get so turned on sexually, he said, that they would kiss all the way home in the taxi and then have wonderful sex together.

Platt would often share his family photographs with Isabel after he picked them up at the photo store in Brentwood. Many photos showed Noël in romantic poses. They were always happy pictures: Noël in the garden, Emily on her mother's knee, Noël leaning against a tree.

"I wish she wouldn't wear dirty jeans, because she doesn't look pretty."

Once he showed Isabel a photograph of Noël nearly naked after she had just come out of the shower. Again, his failure to appreciate boundaries and privacy was evident.

"She's such a beautiful woman, isn't she?" he

said. "You know, her body is actually getting better with age. She looks too young for me, doesn't she?"

Isabel agreed, but she didn't say so. That was his business.

Paradoxically, Platt seemed frustrated with his wife's youth. "Can you try to think of her as older than she looks in that picture, 'cause she looks far too young."

Isabel thought Platt couldn't quite make up his mind what he wanted out of his wife. On the one hand he demanded a sex goddess, but on the other hand he still wanted her to be a girl.

When Lily was born in January 1996, Platt hardly missed a beat and was back at work within days. He told Isabel he had witnessed Lily's birth and it was "awesome."

"Is Noël okay?" she asked out of concern.

"Yeah, apart from the fact she's going to lose her breasts."

Isabel sat bolt upright, wondering what kind of faux pas she had made. Heavens, what had happened to Noël during labour? She sat for a moment in stunned silence.

"Oh, goodness, is it really bad?" she ventured.

"No, no," he mocked. "They're nice and big, but now they'll shrink to nothing again."

Isabel could not believe he would make such a crude statement about the woman he professed to love. It was obvious that Platt's sexual sense of self was separated starkly from his emotional side. Isabel also noted that his intellectual life was separate from everything else and concluded that Platt liked to keep her around for intellectual entertainment, something that he obviously didn't have with Noël. The only things he ever said about Noël, it seemed, revolved around their great sex and her apparent inability to look after the kids. While he often chided Noël for her lack of knowledge about child rearing, he considered himself an expert because of his previous marriage. It was strange, Isabel recalled, that if the girls even had a stomach upset Noël would be on the telephone asking Ron what to do. It was all so strange to Isabel. Platt had often commented that kids were all that Noël had wanted from life. As long as she had her kids she would be happy. She wanted four.

Looking at Noël's lot, Isabel wondered aloud one day that maybe she was too immature to take on such a thankless and constant job with the children. She asked Platt whether he was afraid Noël might opt for a younger man and throw the tedium away.

"She can see who she wants to see," he answered. "I wouldn't stop her seeing somebody."

"Even though she is married to you?" Isabel asked. "And she has your children?"

"No, we have quite an open relationship."

That was not what Isabel had seen. While Ron had described his young wife as self-possessed and strong and his equal, Isabel saw her as demure, a wallflower, almost mouse-like. He very much wanted her to be a self-reliant, sophisticated, worldly woman, but the reality was that Noël was a quiet, passive, home-body. Change would come only if there were major trauma in her life that forced her to make decisions for herself. Barring a big upset of the Platt apple cart, that wasn't going to happen.

Ten

THEY DO IT WITH MIRRORS

RON PLATT CAME cheerily into the office one day and told Isabel about a terrific book he had picked up in a store down the Brentwood high street. He would have given her his copy of Jostein Gaarder's *Sophie's World* if he hadn't lent it to a client who was having trouble understanding his identity. He urged her to get her own copy.

"It is really great and you have to read it," he told her, explaining that it was a fascinating study of philosophy with the message that people have it within themselves to interpret their life the way they want to. "I read the book in my reading chair — you know, the one in the dining room. I've been concentrating deeply on it, trying to understand all of it."

Gaarder's thought-provoking best-seller explores Western philosophy through a fairy-tale-like story in which the mysterious and shadowy Alberto teaches a young girl, Sophie, about the origin of life. Each of the great philosophers and their teachings are revealed to Sophie in his historical context, but

Gaarder deftly uses everyday experiences as common-sense analogies so that Sophie, and the reader, will understand. In the end, Gaarder's point is that if humans know who they are and where they've come from then they can become whoever they want to be. He notes that in a person's mind there can be little difference between objective and subjective reality. Platt raved about the book day after day, saying to Isabel, "Why shouldn't we all have our lives to perceive in the way we want to perceive them?"

In discussing the book with Isabel over more wine-fuelled lunches at the Café Rouge, Platt didn't seem to pay any attention to Gaarder's vignettes of the great philosophers. Rather, he dwelled on the topic of identity. He talked about people who can take on an identity and fool not only the people around them but themselves too, even to the point of believing that they are someone else and that their invention is their reality.

"I've met people who can put up one facade for some people and another facade for others," he stated. "They can live two lives at the same time to the extent that they end up believing themselves and at times have to shake themselves out of their adopted reality."

But things changed in the spring of 1996. Isabel noted that Platt was dissociating himself from work. Again and again he would ask her to cover for him. She soon found herself going into the office daily. She was the one doing the work, setting up the seminars;

Isabel had become "the Voice" of Solutions In Therapy. One day when Platt called in to ask her what was happening, Isabel lamented that so many advertisers had called up with urgent requests to speak with him. He arbitrarily gave her the title of advertising manager. Sometimes one of the partners would call, innocently praising Ron Platt for the good job he had done putting together this seminar and that conference. Isabel couldn't believe her ears: she was the one who had done the work and Platt had passed it off as his own. "Hang on a minute," she asserted finally. "I did that!"

Right in front of Isabel's eyes, Ron Platt seemed to be undergoing a fundamental personality change. Gone was the happy-go-lucky, mature, self-possessed man she had met at her first therapy session. That Ron Platt had been replaced by a man who was under great stress and could not cope well. Bit by bit, his professionalism was slipping away. He began to miss appointments, and his reliability and punctuality deteriorated. Clients would arrive for a therapy session and their therapist wouldn't show. Isabel had to apologize profusely, always trying to offer some plausible reason for Platt's absence. And some of the decisions Platt made lacked integrity. But when she confronted him he would angrily tell her there was enough pressure on him without her putting on more. "I'll do what I like. Don't argue," he would command. Twice he broke down and apologized for taking his frustrations out on Isabel.

Around this same time, Platt's fantasy of expanding the therapy business got a serious reality check. One of the partners, Ian Marsh, began to challenge the office manager. Marsh had eagerly embraced Platt when he'd first approached the partners in August 1995, but nobody had been more surprised than Marsh when, within a couple of months, Platt had suddenly moved lock, stock and barrel from Tiverton in Devon up to Woodham Walter in Essex. Still, it had been a sure-fire proposition for the three partners, who had done nothing but lose money in a series of workshops they had taught in Britain and the United States. With Platt looking after the business end of things, the partners could get on with their "day job" practices and then make the most of this work when it came time for therapy teaching. Platt touted himself as a religious man, a family man, an honest man. And at first, Marsh and his colleagues believed he had behaved credibly. But problems surfaced when Platt started to run the partnership as if he were in charge. The partners considered Platt a bit of an oddball as well.

Platt's wheels began to fall off the track when he suggested to the partners that they should set up a diploma program for him that would enable him to become a fully qualified therapist.

"That's not ethical, Ron, because you are part of the company," Marsh told him. "You can get the diploma, sure, but it will have to be through somebody else, elsewhere."

At this, Platt went into a rage. He screamed at Marsh that sometimes in the early stages of a business you had to take ethical risks in order to survive. He'd done that in financing, he reminded them, and had gone on to a successful life. The partners, he said, should do it here and now.

"I used to sell lousy bonds and made a big profit on them because people believed they were good," Platt yelled. "The reason for my success was that I took risks."

As a therapist, Marsh knew the signs of a disturbed mind, and suddenly he was seeing them in Platt, his business partner. "What kind of person are we associating with here?" he asked himself and his colleagues.

The two also squared off in philosophical debates. Platt made the proposition at one meeting that a person could just forget about the past and all its pains and letdowns and move on with the future.

"You are never cured until you can come to terms with your own hatred," said Marsh, stating a fundamental precept of psychotherapy.

Platt refused to accept it. Marsh realized he disliked not just what Platt was saying but also the way he was saying it. He had a bizarre manner of sneering at you that let you know he thought you were a fool.

Platt had shared with the partners his views of a quasi-religious community based on therapy. It was clear to Marsh that Platt wanted to be the guru, and the partners were to be his acolytes. Marsh thereafter felt such strong revulsion for Platt that he didn't even want to talk to him. In conversations with the others he referred to Platt as "the bastard" and that "tacky" man.

Soon after the row with Marsh, Platt dragged Isabel into the fray. "Get the locks changed," he told her in an early-morning telephone call to the office one Friday in June 1996.

"What's happened?" she asked.

"Don't question me!"

"There hasn't been a break-in, has there?"

He raised his voice a pitch. "Just get the locks changed. I don't want to talk about it any more. Get the lock guy around right now and get the locks changed. I want two keys only."

Half an hour later the telephone rang. It was Platt again. "Have you done it?"

"I've been busy for the past half-hour," Isabel protested, "but I'll get straight to it." She sensed Platt's anger. The locks had been changed by the time Platt appeared at the office later that afternoon.

"What's all this about?" asked Isabel.

"Look, this is your key and this is my key, and I don't want anybody else in here. Do you understand?" He paused for breath and then blurted out his issue: "I've had enough. One of the guys has been using the computer again. I don't like them being in there when I'm not there, snooping around. They're taking phone messages off the answering machine — that's your job!" His rage was boiling over. He was so defensive and protective of his space.

When Isabel finally spoke with the partners they

filled her in on Platt's idea for his diploma. His wanting to cross this ethical boundary angered her. It seemed that he just wanted to make a lot of money and didn't give a damn about the meaning of the diploma, the work that went into it or any belief in therapy. Isabel felt cheapened that she had worked so hard for her diploma and Platt felt he could just come along and have one for nothing.

But getting a diploma wasn't the only thing on Platt's mind. Shortly after the row with the partners, he turned from being just an oddball into someone who was rude, unpredictable, even scary. More than once Isabel became frightened during Platt's now-typical outbursts, and while he raged she comforted herself knowing there were other people in the building and help was not far away.

One day, sensing his despair, Isabel walked over to her boss and gently asked him, "What is it? What's wrong?"

Platt revealed in an angry and tearful confession that he was going through a hassle with somebody.

"People are doing things that might prevent me from seeing my kids," he told her in a depressed tone. As he continued to talk he broke down and wept. "I love my kids and I don't want anybody to stop me from seeing them. I love the girls dearly and I can't bear to think what it would be like not to have them. I love you, too. Oh, God, sometimes I feel so alone." He pulled out his photographs of Noël with Emily and Lily. "The thought of losing them frightens me."

Something or someone was wrenching at his heart. He didn't name anyone, but Isabel assumed he was having problems with his ex-wife.

There were amazing mood swings. One moment he would be perfectly pleasant; the next, he would shout at Isabel for no reason. Whenever she told Platt about a telephone conversation with Ian Marsh, he would almost go berserk.

"I know what it takes to make every single one of them bankrupt," he would rant, and he would reassure Isabel, "And then we can take this and do it our own way." But at the same time he lamented, "If things get bad I'll skip off somewhere else, like I've always done."

He also seemed perturbed by a series of telephone calls by a man asking for David.

Through the spring and summer of 1996, Isabel took numerous calls at the business for "David." It was always a man. "Do you mean David Hawkes?" she queried.

"No," came the surprised answer.

"That's the only David we have here. Could Mr. Platt help you? He's the business manager."

One day a befuddled caller rang three times in succession. Again Isabel said that no one called David worked there. Another day, Platt was in the office when a call came in for David Platt.

"There isn't a David Platt here, only a Ron Platt," Isabel offered. "You must have a wrong number," she said and put the phone down.

"No, no, that call was for me," said Platt, itching

in his chair. He explained that both his brother and his cousin were named David Platt, so some people would get mixed up and call him David. He added that he didn't correct them, just to make it easier to do business. After all, why make a fuss when it wasn't necessary? Isabel recalled that six months earlier Platt had claimed that the English international and Arsenal footballer David Platt was a relative, but she hadn't believed it then and didn't believe it now. She also recalled that back in February he had told the partners that a cousin from Vermont, named David, was in town. He referred to his cousin as a "no-hoper" and said he was trying to help him find work. One of the partners suggested Platt should send him to France. There was lots of work there and that would also remove him from his hair.

Often Isabel would be in the office when Platt took calls on his mobile phone. He would quickly duck out of the building to conduct the call or he would ask Isabel for privacy, perhaps suggesting that she bring them coffee.

In late June of 1996, Platt announced it was time to take a vacation in Devon. Isabel was relieved: she would finally have some peace in the office. He said he would go sailing on his yacht, the *Lady Jane*, with a friend who lived in Devon, and at the same time take Noël and the girls. Platt ordered Isabel that if anyone called she should not tell them where he was, just take a message and he would call back. He reminded her that she was working for him, not the partnership. In July, he was off to Devon. He knew that Isabel would be in the office on Fridays and demanded that each Friday she call him on his cellular phone and advise him of any developments.

Eleven

EVIL UNDER
THE SUN

IT WAS FRIDAY, July 19, 1996. Isabel was loath to call Platt during his Devon vacation. His turbulent moods of late had been frustrating and aggravating. Whenever she talked with Platt she felt she was walking on eggshells. She thought that if anybody needed therapy it was him. Still, he had insisted that she call him each Friday to update him on the office business and telephone messages, so call him she must.

"Hi, Ron, it's me," she said, trying her best to put on a cheery front.

"Not now!" Platt snapped, spitting venom. "I can't talk now."

As Isabel instinctively pulled the telephone away from her ear, Platt's voice muffled by the hand he placed over the mouthpiece. His tone was angry when he came back on the phone and haughtily told Isabel he would call her back. As he said this, another man was talking angrily, almost shouting, in the background. After Platt hung up, Isabel dwelled for a while on the call. But regardless of what he was involved in, she felt put out by his reaction. After all, he was the one who had insisted she call.

Platt returned Isabel's call the next day, Saturday, July 20, 1996. It was obvious from the clear line that he wasn't on his cell phone. After a bit of chit-chat he complained to her that he had some kind of problem with his boat. Not being a nautical type, Isabel didn't really listen to his whining and bellyaching. And she was still miffed at the cold reception he had given her only the day before. They didn't talk about much. After Isabel filled him in on the calls to the office, they hung up. She didn't expect to hear from him until late Sunday, after his return from Devon, when they were to touch base on the workshop they were due to co-host Monday at lunchtime in a town just outside London. But early on Sunday morning, July 21, as she was enjoying a quiet day at home, her telephone rang.

"I've had an accident, a very bad accident," Ron told her, huffing and puffing between words as he tried to catch his breath and pump out an explanation. "I've slipped on the boat and banged my chest badly. I don't know what to do!"

Isabel heard the panic in his voice. It was most unlike Ron to panic; he was normally so reserved, so in control. Even in his wackier moments — for example, whenever Isabel brought up Ian Marsh's name — he had always kept a tight rein on his emotions.

Platt wheezed out an explanation that he had hurt his back trying to drag something heavy off the yacht. He said he'd had such a problem getting the boat back to shore on his own. He sounded like he'd had a heart attack.

"Isn't anyone with you?" asked Isabel.

"Noël is up at the hotel. I came out on my own. There wasn't anybody with me . . . I feel so all alone." He couldn't get back to Essex that night, he explained, because he was hurting so much he couldn't drive the three hours or so. "I can't get the car out of the drive," he said.

"Noël can — "Isabel started, but then he spoke her thought.

"Oh, Noël doesn't drive."

"Ron, you sound in a bad way. Have you been to the hospital?" Isabel inquired.

"No," said Platt. "I don't want to bother them on a Sunday. I don't like putting people out on a Sunday."

Isabel felt the anger rising. She thought, yeah, right, you don't want to bother people on a Sunday yet here you are waking me up so early on a Sunday morning!

"What are you doing today?" he asked, and she took the implication that he wanted her to get to Devon somehow and then bring the Platts back to Essex.

"I'm very busy," she said, which was the truth.

Platt told her she should get one of the other partners to do the workshop with her. Not a bad idea, thought Isabel, who by now was tired of listening to his complaints and excuses. Later in the day he called

Isabel again to see whether she had made arrangements with another partner, which she had not managed to do. This time he seemed calmer, yet there was
still a hint of concern in his voice. Isabel didn't press
Platt for the details of what had happened or seek to
know more about the angry exchange she had heard
on the phone. Not only was it none of her business,
but by this point she didn't care that much what did
or didn't happen to Ron Platt.

At 1:20 p.m. Platt called David Hawkes. "I slipped
on a newly varnished deck on the boat and hit my
chest on a locker," he said. He then asked Hawkes to
help Isabel do the workshop. Hawkes asked how his
vacation had been. "The whole week was a nightmare.
Everyone had colds!"

Platt called Isabel later to tell her that one of the
partners would take his place.

Twelve

CROOKED HOUSE

THE AFTERNOON SUN bathed the pastoral Essex countryside in a golden blanket as Isabel and Neil drove to Woodham Walter on Sunday, August 25, 1996, and made the quick turns onto West Bowers Road and Raven Hall Lane. As the betrothed couple pulled into the driveway of the Little London Farmhouse, they were relieved that their hosts hadn't called off the dinner at the last moment as they had in March, when Platt phoned Isabel an hour before mealtime and told her that she and Neil couldn't come because Noël was "really ill." Oddly, when Noël called the office looking for her husband the next day and instead got only Isabel, she had responded with a puzzled "What do you mean?" after Isabel asked how she was feeling. This time, it appeared that Platt would actually carry through on his promise to be the congenial host. Isabel wanted to show Platt that he was wrong about Neil. It no longer mattered to her what Platt thought about him, but having Neil and Platt meet would be in the best interests of office politics, which, to say the least, were somewhat strained.

When she entered the Platt family home for the second time, Isabel found it even gloomier than on the first visit. The atmosphere to her was cold and soulless. Upon greeting her guests, Noël again appeared very shy, demure, almost speechless. Isabel noted the absence of any visible chemistry between Noël and her husband; they lacked the affectionate bond of a loving couple. There were no kisses, no hugs, no touches, no meeting of eyes across the room, no lovers' teasing. It wasn't what was said or done that made Isabel uncomfortable, but what wasn't spoken and didn't happen. She had felt both envy and warmth when Platt had told her on so many occasions how every morning Emily would get out of bed, run into her parents' bedroom, jump into the bed and snuggle up with them. But when Platt insisted on giving Isabel a tour of the house, she found the couple's bedroom stark and frigid. For one thing, the bed was barely big enough to sleep one person, let alone the six-foot-one Platt, Noël and the morning child all together. The room also seemed to have only the touch of a man. Noël was so feminine, and yet the bedroom — surely an important place in the type of relationship Platt had described — showed only masculine flair. During the tour, Platt didn't open the door to Emily's room, which he had once described to Isabel as a beautiful child's room. Isabel was struck by the total absence of toys in the house, especially in the bathroom. There were no little boats, no rubber ducks. She wondered if these playthings of every child were all hoarded away in Emily's room. Maybe Platt had avoided showing her the little girl's room because Emily, in her child's exuberance, had strewn the contents of her toy box across the bedroom floor. A conscientious parent, Isabel reconciled, wouldn't want to show an untidy room.

Before starting dinner, the four adults and Emily, with baby Lily in the push chair, went for a short walk along the lane. It was a lovely night and Platt rejoiced at life in the country. Through it all, Noël was quiet. There was no reason for Noël to be shy, thought Isabel, because they had talked with each other so frequently on the phone. Yet here she was, more diffident than on Isabel's first visit. Platt, however, was as full of himself as ever. Insisting that he should cook dinner, when they got home he went to pull some home-grown vegetables from the garden. Platt demanded that Isabel help him.

"No, I'll stay and help Noël," said Isabel as she looked over at the overburdened woman. But he grabbed her arm and gave a joking "Come on." As if he were her father! As he opened the garden shed, he pushed Isabel back and told her, "Women can't come in the shed." He grabbed a spade and dug into the earth around the potatoes, then flatly refused her help in pulling the plants, telling her tersely, "Just hold the bag." In an obvious effort to gain favour with her father, Emily, too, offered to help. As Platt turned the spade to unearth the vegetables, Emily tugged on his pant leg, shouting, "Can I pick the potatoes? Can I pick the potatoes?" But Platt impatiently brushed the toddler aside.

When Isabel went back into the house with Platt, Emily and the vegetables, Neil pulled her aside and whispered in her ear, "I would never have gotten away with speaking to you like that!" They shared a chuckle.

With Noël on the periphery of the gathering and barely offering any comment, Platt, Isabel and Neil chatted until dinnertime. When dinner was served, Platt made three-year-old Emily say grace. Emily's efforts were cute, and at first Isabel thought Platt truly was an instructive father. But soon Emily took a teaspoon in her hand and quietly began patting the back of the utensil against her cheek.

"Emily, stop!" Platt roared.

The little girl looked at him, wide-eyed, and stopped. The table returned to normal briefly. Emily took a spoonful of food and put it in her mouth, then, unconsciously, she patted her cheek with the spoon again.

It was Noël who spoke this time. "You had better go and ask Daddy what happens now."

A forlorn look on her face, Emily climbed down from her chair and walked over to her father. "What now, Daddy?" she whispered sorrowfully.

"Now you go upstairs," Platt told her.

With this, Emily trudged up the stairs and disappeared from view.

Isabel and Neil thought their host had overreacted in meting out such harsh punishment for a minor breach of table manners.

After dinner, Isabel excused herself from the table to visit the upstairs washroom. At the top of the stairs, she paused upon hearing muffled sobbing from Emily's room. The door was ajar, and Isabel pushed it open just to make sure the child was safe. Emily had buried her head in her pillow and was weeping. Isabel felt despair. At such an early age, this little girl had resisted crying in front of the others and had hidden her emotions until she was alone. Yet from her studies, Isabel knew that children of this age were so eager to please their parents that when chastised they burst into tears.

To Isabel's surprise, the bedroom was devoid of anything but the essential furniture and there were no toys, as she had conjectured. Isabel quickly moved into the bathroom when she heard footsteps on the stairs. It was Noël, coming to check on Emily. Later, when both Isabel and Noël had rejoined the table, Noël asked Platt if she could retrieve Emily and feed her some dinner. With Platt's permission, Noël brought Emily downstairs. Emily immediately approached Platt and asked him, "Please may I come down and eat?"

As the evening progressed, so did Noël's near-speechless condition. It struck Isabel and Neil that Platt never involved her in any decisions or conversations and she never questioned him. She appeared totally subservient to him. The evening revolved around Platt talking about himself, recounting his exploits as a businessman and pontificating about psychotherapy. Not once did he ask Neil about his work as a police officer and the plans that he and Isabel had for their life together.

There was something odd between the Platts. Noël came across as so helpless. "Should I feed the baby now?" she had asked. "Should I put the baby to bed?" She seemed as dependent and obedient as Emily. At one point, Platt berated her because she hadn't made a pineapple cake for dessert.

"I didn't have time," she said softly, then, speaking rare words, apologized profusely to her guests.

"You should have made one. I told you to make one," scolded Platt.

The meal had been cleared away and the children put to bed when Platt suddenly announced to Isabel and Neil that he wouldn't be in the office for the next couple of weeks. "It's Noël's father." He paused. "He's suffered a heart attack. Noël and I will have to fly to New York."

Isabel looked uncomfortably towards Neil and then they both eyed Noël.

"Yeah, he's not well," said the girl who rarely talked. "I don't know what's going to happen." Tears rolled down her face. "E-xcuse me . . ." she sputtered, and walked quickly from the dining room.

Platt looked across at his guests. He wore a solemn face. "I'm sorry," he said, arms stretched out. "It's really hard for her, and for me, too. Her father and I have been such good friends for so long. It's sobering to realize how many friends my age are dying off."

Noël hobbled back into the room and managed to find her seat. "We're flying to New York on Friday."

Isabel offered her sympathy to her hosts. She respectfully reminded Platt that they were to give a workshop at Barking College starting in a couple of weeks. Platt promised he would make it.

In their car as they were leaving for home, Neil turned to Isabel and stated his disbelief at what he had observed about Noël. "She might as well be his daughter, too."

A week or so later Platt called Isabel at home. He said he was in New York and that Noël's father had died the night before. "Thankfully, Noël was there at his side. I'm going to have to leave her here in New York and fly back to England for the college course. I'm very committed to the course, Isabel. This whole thing has gutted me, but I'll be back."

After she hung up, Isabel pondered the call. Platt had sounded so melodramatic and yet there hadn't been a hint of emotion in his voice. There had been no feeling. He was becoming colder with each passing day.

Thirteen

AFTER THE FUNERAL

AUDREY AND FRANK bumped into Ron Platt in the lane one day at the beginning of September. He told them Noël's father had died, so she was staying in the United States for a little while with the kids but would soon return. Platt seemed unhappy. He said he was lonely without Noël and the children. For the next few nights he didn't return to the house. Audrey believed he had chosen to rent a hotel room in Brentwood or was away on business. Less than a week after that, Noël was at Audrey and Frank's door. The girls were in tow and Ron was in the car. "We're back," she announced, in an almost cheery voice.

Despite his misgivings about the young woman, Frank felt his heart go out to her. "Noël, I'm sorry to hear about your father. It must be hard for you."

Noël gave him an empty look and didn't say anything.

Shortly thereafter, she strode over to Orchard Bungalow and told Marion of her father's death and the funeral. Marion took flowers to Noël later that afternoon. She was toiling at cutting the grass as Marion approached. Emily played outside, and Lily was asleep inside. As they talked, Marion was shocked at Noël's lack of feeling over her father's death. She herself had nursed people with cancer and had seen whole families go to pieces even when they expected the death. She concluded that Noël was either incredibly stoic or just utterly unbelievable.

After this episode, the Platts began to leave the house more and more.

"We're going away for the weekend, and I'm going with my husband this time," said Noël, who previously had always referred to her husband as Ron.

In early October a woman who canvassed for Maldon council gave Audrey an electoral form and asked her to pass it on to the residents at the Little London Farmhouse, who weren't home. It was the second form the town had dropped off, explained the canvasser, and if it was not returned the occupants would not get to vote in the upcoming election. "I'll be sure they get it," Audrey had told her. The form bore the names of Ronald Platt and someone called Elaine Boyes.

What's this? she said to herself, then showed Frank her interesting find.

They puzzled over the new name. Did Noël go by the name Elaine? Maybe Boyes was her maiden name, but if so, why wasn't she listed as Noël Boyes? Frank waved the issue aside. He couldn't believe a high-minded man like Ronald Platt would miss an opportunity to exercise his right to vote, and he wondered why Platt had not signed the form the first time canvassers dropped it off. Then they pondered whether Noël could vote in Britain at all if she was still an American citizen.

Audrey decided something fishy was going on and it was time to play detective. While Platt was away at the office one day, she went over to see the young woman. "Noël, I suppose you have an American passport."

"I'm getting one," she answered.

Well, thought Audrey, then she wasn't eligible to vote. "And look at this," she said, slipping the voting form across to Noël. "Look, Ron Platt and Elaine Boyes. Who's Elaine Boyes?"

Noël was visibly startled. She was lost for an answer, but then she blurted out, "There was a girl here before with that name."

Rubbish, Audrey thought. She had known the previous neighbours for decades. No Elaine Boyes had ever lived in Woodham Walter, never mind next door at the Little London Farmhouse. Leaving Noël in a fluster, Audrey returned home to recount her escapade to Frank. "I knew it. They're not really married," she declared.

This stuck in Frank's throat like a bone. He recalled telling his next-door neighbours at their first meeting that he and Audrey were not married. For two years they'd lived here and they'd never admitted they weren't married? How wonderful!

Another time, Frank mentioned to Noël that he had seen a car go past their house and he thought it must have been Ron. Noël assured him it wasn't. And then in a move quite out of her quiet character, Noël asked, "Have you seen any strange cars hanging around?"

Isabel Rogers, meanwhile, was learning more about Platt. They were about to host the workshop they had put together for prospective counsellors at Barking College. Isabel had naturally assumed that she, as the most experienced and educated therapist, would be the lead tutor and Platt would assist. In the days leading up to the workshop Platt decided he did not want to give the students a syllabus because he didn't want to relinquish control over the workshop. Isabel was dumbfounded. These people had paid a lot of money for the course and deserved to know how it would be structured and what they would learn. By this time, Isabel had talked about Platt with the other partners and was becoming more suspicious of his motives and ethics. As well, Ian Marsh had confided to Isabel his absolute distaste for Platt.

Her concerns about Platt were cemented only minutes into the workshop. Platt not only made the introductions but went straight into teaching mode, relegating Isabel to mere spectator. She was powerless to stop him because it would have meant causing a scene in front of the entire class.

Afterwards, she pulled Platt aside and discreetly told him off. "I don't appreciate the way you dealt with this. You were very derogatory towards me and I don't appreciate it!"

Platt gave her a look that could kill, then he blurted out, "Where's your compassion? My father-in-law just died. I've got to get back out there. He was my best friend. He was the same age as me. It's like me dying." Platt then told her he would be away doing workshops for the next two weeks.

After sleeping on the issue, Isabel decided he was using the death of Noël's father as an excuse to cover up the workshop debacle. That said, there was something about the death that just didn't add up. Isabel sensed a detachment in Platt. He had no real compassion for his father-in-law. She detected a sham of some sort and she was angry. Still, it was apparent that some kind of stress was affecting Platt and he couldn't cope; his behaviour had become intolerable. She just wanted to walk away from the job, no matter the cost to her career. She was exhausted. He was on a steep road downwards and she wasn't going to let him take her along for the ride. Isabel saw no alternative. In early October, in his absence, she left three messages on the office answering machine and wrote him a letter of resignation.

Platt responded with a message on Isabel's home answering machine. He desperately asked her to call him at the office and they would talk things out. He wasn't there when Isabel phoned back, so she left another message: "You're a fraud! I can see through you and I want nothing to do with you. You're pulling yourself down and you're going to take the practice down with you."

Then Platt wrote a letter: "Can we work it out — can we make a go of it?" To Isabel's chagrin, he signed the letter "Love, your friend Ron."

Isabel warned Marsh and the others about Platt's bizarre behaviour and recommended that they confront him.

A secretary who worked in the office next door to Platt's told Isabel that only a few days after Isabel resigned, she had seen Platt in the hall and he was upset at Isabel, saying she had let him down in his time of need. Isabel didn't feel much sorrow for him. As she saw it, he'd let himself down, never mind everyone associated with him.

Now aware of Platt's apparent meltdown, the office partners were concerned about the ramifications for themselves and wanted dearly to ditch him. But at the same time, they feared he would come after them with a hefty lawsuit. They knew from his boasting that he might have a stack of money behind him, and he might be able to tie everything up in legal moves and put a stranglehold on their seminar business. They consulted a lawyer to see how they could dump him with a minimum amount of fuss. It would be difficult, they were told.

Despite his reservations about Platt, Marsh continued to teach the Barking College course with him. After all, there was a contract to fulfil, and besides, he couldn't let the therapy students down after they'd placed their trust in him. On Wednesday, October 30, 1996, Platt was to assist Marsh but pulled out at the last minute, calling Marsh to say he was stuck in a traffic jam on the M25 and he wouldn't be able to make it in time.

Fourteen

HALLOWE'EN PARTY

A THICK AND unrelenting drizzle had descended like a dark blanket over the land as Det. Sgt. Peter Redman drove his unmarked car along Raven Hall Lane and past the Little London Farmhouse at about 6:35 on the morning of Thursday, October 31 — Hallowe'en, such a fitting day to arrest a man of disguises.

It had been just over two weeks since Redman knocked on the wrong door and discovered that David Davis was masquerading as Ronald Platt, but a lot had happened in that short time, including Ian Clenahan's interview with Elaine Boyes, followed by Davis's sudden trip to Harrogate the previous day.

Davis's little silver Metro was parked in the driveway, which meant he hadn't flown the coop. Redman used his cellular phone and awakened Det. Sgt. Bill MacDonald at the County Hotel in Chelmsford. "The car's still here. We're in," said Redman.

Redman would take care of Davis and the woman, whoever she was, and supervise the initial search of the house. MacDonald, meanwhile, would arrange transportation of the suspects to Devon and the subsequent interrogations. If Davis was going to flee, Redman had reasoned, it would be this day — the day of his afternoon appointment at Chelmsford police station. Redman didn't want to go knocking on Davis's door without a full squad behind him. It could get ugly, especially with children in the house.

He parked on the verge where Raven Hall Lane meets West Bowers Road. Redman could not see the Little London Farmhouse from his position, but Const. Mike Barlow, another Essex detective, set up on West Bowers Road with a clear view of the backyard. There was no sign of stirring in the house. They would just wait now until more officers arrived. Redman wanted to get enough manpower together so that when they knocked on the front door Davis would realize resistance was futile. Const. Steve Terry, authorized to carry tactical firearms in his Jeep Cherokee cruiser and on this occasion shouldering a pistol, took up position nearby. Redman felt Terry and his gun were necessary; they had few clues as to who Davis might be and what they were dealing with. After all, he was an American and might have his own gun. Redman was glad it was Terry and not he . . . he'd always hated guns.

Some three hours later, as the final details of the takedown were being worked out, Redman peered through the misted car windows and the rain that now pelted those outside to see a white Allied Taxi pull into Raven Hall Lane. He called Barlow on the cell phone and Barlow gave him a play-by-play on the cab's progress. Just as Redman himself had done on that fateful day of October 14, the cab drove past the Little London Farmhouse, possibly mistaking Frank and Audrey's house for it, as Redman had done. The cab reversed and stopped between the Mossman and the Platt house. "It's on its way out now," said Barlow. Moments later, the cab turned out of the lane with a passenger in the front seat. Redman cursed the mist as he tried but failed to ascertain if the passenger was Davis. Yet who else could it be? He knew that Frank had driven Audrey to the train station that morning — she was going to London — so it couldn't be either of them.

Redman followed the taxi as it made its way along the winding country roads to Danbury and onto the A414 towards Chelmsford. They could no longer take any chances with their mysterious quarry. Redman called Terry on his mobile and gave the go-ahead for the arrest. Redman was some distance behind the taxi when it turned onto the Chelmsford road. Just then, Steve Terry's police Jeep roared past Redman's car. Terry had already pulled over the taxi and was ordering its passenger out of the car as Redman drove up behind the cruiser. A tall figure emerged. It was Davis, all right.

Redman parked his car but stood back as Terry, his coat open to reveal his holstered gun, ordered Davis to the back of the vehicle and told him to spread-eagle himself face down over the taxi's trunk.

As Terry readied himself to place handcuffs on Davis, Redman stepped forward.

"Good morning, Mr. Davis. Do you remember me?"

"Yes, of course." Davis was showing some surprise. "What's this all about?"

"I'm arresting you on suspicion of the murder of Ronald Platt in Devon on or about July 21, 1996," said Redman.

"Okay," said Davis.

Redman went into the mandatory spiel that told Davis his rights. "Do you understand?" he finished.

"Okay," Davis said again, and nodded.

With this, Davis put his hands behind his back and seemed to accept his fate. Redman was surprised at the man's coolness.

Terry handcuffed Davis, took four keys from him and then drove him to the Chelmsford police station. Redman apologized to the bewildered cab driver. The driver just shrugged and pushed a button; the accumulated fare of £1.40 vanished from the meter. Satisfied at this smooth apprehension, Redman returned to the Little London Farmhouse and met up with other officers as they prepared to execute the search warrant. They knocked on the front door.

A young, attractive woman opened the door. Redman was taken aback. She was so much younger than her husband. A look of shock came across the woman's face as she saw police officer Susan Tyler in her uniform.

"Is it Elaine?" Redman ventured, not sure what to call her.

"No . . . Noël," she said. After taking a few moments to gather her thoughts, she asked, "What's this all about?"

"I'm arresting you on suspicion of murdering Ronald Platt in Devon on or about July 21, 1996," said Redman.

The young woman said nothing for a moment, showed nothing, then asked, "What about my children?"

Redman could see the toddler and the infant in the lobby behind her. "Arrangements can be made for the baby, but it will be best if you get care for the older child."

When Redman walked into the house, Noël explained that she was breast feeding so the baby would have to go with her. Redman didn't want to say too much or ask any questions. It is standard procedure not to talk unnecessarily during an arrest; it can only cause problems when the case gets to court. He looked around the house and saw that it was as bare inside as outside, and devoid of soul, as if it wasn't being lived in. With Redman nearby, Noël made a phone call to get care for Emily.

At Orchard Bungalow, the events of the morning had escaped Ed and Marion Jones as they prepared to meet with one of Ed's close business contacts. The telephone rang at about 10:30.

"Marion, it's Noël. Can you come over?"

"Oh, hello. Do you want to have coffee?"

"No. Will you come over?"

Marion sensed an urgency in the young woman's voice. Noël had never made demands on her before.

"Is it an emergency?" she ventured.

"Yes, it is."

Same old Noël, yes or no — that was it. Marion wondered if Noël wanted to get something for the children, go grocery shopping, perhaps take Emily to nursery school. "Can I give you a lift somewhere?" she offered.

"It's Ron." Noël's soft voice trailed off. She sighed.

"Is it a hospital? Can I give you a lift?" Marion offered again, trying to pry from Noël the words the young woman obviously wanted to say but couldn't.

"No. Marion, can you just come over?" Noël begged, almost out of breath now.

"I'll be right there."

Marion explained the mystery situation to Ed and told him she would return in time for the meeting. Then she turned her Volvo out of the driveway onto West Bowers Road and made a quick right again onto Raven Hall Lane. Across the farm fields ahead and around the bend in the lane, she could see an assortment of cars outside Ron Platt's house, among them a police cruiser. Because of her experience as a counsellor, Marion didn't get too excited by the sight; she had witnessed this scenario again and again. She pulled up outside and entered the house through the open door to find four uniformed police officers in the sitting room. They stared at her. A husky officer, whom she sensed was the superior, gave her a name she didn't catch and asked her to identify herself.

"I'm a friend of Noël's. I'm a responsible person. May I help?"

As though on cue, Noël came from another room. She had a half-packed bag in her hands. Clearly, she was being taken from the house.

"Oh, Marion," said Noël, somewhat stunned. And that was all she said.

Marion heard the chatter of children upstairs, then the clip-clop of someone coming down the stairs. Susan Tyler, the uniformed female officer, appeared and went up to the senior officer.

"Sir!" With this, she raised a hand. In it she held several gleaming gold bars. Everyone took a deep breath, then fell silent, pondering the find. Interrupting the bewilderment with another "Sir!" Tyler raised her other hand. In it she clasped a wad of brightly coloured Scottish £20 notes. The officer counted the notes on the spot. Marion lost track when he reached the £10,000 mark. She focused on Noël. The young woman moved like a zombie as she continued to pack her bag. She avoided eye contact with anyone, including Marion. When she finally did look over, her face was ashen as she asked if Marion could take care of Emily for a while.

"Oh, lovely, yes," replied Marion.

Noël didn't talk any further.

"And who are you?" asked Peter Redman, after witnessing the fleeting exchange.

"I'm Marion Jones. I'm a neighbour and a friend."

"Good," he said, handing Marion a card, then added, "I'm not at liberty to say anything at this point."

Marion took Emily outside to her car and under the watchful eye of a police officer tried to fit the little girl into the seatbelt. Her three-year-old frame wouldn't quite fill up the belt. After fussing and flapping, Marion finally decided to make do with what she had and drove off.

As she did so, officers drove Noël away in an unmarked car. Arrangements had been made to leave Lily with social services. It would be easier to question Noël without an infant around.

Inside at the Little London Farmhouse, police uncovered a veritable treasure chest. A suitcase contained £4,020 in English £20 notes; another stack of £20 notes totalled £2,900. The rucksack Noël had been packing, allegedly with items for the baby, held five gold bars and £4,100 in banknotes. Tyler found five more gold bars and various investment certificates in a bedroom. From a wallet police found a driver's licence, birth certificate, tetanus injection card and other documents in the name of R. J. Platt. Noël had already provided a birth certificate for Emily Jane Platt, born September 1993. As well, police came across a receipt from the Dittisham sailing school in Devon.

With Davis and Noël on their way, separately, to jail for post-arrest interviews, Redman slumped in his car seat and gave a sigh of relief: he would wait until the forensics team from Devon and Cornwall arrived to do a full search of the house. As the rain continued to thump on the car windows, his mind raced through what they'd just found. "Where did all that gold and all that money come from? What's that got to do with it?"

Meanwhile, at Chelmsford police station, Const. Mike Barlow searched the man who called himself Ron Platt and found British Telecom and Harrogate library cards, plus a birth certificate, all in the name of David Davis. But the man also had various bank cards in the names of R. J. Platt and R. L. Platt. This evidence accompanied Davis when he was taken to the Torquay police station later that day.

At 10:10 the next morning, Det. Sgt. Bill MacDonald and Det. Ian Clenahan conducted a tape-recorded interview with David Davis in the presence of his lawyer, Roger Bryce, from Gepp and Sons of Chelmsford. For eight minutes MacDonald and Clenahan barraged Davis with questions about his use of Ron Platt's name and the last time he'd seen Platt. They even asked, "Was it an accident?" But all they got from him was his name, David Walliss Davis, and his birthdate, February 17, 1944. Still, by his silence Davis told them there was even more to this bizarre tale than met the eye.

That afternoon in Torquay, Bryce was talking with Davis in his cell when Det. Const. Paul Lavis asked Davis for pubic hair, saliva, head hair and blood samples, warning Davis that if he did not comply, the fact of refusal could be used at his trial. Davis steadfastly refused, but Bryce hushed him and asked Lavis for clarification. The officer returned a few minutes later and said pubic hair had been requested under legal authority. Bryce asked for a few minutes to speak with his client, and when the officer returned Bryce told him Davis would comply only with the request for head hair and saliva. Lavis took a mouth swab and pulled two scalp hairs. They were put in sterile containers for testing.

As the law allows in a formal investigation, police fingerprinted Davis and took a file photograph. "Do you want me to smile?" Davis playfully asked as an officer prepared to take his mug shot.

On Monday, Davis was interviewed four times by MacDonald and Clenahan in Bryce's presence. Again, the usually garrulous bon vivant had nothing to say.

At the Little London Farmhouse, however, the forensic search uncovered all kinds of goodies. A briefcase contained a credit card, a diploma in the name of Ronald Platt, a diploma in the name of David Davis, rubber stamps depicting the signatures of Ronald Platt and Elaine Boyes and returned cheques with Platt's name on them. In a suitcase, detectives found more cash and business cards and other documents in the name of David Davis. A sports bag in a rear bedroom was stuffed with five more gold bars and four envelopes containing a total of £8,000 in cash. In Noël's handbag, searchers discovered medical documents, bank papers and credit cards in the name of Elaine Boyes. One business card purported to be that of financial consultant James B. Hilton of Belgravia, London. Throughout the Little London Farmhouse sat several Pickford moving boxes. One of the bedrooms was empty, and it appeared that someone had been sleeping rough on a downstairs couch. "The Platts," it seemed, had been ready to move.

Fifteen

DEAD MAN'S FOLLY

AS DAVIS COOLED his heels in prison, detectives began to pull together a case against the bizarre character in their custody who for three years had masqueraded as Ronald Platt while the unbelievably demure woman at his side had posed as Mrs. Noël Platt. The project was titled Operation Farrier.

Given Davis's web of deception in Britain, the police team felt there was a good chance he was up to his eyeballs in crime elsewhere and Interpol might already have his fingerprints on file. Immediately after getting prints from Davis, Devon detectives sent them to Interpol to be checked out. But because the worldwide fingerprint bank services so many countries and is perennially understaffed, results can take weeks, even months, to come back. Meanwhile, the detectives set about investigating a paper trail and interviewing witnesses.

In Devon, detectives followed up numbers listed on Davis's cell phone bills. They were ecstatic when they reached Frank Kirk Davis and a ferrymaster on the River Dart between Greenaway Quay and the village of Dittisham, and he confirmed he knew the bogus Platt and that Platt not only had a boat but kept it moored near Kirk's quay — a few miles upriver from Brixham, where trawler skipper John Copik had brought the real Ron Platt's body ashore.

When officers asked about two telephone calls the phoney Platt made to him one morning in July 1996, Kirk couldn't recollect either call. But he did remember first taking Mr. Platt and a male friend out to the mooring sometime in 1995. A brisk wind had turned the water rough that day, and the man now recognized from a police photo as the real Ron Platt sat on the bottom of the ferry and braced himself, afraid the ferry would tip over if he remained on the seat. Not much was spoken between the two men that day, Kirk remembered. The shorter fellow talked only when prompted by his friend.

The next time Mr. Platt used Kirk's ferry was when he came with the young lady — whom Kirk assumed was his wife or mistress — and the children. This was sometime in 1996, maybe ten months after the fake Platt had brought the real Platt. The woman smiled and said good morning, but like Platt's male friend she hardly uttered a word, either. The dynamics between the two were odd, Kirk thought. They shared none of the rapport you expect in a couple. Intuition told Kirk something was a little strange about them.

Sarcastically, Kirk recounted that one busy, sunny

day several yachters came back to Greenaway telling him of a bizarre sight — a boat going backward. Sure enough, a few hours later the *Lady Jane* streamed by Greenaway Quay in reverse.

John Foale, owner of a wharfside yacht service operation named Simanda Yacht Sales in the town of Totnes, also a few miles up the River Dart from Brixham, came forward voluntarily to police. Foale couldn't believe his ears in early November when the radio blasted out news that a businessman from Essex had been arrested for the summertime murder of Ron Platt — the Rolex Man, as he was initially known to Devon residents. The businessman, the announcer went on to say, had pretended to be Ron Platt.

"Which one is our Ron?" Foale had asked his business associates, Amanda and Simon Baker, and his marine mechanic, Stewart Williams. An American named Ron Platt had bought a sailboat from the Bakers and, mostly because of his own incompetence, had had all kinds of mechanical problems with it. Foale called Devon police, who confirmed that the man under arrest was that Ron Platt. In short order a team of detectives arrived in Totnes to take statements and pore over Simanda's business records.

It was in March 1994, the Bakers told police, that Platt had bought the sailboat, a twenty-four-foot Trident through them. When the Bakers first met Platt, he told them he was living in the tiny, secluded Devon village of Oakford, near Tiverton. Platt quickly changed the name of the sailboat from *Peach* to *Lady*

Jane. Amanda recalled that the fake Platt wanted to teach his young wife how to sail. It struck Amanda that the age gap between the so-called Platt and his wife was enormous. But the young woman seemed happy, albeit reserved, and she lavished affection on the baby daughter she carried along wherever she went. Amanda once tried to strike up a conversation with her, but when the shy young woman gave only yes and no answers, Amanda gave up.

Platt told Amanda he wanted to add equipment to the boat, specifically a satellite navigational system. John Foale saw to it that the *Lady Jane* was equipped with an Apelco Global Positioning System, a device that bounces signals off twenty satellites that orbit the earth and allows a mariner to pinpoint his position to within a hundred yards, provided the system can get a fix on three satellites. The system comes with a separate aerial that attaches to a railing on the deck. Simon Baker just shook his head. He didn't think much of Platt's sailing. In fact, he didn't think much of Platt. First, he had the most foul breath, and second, when he talked he was one of the most boring men on the planet.

In the spring of 1995, Platt again showed up with his wife and child to go sailing. He announced that he had moved to Essex for a job. After having problems with the *Lady Jane*'s engine, he installed another one, but when he attempted to sail from Devon to Essex the engine mounting fell apart because the wood was rotten; the boat got stranded near

Lymington, only halfway to Platt's destination on the Blackwater Estuary.

Still, when sailing weather arrived in the spring of 1996, Platt turned up once more. This time he brought not only his wife, their daughter and another new baby, but a male friend. The man was so quiet and unimpressive that nobody could say for certain what he looked like. Off they went with the boat. Fitted with a new engine, the *Lady Jane* should have worked like a charm. It didn't.

"I can't get it into forward gear. It will only go in reverse!" Platt moaned to John Foale on the phone in the late summer. He needed to get it fixed right away because he was coming to Devon for the weekend and wanted to go sailing. When Foale inspected the *Lady Jane* he found someone had slammed a gear into position rather than smoothly moving it, and this bent the control cable from the gear lever to the gearbox.

Both in their early thirties, John Foale and Simon Baker were amazed at how such a decidedly boring middle-aged man could hook such a young, beautiful woman. John and Simon chuckled about the odd couple and wondered how Platt had managed to "rob the cradle." In June or July 1996, they popped the question.

"What's the secret, Ron?" John asked. "How did you catch such a lovely wife? She's young enough to be your daughter!"

Platt responded with a chuckle and a cheesy

grin. "I'm just a very lucky man. I have two gorgeous children and a very beautiful wife."

Some weeks afterward, Platt suddenly asked John to look at the gear cable, repair a dent in the *Lady Jane*'s propeller and deliver the craft to a marina in Essex. John sent Platt a bill at the Little London Farmhouse for about £530, and Platt paid up. No one at Simanda heard from him after that.

Detectives, chasing other leads from Davis's phone records, moved around Totnes and downriver as far as Dartmouth, trying to connect Davis and Platt in the weeks leading up to Platt's death. In speaking with publican Ed Thomas and his son Paul at the Steam Packet Inn, only a few hundred yards along the wharf from Simanda Yacht Sales, detectives found a damning link between Davis and the real Ron Platt. From the night of July 6 to the morning of July 9, the inn's records showed, a Ronald Platt and a David Platt stayed in a second-floor studio apartment. The odd thing was, noted Ed, that the man he recognized from a photograph as Davis had called himself Ron Platt and had introduced his shorter, thinner companion — whom Ed recognized as the real Ronald Platt — as his cousin David. This injected an entirely new element into police equation: clearly the real Ron Platt knew Davis was using his name! Detectives now had to consider the possibility of blackmail.

On July 10, the bogus Platt booked a room for David Platt at the Steam Packet; David Platt stayed until the morning of July 18. Even though summer traffic in Totnes meant full houses for the Steam Packet, Paul Thomas not only remembered the congenial, meticulously turned out North American Ron Platt and the man he introduced as his cousin but also two earlier visits when Ron Platt had taken the studio with his young wife and their children. Paul guessed from his accent that Ron Platt was Canadian; the noticeable maple leaf tattoo on his cousin's hand suggested that he, too, was Canadian. Ron and David Platt always seemed to get along well and looked quite at home in the comfortable Tudor-style bar. They either sat directly in front of the towering beer taps huddled in a tight corner nook. Most of the time they kept to themselves. They would eat breakfast at the inn, leave, then return for supper but never for lunch. Ron Platt always paid the bills with cash. Ron, noted Paul, was a bit of a braggart and the more dominant of the two; in contrast, the shorter man was almost mute, much like Ron Platt's young wife. Thomas also noted that when he last saw Ron and David Platt in mid-July, their friendship appeared to have chilled.

Police learned from Steam Packet patrons Geraldine Thompson and Janet Barr that while they were drinking at the bar in July they met two men, whom they now recognized as Davis and Platt. Davis, the women said, did all the talking, telling them he was a Canadian but that he had lived recently in Scotland. He and his friend were sailing to France, he volunteered, where they had just bought a farm and would start a new life. The women inquired if they were married. "We were," Davis said, "but we're not any more!"

Tracking Davis and Platt after they left the Steam Packet Inn, detectives spoke with manager, Ken Stone of the Royal Seven Stars Hotel in the busy pub of Totnes. After checking his records, Stone confirmed that a man named Platt took two rooms on July 9, but stayed only one night. Stone remembered the booking because it was unusual. First, a man called from a cell phone that evening to reserve a room, he and his party would arrive late because they had to wait for the tide to rise to dock, he explained. He called again just after 11 p.m. to say they were on their way, and not long after, two men appeared in the lobby. As Stone prepared to take the booking, the taller of the pair told him in a saddened voice, "I've just run over a cat." The other fellow stayed in the background and didn't utter a word. Stone could only tell police that both men booked in under the name Platt but didn't use first names.

While the real Ron Platt was at the Steam Packet, the bogus Ron Platt, it seemed, had stayed downriver in the pretty hamlet of Dittisham. A bed-and-breakfast operator, Mary Quick, confirmed that her Potter's Loft cottage was rented to Mr. and Mrs. Platt from July 12 to 19. She said the man police knew as Davis had identified himself as Ron Platt and had introduced Noël as his wife.

During a door-to-door campaign, detectives found that the real Ron Platt had spent the last known days of his existence at a bed-and-breakfast called the Anchorage. Owner Joan Wintle's records showed that on July 18 and 19 a Mr. Platt rented a room there. Shown a photo of the real Platt, Mrs. Wintle could not say if it was him, but she recalled that he was a quiet and gentle man, a loner.

On July 19, the bogus Platt and his family wanted to stay at Potter's Loft longer, but the property was already booked. They rented another Dittisham cottage, the Old Brewhouse, from July 19 until July 26, but left early on July 23.

The detectives were elated: they had placed Davis and Platt together in Devon from July 6 to July 10. And while there was no direct link between the two men from July 10 on, police could place them only miles apart — with certainty — until the morning of July 20, 1996, eight days before Platt's body was found.

When interviewed by Detectives MacDonald and Clenahan at Torquay police station shortly after her arrest, the young woman who called herself Noël Platt looked the interrogators straight in the eye and confidently told them she was Noël and that she came from New York — basically the same story Davis had told others over the years. Yes, she went by the name of Davis as well, as did Ronald, or David. By this time, MacDonald and Clenahan were fully aware that their main suspect and this woman were certainly not who they claimed to be. She tried her best to bluff them, but while Noël had been well rehearsed and could give the basic facts of who she was and where she was from, she stumbled and stuttered when asked to supply names for her math teacher and others. The background information was important to police, but what they really wanted to talk about was the Devon holiday that she and her husband took in July. As Noël spoke freely about their vacation, it became painfully apparent that she didn't have a clue that the real Ron Platt had been in Devon with the so-called Davis in July. As far as she knew, Ron Platt had gone to France. As far as she was concerned, he had probably committed suicide. On three separate occasions detectives quizzed her in fine detail on the Devon trip. She could lie all she wanted about her past, but it would be these specifics about the Devon Trip that would nail Davis.

Sixteen

A MURDER IS ANNOUNCED

BACK IN ESSEX, the probe moved along at a furious pace. Detectives tracing the real Ronald Platt's movements after he left Beardsley Drive on June 21, 1996, found startling evidence at a Chelmsford storage firm. After renting a unit the same day that he left Beardsley Drive, Platt and Davis showed up at Chelmsford Storage Ltd. with Platt's furniture and belongings. Following a big discussion, Platt and Davis took away three Samsonite suitcases. But in an odd twist, Davis returned the three suitcases on July 31, three days after Platt's body was found, and asked that they be put with the rest of Platt's goods. Opening the cases, detectives found Platt's Canadian citizenship card, a cheque book and forty-six items of clothing, as well as other personal effects. It raised the question, Why would Platt go to France without his suitcases and some key personal belongings? Also on June 21, Platt had checked into the Tanunda Hotel in Chelmsford and stayed there until the morning of July 6, the same day that Ronald Platt and his "cousin" checked into the Steam Packet in Totnes. As usual, Davis had paid. Had Davis put Platt into the hotel as an interim measure until he could carry out his plan to kill him? Cleaning staff at the Tenunda recalled that Platt had very little luggage. They also recalled that almost every morning they found an empty wine or sherry bottle in Platt's room.

The Essex arm of the probe also took police to the Blackwater Marina. There, on November 1, 1996, a forensic officer boarded the moored *Lady Jane* and removed various items for analysis. Of special interest was the GPS navigational aerial on the boat's back rail. The navigational unit itself, however, had been dismantled from the cockpit. Detectives knew the GPS unit must be somewhere. Perhaps the aerial and, if they could find it, the unit paper could help them trace the *Lady Jane*'s movements.

Three head hairs linked by a trace of human skin were found on a cushion in the cabin. These were bagged for DNA testing before the *Lady Jane* was taken to the Forensic Sciences Centre in Chepstow for further tests.

Checks with car rental companies revealed damning evidence that on August 24, 1996, two days after Detective Sergeant Redman had informed Davis of his best friend Ronald Platt's drowning death, Davis, under the name of R. J. Platt and paying with a Visa card in Platt's name, rented a Ford Transit van from Chelmsford-based Blue Line Hire, through August 28. The lease was later extended as the so-called Mr. Platt kept the van until August 30. Earlier Transit rentals coincided with the days that Platt moved to Chelmsford and checked into the Tenunda Hotel.

Checks with financial companies showed that in late August and September of 1996, Davis was buying gold bars in large quantities. On August 27, five days after he'd learned of Platt's death from police, the fake Platt showed up at London bullion dealer Metalor, seeking to buy twelve half-kilo bars of gold. He was quoted £57,880 by Metalor staff, but the deal wasn't completed because Metalor's gold supplier didn't want to trade. A London jeweller recalled that a man calling himself Platt wanted to buy £50,000 in loose diamonds but then switched his focus to gold when the jeweller advised him it had more liquidity. An agreement to buy £19,994 worth of gold fell through in August, but on September 12 Platt bought two 1-kilogram bars for £18,936. Later in September, "Ronald Platt" bought five 500-gram gold bars from a Credit Suisse branch for £23,607.

Clearly, Davis had been spooked by the police probe and he was on the move.

Oblivious to all the police commotion, Isabel Rogers was at home November 1, 1996, when a friend phoned her.

"When was the last time you saw that American, Ron Platt?"

"Three or four weeks ago," said Isabel. "Why?

The friend paused. "He's been murdered. It was on the news. Ronald Platt, fifty-one, from Woodham Walter. He's been murdered. I heard it on the radio."

Isabel called the police and told them about her dealings with Platt.

Detectives hadn't known much about the therapy business and said they would dispatch someone to talk with her immediately. They explained that the Ron Platt she knew was still alive but was facing murder charges.

Isabel promptly called Ian Marsh. "When did you last hear from Ron Platt?" she asked after a few pleasantries.

"He called me Wednesday night. He was supposed to teach with me at Barking, but he was stuck on the M25 and couldn't make it. Why do you ask?"

"He's either dead or he's murdered somebody," she stated bluntly.

"Murder? Ron?"

"Yes, murder. One man called Ron Platt is dead and another man named Ron Platt is in custody, charged with murder. The guy we know as Ron Platt — apparently, he doesn't exist!"

When police interviewed Isabel they were stunned. "You know him much better than anyone," one detective said. The officers came back again and again, asking for more and more details.

As police continued their probe over the weekend, Marsh and the partners checked the ledgers at the therapy office and found that a lot of money

Ron the Voice had bragged was on the books wasn't accounted for. Marsh and the others were devastated.

"Bloody hell," Marsh said, head in hands. "This can't be happening."

The trio were more concerned about their integrity and their overall careers than about extra money in their pockets from their side business. Isabel thought it so unfair. Ian, David and the other Ron were such decent, ethical and trusting people, who had for years been dedicated to helping others.

Marsh begged Isabel to accompany him to the upcoming night class at Barking College. It would be the biggest, most stressful therapy session of their lives. Marsh was almost green with sickness as he waited in the classroom for the students to arrive.

Eventually they told the students that Mr. Platt had been arrested and was being questioned for murder.

After the shock, Marsh and Isabel explained what they knew of the two Ronnies. Barking almost cancelled the course at the news, but the students rallied around their teachers and the course was saved. Isabel was furious at Platt, or whoever he really was. This was such a betrayal by the man the students had counted on to give them a grounding in therapy, a method that depends so heavily on trust. He had pretended to teach the students honesty; instead, he sold them a pack of lies.

Seventeen

CARDS ON
THE TABLE

ON NOVEMBER 6, 1996, fisherman John Copik called the Devon and Cornwall police.

"What about the anchor?" he asked.

"What anchor?" quizzed the detective.

"The anchor that came up in the net with the body!" Copik went on to say that the only way the 10-pound plough anchor could have gotten into the net was if it had been attached to something — a body, for instance.

"Where is the anchor now?" the policeman asked hopefully.

"I gave it away."

Copik told police he had handed the anchor to Derek Meredith at Brixham Harbour; if they were lucky, he still might have it. Meredith's wife, Susan Johnson, informed police that when she went to an August 4 car boot sale, Meredith gave her an anchor from the garage and asked her to sell it. She tried to flog it for £15, but nobody bought it. After the sale she had taken the anchor to her mother's house.

Detectives breathed a sigh of relief when Pam Johnson confirmed she still had the anchor. The tag for the £15 asking price was still on it.

Checking through credit card records, detectives found that on July 8, only twelve days before Platt was last seen at the Anchorage bed-and-breakfast, Davis had used his Ronald Platt card to buy a 10-pound Sewester plough anchor, a length of polyester rope and half a dozen other marine items at the Sport Nautique store in Dartmouth. There was great rejoicing among the Operation Farrier brass — it must be, had to be, the very anchor that came up in John Copik's net! The anchor would be tested at the Chepstow forensics lab.

Success, as they say, follows success. Detectives were still rejoicing over the anchor when, on November 13, after tracking a receipt found at Little London Farmhouse, they recovered the GPS unit from a Genstar storage unit in Northampton, Northamptonshire. It was sent off with the *Lady Jane*'s aerial to a specialist in Portsmouth. The GPS system wasn't the only haul at Genstar. Five 10-ounce gold bars, and two 1-kilo gold bars, £8,000 in cash, a National Insurance card in David Davis's name and an application for a birth certificate in Elaine Boyes's name were also found, as well as the company papers for Cavendish Corporation. Genstar records showed that a David W. Davis and Elaine Boyes rented the Genstar unit on August 26, 1996. A month later, the so-called Boyes paid for more rental time, and a month after that, on October 20, the couple returned again.

As Davis spent his third week in custody, scientists at Chepstow Forensics made swift progress analysing the evidence before them. Dr. Alexander Grant was asked to determine if the plough anchor had ever been used and if it had had any prolonged contact with the leather belt Platt had been wearing. Grant found the zinc-coated steel anchor had hardly any surface wear and only minimal corrosion. Even the steel flash from the casting process, which had remained inside the anchor's chain slot, was intact. This suggested to Grant that the anchor had not been used for normal purposes. Examining the belt, Grant noted several diagonal marks on the inside, about a foot from the buckle. Under a microscope, he saw that the marks had been lightly etched into the leather. Analysis found the marks contained significant levels of zinc. Using the police proposition that the anchor and belt had been on a corpse at the bottom of the sea for a week, Grant concluded that the zinc deposits on the belt could have come from the anchor. The corrosive action of salt water, he said, would have hastened the transfer.

Around the same time, the Rolex watch pulled from Platt's body three months earlier was taken to Rolex headquarters in Bexley, Kent. The watch still showed the same date and time it had when police first looked at it in Brixham Harbour and later at the Torbay Hospital morgue — 11:35 on the twenty-second day.

Rolex's chief technician, Trevor Pilkinton, ascertained that the watch was fully waterproof and fully functional. It would take, he concluded, eight to 10 hours of daily wrist movement to keep it fully wound. But more important, as far as police were concerned, he estimated that if the watch were fully wound but then left stationary, it would stop after about four or five hours. The Operation Farrier squad were ecstatic. Working backwards, they deduced that if the watch had stopped on July 22, 1996, at either 11:35 a.m. or 11:35 p.m., Platt likely met his end on July 20–July 21 at the latest. Given that he was last seen alive in Dartmouth the morning of July 20, this finding was big!

A water hydraulics expert later confirmed that if a 10-pound anchor was attached to a body on the sea bed, the body would not move. Thus, the wound-down watch theory was supported.

From the evidence before them so far, police developed their hypothesis of how Platt had met his end. With the motive and the means to kill Platt, Davis took him out on the *Lady Jane*, struck him on the back of the head with a blunt instrument, perhaps even the anchor, then attached the anchor to Platt's body and dumped him overboard.

Two more results were still to come in: a second post-mortem and the analysis of the *Lady Jane*'s Global Positioning System.

On November 25, Dr. Gyan Fernando examined Platt's body for the second time. Before this post-mortem, police gave Fernando an anchor and suggested that it might have been attached to the body, perhaps from the left-side waistband of the trousers. Placing the anchor alongside the leg where it would have fitted into the belt, Fernando saw that the bruises on the hip and knee aligned perfectly with the contacting edges of the anchor. It was obvious to Fernando that the anchor could have caused the bruises. Both Fernando and a defence pathologist who examined the body the same day reasoned that the injuries were caused before death. Putting it all together, police determined that after knocking Platt unconscious, Davis tucked the anchor into his belt and tossed him into the sea.

Over the next week, all of the work that had gone into Operation Farrier paid off. With a police video-camera rolling, Ian Roalf and Robert Thompson of Rathion Marine in Portsmouth examined both the GPS display unit and the GPS antenna, Roalf and Thompson were familiar with the Apelco GPS system because their company marketed the units.

Downloading the display unit, they found the last recorded time and date to be 19:59 Greenwich Mean Time on July 20, 1996. Given an advance in one hour for British Summer time, this meant the GPS was turned off at 8:59 p.m. on July 20, 1996. Subsequent examination of the memory in the antenna revealed that the last reported position matched that in the display unit.

More important, though, the GPS showed that

at that time on that date — the suspected day of Platt's murder — the *Lady Jane* was at sea off Hope's Nose — only 3.78 nautical miles from where John and Craig Copik pulled up Ronald Platt's body eight days later.

While all these investigations were in progress, the Interpol fingerprint inquiry came back, matched to a man wanted by the Ontario Provincial Police in Canada and by the United States Marshals. The Interpol information sheet gave not one but two biographies:

> WANTED: Walker, Albert Johnson . . . it is unknown what name the subject has assumed . . . 6-foot-1, 170 pounds, hair brown with grey streaks, eyes brown . . . subject will probably be in the company of his daughter Sheena. Sheena is not a wanted fugitive. She is a missing person from Canada. Wanted on theft and fraud offences totalling $3.5 million.

> MISSING PERSON: Walker, Sheena . . . 5-foot-7, 130 pounds, brown hair, brown eyes . . . Sheena Walker left Canada in December 1990 with her father, Albert Johnson Walker, and there has been no known contact with friends or family since then.

And except for the dyed hair, his black, hers blonde, and a few years on each face, there in the Interpol photographs were the bogus David and Noël Davis —

and for the first time confirmation that she was not his wife but his daughter.

Now police had their answer to the perplexing riddle of David Davis and his manipulation of Ron Platt and Elaine Boyes. He had used them to move money through the Cavendish Corporation because it was stolen money, all $3.5 million of it. And then, detectives theorized, after the man they now knew as Albert Walker had successfully used Platt and Boyes to launder his dirty money into a variety of bank accounts in such a way that he could never be traced, Walker packed them off to Canada — Calgary, Alberta. From February 1993 on, it appeared, all British bank accounts bearing the names of Ron Platt and Elaine Boyes were in fact controlled by Walker. Whenever Walker wanted to use Platt's or Boyes's signature to verify an official record, he would simply use the rubber stamp signature he had made up in 1991, purportedly for convenience but actually so that after they left he could keep up business as usual.

With the truth out, Noël Platt acknowledged in an interview with Clenahan and MacDonald that she was Sheena Walker and that her father, Albert Walker, was the man being held in custody. Despite grilling Sheena about Ronald Platt, the British detectives could not break her down and quickly determined that she knew him as her father's friend but beyond that knew little about Platt's life and nothing about his death. The implications of the father-daughter marital combination, however, were staggering. Were the children born through incest? When the detectives asked Sheena who had fathered the children, she held her head low, began crying and wouldn't answer their question. Short of Sheena's confession to the paternity issue, there was no way police could ascertain once and for all if Albert Walker was the father. Although they had blood and saliva samples from Sheena and Walker, there were no legal grounds to take samples from the children for a comparison. Even as babies they had a full right to privacy under the law. As incredible as the truth might be, the question of paternity would not help the case in court. The issue would be simple: did Walker murder Ronald Platt off Devon in July 1996?

It appeared so. In just over a month, police had compiled a formidable case against Walker. The evidence was all circumstantial but it was incredibly rich. Albert Walker, though considered innocent until proven guilty by the courts, was in hot water, and sinking fast.

Eighteen

CAT AMONG
THE PIGEONS

ALBERT JOHNSON WALKER'S birth in the Ontario steel city of Hamilton came on a day when everyone's focus was on the mass destruction wrought by the atomic bomb the Allies had dropped earlier that day on Nagasaki and on the blast that had levelled Hiroshima three days earlier. When baby Albert's birth finally hit the Announcements page, it took up little more than one line: "WALKER — At Mountain Avenue Hospital on August 9, 1945, to Mr. and Mrs. William G. Walker of Freelton, a son." (Marion Jones didn't know on August 9, 1995, that when the man she knew as Ronald Platt made such a fuss of her fiftieth birthday, he was also celebrating his own.)

Albert was one of five children born to the Walkers, who lived on a farm near Freelton, about thirty miles north of Hamilton and fifty miles west of Toronto. By his own accounts, young Albert was distant from family members. He clearly detested his mother — he thought she treated him harshly — and he had little interaction with his father. In fact, Albert made it his business to stay away from the house as much as he could. While the adult Albert often gave complete strangers nostalgic soliloquies about his childhood on the farm, he told others that his family connection was weak. Perhaps when Albert waxed lyrical about farm life, he was fantasizing about how he had wanted it to be.

Actually, he spent few years in the country. He was about six when his parents sold the 56-acre spread to Canadian army veteran Jim Munday and his wife, Ruby. The Mundays swapped their Hamilton house for the farm, but William Walker quickly turned over the Hamilton property for cash and bought another place outside the city. The Walker farm had looked like a good deal for the Mundays but within weeks of moving in, it quickly became apparent that William Walker had made no improvements in a half-dozen or more years there. Almost every corner of the house had been neglected in some way and years later Munday found out the barn's main beams were rotting because Walker had ignored a leaking roof. About ten years after the Mundays took over, a teenage boy stopped by and asked if he could look around. He said he'd lived there once and really missed the old place. The boy stayed for an hour or so, just wandering around the barn and the fields. Then he thanked the Mundays and left. Now, upon reflection, they believe the young visitor was Albert Walker.

Tracking more about Albert's childhood is difficult. Many people connected with Albert have wanted little to do with the man for years and want even less to do with him now. But even with the scant details that are known, it doesn't take much imagination to conclude that there were many problems in Walker's family. Either Albert rejected them, or they collectively spurned him. Given Albert Walker's character, the latter is a more plausible explanation.

In contrast, the family of Barbara McDonald, the woman Albert was to marry, was close-knit, trusting and, for the most part, nonjudgemental. The McDonald clan once loved the newspaper spotlight, at least at the community level. When Barbara was a little girl in the Ontario town of Ayr, her parents frequently ensured they made the gossip column in the *Ayr News*. Called Town Talk, the chatty column was a fixture on the paper's front page. The first-ever mention of Barbara is on the front page of the July 11, 1946 edition. Births: "McDonald — To Mr. and Mrs. John McDonald in Galt Hospital, on Sunday July 7, twins, a boy and a girl [Donald Robert, or Bob, and Barbara Mary Anne]."

According to the *Ayr News*, the tiny town of Ayr was the centre of the universe. On its front page, the *News* showed a map of Southern Ontario. A black dot pinpointed the location of each city and town in the province. The relatively large cities of Kitchener-

Waterloo, Galt and Woodstock, each with populations in the tens of thousands, were represented by small dots. Ayr, in contrast, was represented by the biggest black dot, with radar-style rings radiating from it in all directions. Local pride notwithstanding, it was hardly a place that stuck out in the consciousness of Ontario residents. Basically, Ayr was a staunch Scottish Presbyterian farming community filled with humble, hard-working people who had to grind out a tough living in the dairy and cash crop business.

The McDonald clan had been an Ayr fixture for decades. Like most of their farming neighbours, the McDonalds were salt-of-the-earth folks, generous to family, friends and the community. Jack McDonald and his wife, Hilda, Barbara's parents, were known to be respectful, courteous and considerate. Local business people never had a problem with any of the McDonalds. Their word was their bond.

The first public linking of Albert Walker and Barbara McDonald was in the Town Talk column of Thursday, October 3, 1968: "Sunday guests of Mr. and Mrs. Jack McDonald were their daughter Barb of Downsview and Al Walker of Galt." Four weeks later the *Hamilton Spectator* Weddings column noted: "WALKER–McDONALD — The wedding of Barbara McDonald, daughter of Mr. and Mrs. J. D. McDonald, Hall St., Ayr, and Albert Walker, Galt, took place quietly at St. Paul's Chapel at the University of

Waterloo, Friday evening, October 25. The candle-light service was attended by parents, brothers and sisters of the bride and groom from Oakville, Water-down, Hamilton, Hespeler, Galt, Los Angeles and Ayr. The bride and groom wish to express their sincere thanks to Bob Marshall for the beautiful rendition of the wedding music and to Reverend D. E. Willis for conducting the service in such a meaningful and reverent manner."

Doug Willis, minister of Knox United Church in Ayr, recalled how Albert and Barbara had met through a youth group while attending the University of Waterloo. Willis, who counselled the couple before their wedding, said the homely and naive Barbara had taken a great interest in the energetic and well-groomed Albert, and without much, if any, experience in matters of the heart, suddenly found herself "swept off her feet." Lacking any close family connection himself — or close friends, for that matter — Albert was quickly absorbed into the McDonald clan. While still at university, Barbara and her new husband were frequent visitors to Ayr. Barbara's mother embraced her son-in-law as one of her own, and in many ways treated him better than her son Bob, a gentle and kind soul. With Hilda's help and encouragement, Albert joined the Ayr community and carried the pride of being a McDonald.

After getting married, Barbara and Albert con-tinued with school. It seems, though, that they had different academic abilities. Barbara pushed ahead and easily earned her degree; Albert, who had dropped out of high school at sixteen, earned only two years of credits in five years as an adult student, passing a course in literary criticism and a course in business administration. Even then he had low marks.

Albert's first traceable job was at Zellers department stores, where he found the expected labours of a trainee manager — checking stock, stocking shelves and arranging displays — a bit beneath his pedigree. He had expected a manager to manage, but at Zellers and stores like it, trainee managers, he lamented, were essentially glorified stock clerks. His time at Zellers was short.

In 1970, Barb and Albert lived for a while in Scotland. Albert worked as a health insurance salesman for the Combined Insurance Company of America, selling policies through various contacts and by knocking on doors. He would later tell business associates that he had a degree from the University of Edinburgh, but given his limited high-school education and his stay of less than two years in Scotland, this claim is highly suspect. Records compiled by OPP detectives showed that while in Scotland he completed only two postsecondary courses: creative writing at the University of Edinburgh and computer training at Heriot-Watt University.

In 1971 Al, as he was known, worked at the Dana Porter Library, at the University of Waterloo stacking books and supervising the part-time students shelving them. Barbara, meanwhile, was a librarian at a small branch in the Kitchener-Waterloo suburbs. Library workers recall Al Walker as a "serious person" and "a man with a plan." Each day he showed up for work dressed in a trademark tweed suit, with a pressed shirt and stiff collar and tie. There was never a hair out of place and he was always clean-shaven. The attire seemed entirely inappropriate to other student workers, if for no other reason than Albert was basically stacking and carrying dusty library books that tended to dirty clothes.

"Al, what are you doing dressed like that?" co-workers would ask.

"You have to dress well to get ahead," Walker would assure them, adding that he had his eyes set on management.

"But, Al," they would say in disbelief, "you don't have a library science degree. You can't be a librarian without a library science degree!"

Walker would shrug off their sage observation. He stubbornly held out that good dress, hard work and gaining the favour of people in the right places would get him ahead. He told doubters to watch him: he had a dream to retire to Scotland at fifty and he would make sure that dream came true.

For about six years Albert tried to ingratiate himself with library management, showing his prowess and knowledge at every possible opportunity. Some employees tagged him a "butt-kisser." Yet he was always charming and pleasant, especially to the women, often complimenting them on the way they looked and the nice smell of their perfume. But his ambition was so nakedly obvious that his superiors came to view him as a pest. Ultimately, colleagues saw him as an object of ridicule. His boasting and exaggerating were typically passed off with a shake of the head and an "Oh, come on, Al."

While still holding down their library jobs, Albert and Barb Walker began doing income tax returns and bookkeeping from their house. Locals believed that Barbara was the brains and Albert just the frontman. Their initial clients were friends and acquaintances of Barbara's parents — farmers, mostly. During this time, too, Barbara gave birth to two daughters: Jillian, born January 19, 1972, and Sheena, born July 28, 1975.

Albert left the library in 1975 and tried his hand at market gardening but couldn't cut its varied pressures. For over a year he worked as a general labourer for the Ayr Feed and Supply Company and in 1976 hired out as a cattle herdsman for Ballona Enterprises. Albert was never happy while surrounded by animal feed and cow manure. His ambition for something better saw him again go into the white-collar sector in 1978, when he became a life insurance agent for Mutual Life of Canada. On August 16 that year Al and Barbara registered Walker Financial Services Incorporated. As Walker continued selling insurance, he and Barb offered payroll and income tax services for other companies.

A few months after John McDonald died in 1978, Albert and Barbara bought a century-old farmhouse on rural Watt's Pond Road, on the northern outskirts of Paris, Ontario, a small community only a dozen odd miles south of Ayr. During the next four years, two more kids were added to the Walker household: Duncan James McAllister, born June 25, 1979, and Heather Jane, born on June 14, 1982.

Knox United Church in Ayr continued to be central in the Walkers' lives. Throughout their childhoods, Knox United had been like a home to Barbara and her twin brother, Bob. Jack and Hilda McDonald had been long-time members, and Hilda was among the small but tightly knit group who kept the church working. Knox retained its Presbyterian pedigree and unrepentantly Scottish flavour. Albert Walker, the pseudo-Scot with the tweed jackets, was able to blend into the scenery. In short order, he became a counsellor with the youth group, taught Sunday school and, with his booming bass, was a natural for the choir. When it came time for Reverend Doug Willis to baptize the Walker children, Albert insisted on the full religious regalia. Not a drop of pomp and ceremony was spared, and hardly anyone of social importance was left from the guest list. Albert, it seemed, shouldered the burden of his Christian cross with great ease.

Over time Albert gained some powerful friends in the congregation, in particular Gord and Barb

McRuer and Bob and Betty Staley. The McRuers and the Staleys were also choir members and were closely connected with the Walkers through the 1970s — if only they had known. It wasn't so much that they were Albert's friends but Barbara's. Even after the Ontario Ministry of Natural Resources transferred Bob Staley to the Toronto area in the late 1970s, the Staleys kept in touch with the Walkers. The couples visited Scotland together two or three times and for all intents and purposes could be termed the best of friends. With the support of his close friends in the church congregation, Albert was eventually elected to the prestigious post of church elder.

Reverend Willis's wife, Joan, recalled how Hilda McDonald appeared to treat Albert better than her own family. And Albert, of course, played the part of the doting son-in-law, always complimenting Hilda on her choice of clothes, bringing her flowers and chocolates and making sure that his children fussed over her. Baby Duncan's arrival, for example, earned her a special note in the birth announcements: "First grandson for Grandma Mac!" When Albert was elected elder, Hilda threw a party for him and took the entire family out for dinner; her son Bob's election as an elder, however, passed virtually unnoticed. In Hilda's mind, neither of the twins lived up to the exploits of their elder brother, Ken, who left Ayr for an education and later gained fame as a broadcaster for the Los Angeles Kings. But her son-in-law certainly did.

Albert always dressed like an uppercrust gentleman, wearing flashy navy blue or black pin-striped suits and matching old-school tie. And he could turn on the charm as naturally as others turn on a radio. He wore his religious piety like a badge for all to see, but he was quick to tell anyone who cared to listen that he was a financial whiz-kid.

Reverend Doug Willis saw through the superficial Christian before him. Willis didn't trust Albert or even like him. The cleric believed Albert's position and prestige as a leader was built on the back of the McDonald family's impeccable reputation. He was of the opinion that without the strength of the McDonalds, Albert's world would fall like a house of cards.

Nor was Joan Willis impressed with Albert. She hadn't liked him from the first moment he'd walked into the church: "I don't know why, but I just didn't trust him. He was too smooth. Very debonair. I thought he was pretty cocky. He really thought he was somebody, but he really wasn't anybody . . . He gave you this picture of being a gentleman, wanted to be a gentleman farmer. When he bought the farm he said, Oh, no, I won't have to pay taxes on it. He could write it off . . . He was a chameleon . . . he had a way of saying things . . . would kind of lower his eyelids and speak in that soft voice. Some people just go for that." She recalled, too, that Walker had a "strange sexual side to him." She cannot remember the details of a conversation they once had but concluded from it that Walker had "poor boundaries." She pitied

Barbara Walker, who, she observed, was enchanted by her husband's ways. Albert, it seemed, could do no wrong in Barbara's eyes.

In the early 1980s, Albert Walker bought a book-keeping business in Ayr. While still working his land part-time as a pig farmer, he bragged to the church flock about the returns he was making on investments. The returns seemed good to Willis, but when Albert approached him to invest and make some money, he didn't give the so-called opportunity a second thought because he knew how his wife felt about Walker. "If I had suggested putting $25 in one of his accounts Joan would have had a fit! She just felt he wasn't on the up and up . . . and she told me not to invest a dollar with Al Walker!"

Succeeding Reverend Willis after sixteen years was a difficult task for Reverend George Saunders, a likeable fellow with a quick wit. When he began his mission at the church in July 1982, Saunders didn't find much fun in Albert Walker, whom he found suspiciously slick and slightly condescending. Saunders sensed that Albert consistently heaped lots of subtle put-downs onto the people around him.

"Frankly, I didn't like Albert Walker. I found him very smugly superior. He tended to look down on me. I'm sure he did, although he didn't cross swords with me at all. I can remember one time during a sermon on mid-life crisis and I was saying there comes a time when people realize they have reached their peak. He came up to me afterwards and, in the most condescending way, gave me a little lecture on, 'Oh, never give up.' But it was the tone he took, as if I were somehow weak. He didn't get the point that people reach the point where they cannot go any further. I must say I didn't like it."

Albert was quick to volunteer for anything, but whenever the moment of reckoning came he was never there. In contrast, his brother-in-law Bob McDonald was as solid as a rock. When the time came to prepare for the church's 150th birthday celebrations, Bob was a mainstay; Albert, however, didn't share the enthusiasm, mainly, thought Saunders, because he was not in control. Saunders never likes to judge a man's faith, but in Albert he saw not the simple, seeking Christian but rather a slick salesman with a "think positive" attitude that lacked true spirituality. Albert's interest in the church seemed purely social. During Albert's tenure as an elder, Saunders cannot recall either a constructive suggestion or an obstructive action. The minister believed Walker was serving as an elder purely for the honour and the trust it bestowed upon him.

When Albert requested a transfer to St. Paul's United Church in Paris in 1984, Saunders didn't try to stop him and gladly signed the release papers. His absence at Knox didn't make a bit of difference. This was odd to Saunders, because in most cases a departing elder left a gaping hole in the congregation.

Though Saunders and others questioned Albert's sincerity, people who knew him only casually have had a different impression. Wherever Albert went, his professed Christianity followed him. Anyone who accepted a ride in his car would see the Holy Bible on the front seat, or perhaps an Easter raffia palm on the dashboard or hanging from the rear-view mirror.

Nineteen

HICKORY
DICKORY DOCK

AFTER BUYING THE Ayr bookkeeping business, Albert Walker and Barbara, a guiding hand and a full partner, took over a Brantford bookkeeping company Albert had worked for for a couple of years preparing tax returns and consulting on tax matters. In 1980, he had picked up Oxford Bookkeeping of Woodstock, Ontario. It had been owned by Al Boggs, an elderly gentleman who had served his clients so well over the 1960s and 1970s that most of his business was made up of long-time customers. Maybe Walker bought Oxford Bookkeeping because he saw a great potential in Boggs's business, but perhaps he saw it as a chance to use Boggs's reputation and credibility as the launching pad for his schemes. Whatever the reason, Walker made sure that Boggs was kept around as more than just a part of the furniture. Tried and tested Al Boggs, he figured, would keep his cronies and clients coming back to the company year after year after year. Al Boggs was being used and couldn't see it.

Jim Wilhelm was a twenty-one-year-old junior

Jill Walker, eldest daughter of Albert and Barbara Walker. She was in touch with her father and sister Sheena by letter and phone from 1990 to 1992, but didn't tell police.

Sheena Walker in high school yearbook photo.

The Walkers' matrimonial home in Paris, Ontario, (Mark O'Neill, Toronto Sun)

Barbara Walker.
(Canadian Press)

Myrtle Winter, foreground, died in 1995 of a heart attack. Her husband, Eric, says it was brought on by her dealings with Albert Walker (top).
(Toronto Sun)

Walker used the identity of David Wallis Davis in Britain until he assumed the identity of Ronald Platt in early 1993. Note the close resemblance.
(Stuart Clarke)

Ronald Joseph Platt. Murdered by Albert Walker off the coast of Devon, England in July 1996. Note the Rolex watch and the maple-leaf tattoo on his right hand. (Toronto Sun)

Elaine Boyes, the Yorkshirewoman who was duped by Albert Walker into laundering his cash across Europe. With this done, Walker arranged her emigration to Canada with boyfriend Ronald Platt. (Stuart Clarke)

Albert Walker
photographed under
the Christmas tree of
his Paris, Ontario home.
(*Toronto Sun*)

Sheena Walker photographed
outside her mother's Paris, Ontario
farmhouse after her return from
Britain and before her father's trial.
(Greg Reekie, *Toronto Sun*)

The Little London Farmhouse, near Woodham Walter, where Albert Walker and daughter Sheena lived as Ronald and Noël Platt, husband and wife, until their October 31, 1996 arrest. (Stuart Clarke)

Birth certificate of Lillian Platt showing the parents listed as Ronald Platt and Elaine Boyes, or Noël Platt. (Stuart Clarke)

Ronald J. Platt
BA RSA Cert.
Member: British Association for Counselling

solutions i n *therapy*

Training in solution focussed therapy,
counselling for individuals, couples
and families

Swan House
Suite 3
9 Queens Road
Brentwood, Essex
CM14 4HE

Tel. 01277 229 992
Fax: 01277 261847

*Business card in the name of the
late Ronald Platt which Albert
Walker used to introduce himself.
The card shows a fake BA.*

*Swan House,
where Albert
Walker worked
with Isabel
Rogers as
business
manager
"Ron Platt"
of Solutions
in Therapy.*
(Stuart Clarke)

*Therapist Isabel Rogers was
hired on the spot by Albert
Walker early in 1995 and
worked with him almost daily
until she quit only weeks before
his arrest.* (Stuart Clarke)

Albert Walker's sailboat Lady Jane *as presented to the trial jury at Walker's trial in Exeter. Walker was convicted of using the sailboat to take Ronald Platt out into the English Channel and kill him.* (Paul Slater/Apex Agency)

Brixham fisherman John Copik pulled up Ronald Platt's body off the coast of Devon on July 28, 1996.
(Guy Newman/Apex Agency)

The Rolex.
(Paul Levie/Torbay News Agency)

Det. Sgt. Bill MacDonald (l) and Det. Const. Ian Clenahan (r) with the 10 lb. Sewester plough anchor dragged from the sea with Ronald Platt's body.

(Alan Cairns, *Toronto Sun*)

Former OPP Det. Sgt. Joe Milton holding the photos of Albert and Sheena Walker that he posted with Interpol.

(Fred Thornhill, *Toronto Sun*)

Albert Walker's defence lawyer Richard Ferguson takes a break outside Exeter Crown Court at Walker's murder trial.

(Samantha Pritchard/Apex Agency)

Prosecution lawyer Charles Barton outside Exeter Crown Court.

(Samantha Pritchard, Apex Agency)

broker with Gaulding, Rose and Turner in Woodstock when Walker approached him out of the blue in 1981 and asked for his help in building up Oxford Bookkeeping. Walker offered to swap business, so there would be something in it for Wilhelm as well. Accounting, investments and insurance were fine, noted Walker, but he wanted to go much further. He had an idea for a one-stop financial supermarket that would fill every need for every customer. His first step would be to build up his own mutual fund — he didn't see the point in selling someone else's corporate fund — and offer it to Oxford Bookkeeping clients as a good investment opportunity. When Wilhelm broached the subject with his head office in Toronto they were keen to meet with Walker. For the trip Wilhelm borrowed his father's brand-new Cadillac, an immaculate car that and had every conceivable electric-powered option. Wilhelm didn't let on that the car wasn't his own, and as he drove east on Highway 401 towards Toronto with Walker in the passenger seat, he couldn't help but imagine what the impeccably groomed man in the dark pin-striped suit with matching vest and old-school tie was thinking. Was it "Look at this guy's car. This must be a great business"? Or was it "There's a lot of money in this — a lot for me!"

By his dress, demeanour and vocabulary, Walker gave the impression he was from a blueblood family and had attended private school. To pass the time on the long drive, Wilhelm asked Walker about his background and his schooling, but the questions didn't go anywhere; Walker gave vague answers or changed the subject. Still, the meeting went well. When Walker offered that if the company helped set him up he would give them a fair percentage of his takings, the company grabbed the opportunity. Wilhelm and Walker returned to Woodstock to work on a prospectus that they would file with the Ontario Securities Commission (OSC). Walker was gung-ho on the idea until he realized that he would have to come up with $20,000 to $50,000 to pay for the OSC prospectus fee and publishing costs for a thousand-odd copies of the prospectus and other marketing materials. Then he learned he would make about one half a percentage point on the sales. Walker pulled out without giving reasons, but Wilhelm understood it was purely a question of profit margin. Wilhelm now believed he knew what Walker was all about and amended his thoughts on what Walker must have been thinking. It was "I'm out to make a lot of money and I want to make it fast, and if I don't have to spend anything in the process, all the better!"

But Walker was back on Wilhelm's doorstep before too long. In 1982, he asked Wilhelm to set him up so he could buy Canada Savings Bonds from the government and sell them to the public. By then Wilhelm had moved to Pitfield, McKay Ross. Walker's plan was all aboveboard, so Wilhelm had no problem helping him. Besides, Wilhelm was mostly helping himself. But one afternoon at Wilhelm's office, after signing the forms that would allow him to sell government bonds, Walker was on his way out when he made a telling comment to Mandy Bee, Wilhelm's business partner.

"All this shit for half a lousy per cent!" he complained.

After that, Wilhelm regarded Walker as the scum of the earth and wanted nothing to do with his schemes. It was obvious to him that Walker wanted to take shortcuts; he wasn't happy with the profit margins everyone else in finance was working with and working hard to get. Clearly, Walker was after much, much more than what the competitive industry paid out to the people who managed it. Wilhelm also noted Walker's interaction with others. It seemed the man was interested only in people who could do something for him. Unless you offered a financial or political advantage, you were not worthy of his time or attention. When Walker had sought out Wilhelm's help, for example, he had spread the charm. He had acted interested and concerned and tried to make Wilhelm feel good about their relationship. Walker had a habit — or maybe it was a habit by design — of asking personal questions that made you feel important and appreciated and made him seem genuinely interested in your welfare. But then he would subtly turn the conversation around until it focused on his problem and what he wanted you to do about it. While Albert talked, Wilhelm didn't listen, but many others soon would.

Walker somehow gathered some capital and set about realizing his dream of building up Oxford

Bookkeeping. First, he rolled Oxford into Walker Financial Services Ltd. The hole-in-the-wall image was next to go. He would dress up the business, make it bigger and brighter and more attractive — essentially a copy of the way he dressed and presented himself. He would take the company from its out-of-the-way Huron Street cubby hole to a bigger, better, newer building that in the years to come would act as a headquarters for the vast chain of one-stop financial supermarkets he would spread across Ontario. With an office already up and running in Brantford, Walker eyed an imposing red brick house at 15 Riddell Street part of which was being offered for rent by its landlord, Larry Roddick, the owner of Oxford Cycle and Sports.

Life hadn't given Larry Roddick any shortcuts. Everything he had he had earned. After his father died when Larry was only three months old, Roddick lived with his mother at their London, Ontario home, and they were alone until she remarried when Larry was eighteen. Four years later Larry's stepfather died of a heart attack. Larry's mom put food on the table by working as a wire installer at the Minchell organ factory and as a candy maker at Keat's confectionery. He started paying attention to a girl who had been in his grade three class, Sharon. Within a few years the two were married. They still are.

After a spell working for Eaton's department store, Larry took over the Oxford Cycle shop from the retiring owner, Victor Muth. At first, Larry didn't have enough cash to buy the business in the Woodstock downtown, but Victor liked Larry and wanted his old business to fall into the hands of someone who cared. Muth formed a partnership that would allow Larry to take over the business when Muth reached sixty-five. Their relationship worked because it was based on mutual trust and respect. Larry toiled at his new business and took full advantage of the North American sports boom of the early 1970s. He was so successful that by the middle of that decade he needed more storage space. He thought of moving to an old Canadian Tire store, but then he heard that old Dr. Colin McPherson wanted to sell his lovely three-storey century-old brick house next door. The house was separated into five apartments, but Larry just needed space. He bought the house and had contractors dig out the land between the basements of the store and house and link the two into a giant cellar, where he did repairs and kept equipment.

Out of the blue, Albert Walker, dressed to the nines as usual, visited Larry and asked about the three-storey house. Without much ado, Walker offered to rent the north side of the main floor, emphasizing that "money's not a problem." Upon striking an agreement, Walker gave him twelve post-dated cheques, all of which were honoured. Walker told Larry the location — just off Dundas Street, Woodstock's main commercial street — was perfect for his business. The downtown city parking lot was across the road from the house. Only a few hundred yards away were the Toronto-Dominion Bank and Montreal Trust. Also close by were the Canadian Imperial Bank of Commerce, the Royal Bank, Woodstock High School and the United church. Larry was impressed with Walker's style. He dressed in great clothes, had an imposing upright posture and was always alert. And it never changed, day in, day out.

About a year later Walker took the south side of the main floor. He knocked down walls, built cupboards and refurbished the whole area. He installed the best carpet and had luxurious wallpaper hung. Outside he erected a large, brightly lit sign for Walker's Financial Services. True to his promise, Oxford Bookkeeping was no longer a hole-in-the-wall operation. As the years passed, Larry never even had to approach Walker with proposed rent hikes. Just as Larry would start thinking about annual increases of 4 or 5 per cent, Walker would visit the sports store and offer him 10 or 12 per cent. In the mid-1980s Walker asked Larry to rent him part of the second floor, which Larry did. Within a couple of months Walker asked for more space. This time, though, Larry turned him down because he didn't want all his eggs in one basket.

As Larry watched Walker's phenomenal growth, he thought the man must be a genius and said as much to his wife. But Sharon had never liked Walker. She would often see him on the street in Woodstock, and despite having been introduced to him on three or four occasions, he would not acknowledge her. She wondered how Walker could be so smooth and

nice in one breath, then in the next forget that you
were alive. She felt he was a phoney. At first Larry tried
to make excuses for his tenant, but he knew deep
down that Sharon might be right. Still, Walker treated
Larry well and bought tennis racquets, balls and bikes
at the sports store for his kids. He had Larry convinced he was a businessman, a family man, and a
church man.

One Friday morning, Walker came by the store.
He approached Larry in his usual cool way.

"It's my minister and his wife's anniversary today
and I'd like to buy them both bikes. Can you deliver
them to Paris?"

"Sure, Al, no problem," said Larry.

Walker chose matching Raleigh five-speeds and
asked Larry to drop them off in his garage. Larry duti-
fully drove the bikes out to Walker's farm and around
to the garage behind the house. He was shocked to
find the garage doors falling off and the garage filled
with all kinds of junk, old newspapers and garbage.
This didn't seem to jibe with the immaculate man
Walker presented to the world.

Those who'd ever entered the Walker house, knew
it was in the same mess as the garage. Walker never
fixed a thing, and the house needed all kinds of repairs.
Barbara Walker tried to cover up the deficiencies with
paint and wallpaper, but beyond these inexpensive,
superficial improvements, Walker would not cough up
the cash to do anything more. Sometimes when the
Walkers hosted guests, Walker would talk of his "big

plans" to renovate the kitchen and return the rest of the farmhouse to its former beauty. Hearing this, his wife would roll her eyes as if to say "Oh, yeah." Over time, friends realized that while Al Walker was posing as the big businessman, Barbara did all the work around the house, from taking care of the kids to making the meals to cleaning. They often wondered why Barbara put up with her husband's laziness, but they realized that she took her marriage vows of "for better or for worse" seriously.

Shortly after their move from Ayr to Paris, Barbara Walker began attending at St. Paul's United Church with her neighbour and new friend Davina Webber. Barbara taught Sunday school and took her kids to St. Paul's, hoping to bring them up in an environment akin to the one her own family had provided for her. Barbara and the kids became known at the church. A year or so after Barbara began attending, Albert suddenly showed up and gave the impression that they were a new family in the congregation. He ingratiated himself with the influential people mainly by telling them that Bob Staley from Ayr was his best friend. On the back of Staley's reputation as a just and honest man, Walker gained instant credibility with St. Paul's members. He told some of them that he left Ayr because he didn't like the minister, George Saunders, but Barbara was never heard to criticize Saunders. Each Sunday, the Walker family sat in the front row of the balcony. Some in the church thought it was likely a tradition that had carried on from

Ayr. In retrospect, they believe it was all Walker's plan to gain a higher profile and with it more investment business.

A church member at Bible study recalled that Walker would show up at only the first and last of the twelve meetings during the year, yet he would have the strongest opinions and the loudest voice of everyone. People felt a great sense of intrusion, but they put up with it. He would also join the Easter and Christmas organizing committees but then wouldn't appear. Every time Walker volunteered, church committee members took it for granted that they couldn't count on him. Yet, despite all this scepticism, Walker again worked his way onto the board of elders and represented St. Paul's at the United Church's presbytery meetings for the Erie region.

The St. Paul's minister, Mark Aitchison, told a confidant that one day he had noticed Walker's raffia cross on his rear-view mirror. When he asked about it, Walker said he felt he should show the world he was a Christian.

"Al, there is more to Christianity than just talking about it all," Aitchison told him.

But Walker just brushed off the remark, got in his car and drove away.

Twenty

A CARIBBEAN MYSTERY

TWO YEARS AFTER incorporating Oxford Book-keeping into Walker's Financial Services and moving into his 15 Riddell Street headquarters, Walker made some major moves to boost his business. Forming an offshore company named United Canvest Corporation Cayman Ltd., Walker advised his tax, bookkeeping and bonds clients that they should put in this tax shelter any extra money they wanted to protect from Revenue Canada's interest earned on money invested with United Canvest would be tax free. He piqued a lot of curiosity when he said that the money was invested in failsafe Canadian government bonds. Interest gained, he said, would be reinvested in government bonds in order to earn even more money. To some clients, United Canvest was a gift horse they could not look in the mouth. Each investor received official investment certificates and statements of interest earned. Al Boggs and other employees of Walker's Financial Services did not deal with United Canvest — the scheme was purely Walker's baby.

In the mid-1980s, Myrtle Winter of Brantford sold her tiny bookkeeping and income tax business to Walker and then invested the money with Walker's company. At the time, Walker told Winter she and her husband, Eric, would be well taken care of in their retirement. Myrtle Winter told Eric, a former jockey and World War Two aircraft gunner who was fast approaching sixty-five, that the money from the business and the sale of the house and about $30,000 in life savings would give them a retirement nest egg and there would even be some left over for the kids. Myrtle Winter thought Walker was a "great guy." She liked the way he looked and the way he did business. Smooth was the word she used.

With this and similar acquisitions, Walker's Financial Services Ltd. grew by leaps and bounds and by 1986 was one of Southern Ontario's most conspicuous finance companies, operating satellite offices in London, Guelph, Paris, Brantford, Stratford and Hagersville. Each office was close to the main street and highly visible, and each advertised short- and long-term investment rates at least a quarter of a point — and often half a point — higher than the banks and trust companies. The day's rates were proclaimed, on outdoor signs or in windows, in big, bold lettering or flashing neon. Each night in the local newspapers, Walker ran ads offering his best rates. And in each case, Walker's Financial Services gave its own in-house guarantee that the funds were safe. The company's phenomenal growth wasn't lost on anyone who was remotely interested in finance and anyone who wanted to push his or her investments just a bit further.

Customers entering a Walker establishment would typically be met by smartly-dressed, friendly young women Walker himself had hired to be the "frontmen" and operators. In Woodstock, anyone who had an appointment with Walker would be chaperoned into a plush office that gave the appearance of success and honesty. On the walls hung copies of fine art. On Walker's desk sat homey photographs of his loving wife and their four beautiful, smiling children. In the company's brochures, Walker stated that he had a degree in business and had studied at the University of Edinburgh and the London School of Economics. He also told of lecturing at various universities. He had grown so fast and so far that nobody ever questioned his credentials.

Walker revelled in his success. As his wealth increased, he dressed in even better suits, bought a green vintage Jaguar XJE for $60,000 and played golf. Always jealous of his friends the McRuers' in-ground pool, Walker had one installed at his Paris farm. At work, he demanded the royal treatment from his employees. One young woman who was a member of St. Paul's United Church and worked for Walker said he insisted, even ordered, that his staff address him as Mr. Walker. It was as though Walker believed himself to be above everybody else and he wanted everybody else to believe it, too.

In the late 1980s, he enrolled himself and the older kids in the Northfield-Doon Racquets Club on the outskirts of Kitchener. Jill and Sheena were part of a Saturday-morning junior clinic taught by new pro Gary Schneider. Walker, who mostly played doubles with men in the "Ayr group" as well as business associates, pulled Schneider aside one day at the junior clinic and asked if he could get introductory tennis lessons for himself. The lessons lasted for a year. Schneider recalls that Walker was not a natural athlete but was able to acquire a certain level of technical skill.

"He could take criticism. He was very knowledgeable about the game. When we tried to pick up style or things, he would ask me how such an action would help him. He always wanted to know the reasons behind it and how it would help him."

After the lessons, Schneider and Walker would go upstairs for a beer or a juice. Walker mentioned finances on more than one occasion, but at that point in his young life, Schneider wasn't interested in investments and retirement.

Over at Pitfield, McKay Ross, meanwhile, Jim Wilhelm watched with interest the unprecedented growth of Walker's Financial Services. Some of Wilhelm's clients had told him how Walker had talked up United Canvest to them and challenged Wilhelm to better the offer.

"They thought this was the cat's ass!" Wilhelm says. But Wilhelm was convinced that Walker was running an illegal scheme. Though Canadian tax laws had once allowed offshore tax shelters that would protect even government bonds, Revenue Canada had prohibited the practice a couple of years earlier. Wilhelm realized that Walker was misleading his clients. Walker could not back up the promises that came with United Canvest; it was likely a sham. One elderly woman was keen on Walker and invested $50,000 with him, until Wilhelm told her that Walker was misrepresenting the truth. The woman took Wilhelm's advice and asked Walker for her money back, insisting that he send it directly to Wilhelm at PMR. She later told Wilhelm that Walker had arranged for her to pick up the money at the bank, and there it was, a $50,000 cashier's cheque written on a Toronto-Dominion bank in Woodstock.

It struck Wilhelm as odd that the cheque wasn't more of a formal affair from the Cayman Islands. He decided to bring Walker to heel.

"You obviously don't know about the tax rules, Al," Wilhelm told him in a terse telephone call. "The rules have changed, and what you are doing isn't right. How can you do this legally?"

Walker gave Wilhelm an abrupt but polite brush-off.

"After that, if the topic of Albert Walker ever came up with any of my clients, I would openly call him a scumball. I knew he couldn't sue me for slander because it was all true."

Wilhelm was angered again in 1987 when he read

Walker Financial newspaper advertisements offering guaranteed investment certificates at top-notch rates. It wasn't the GICs that had Wilhelm concerned but that right next to them Walker would advertise short-term investment rates without supplying details. Walker was giving the impression that the rates were for GICs and therefore guaranteed, when in fact they were investments made directly by Walker's Financial Services without any guarantee other than his own word. Again, it was misleading to the public and against the rules.

Wilhelm photocopied the newspaper ad and faxed it to the Ontario Securities Commission, the stock market and investment watchdog. "How can you allow something like this to go on?" he asked the OSC.

The OSC did not contact Wilhelm; nor, it appears, did they try to rein in Walker, perhaps because he was not a member of any licensed body and was beyond their jurisdiction. The reality was that Walker had set up his business in a way that enabled him to fall through the regulatory cracks: neither GICs nor bookkeeping was controlled. And Walker did not sell mutual funds himself but merely brokered them through others and took a cut. Over time, Wilhelm's dislike of Walker grew into a deep hatred. He noted with interest that Walker didn't seem to have any close friends. He was a loner. Unlike other businessmen who made their living in Woodstock, Walker never joined any facet of the Woodstock community. To

Wilhelm, the man was a dark blot on the landscape, a parasite, but there was nothing he could do.

Larry Roddick, meanwhile, saw only the phenomenal growth and continually had to push off Walker's requests to expand at 15 Riddell Street. Larry was leaving the sports store one day when he bumped into Walker as he returned to his office. Walker flashed a smile.

"Larry, do you want to get in on the ground floor of a super deal?"

"What's going on?" Larry asked.

"Walker Financial Services is going public on the Alberta Stock Exchange. It's a great deal. Go to the Toronto-Dominion Bank. It's all set up. They'll look after you. The company's called Walker's Capital Corporation."

Larry didn't really need to get into any investing, but, despite his wife's dislike of Walker, he felt an allegiance to the tenant who had been so responsible with both the building and the rent. Larry invested $500 in Walker's Capital, buying shares at about 70 cents each. As Walker had said, it was all arranged and delivered by the TD Bank. He later realized that Walker had talked most of the tellers into buying WCC stock.

Barbara Walker has told friends that she was vehemently opposed to Walker's going public with WCC in 1988, yet she was listed as vice-president in the incorporation papers. Shortly afterwards, Barbara quit working in the Walker Financial Brantford office and joined the Brant Business Incentive Council for a lukewarm $30,000 annually. Her move from Walker Financial Corporation appears odd given that at the time, it certainly looked as though her husband was expanding the firm. Why, if she was the boss's wife, couldn't Walker find her a lucrative job in the company?

To help his fledgling company go public, Walker called on some reputable people to serve on his board of directors. Over time, he enlisted Ken Rae, president of AIC Financial in Kitchener and a former executive with Dominion Life Assurance; Mark Aitchison, minister of St. Paul's United Church in Paris; John Moran of Guelph, president of John Moran and Associates and a noted conservative investor; and William Gunn, president of Equi-Ventures, a holding company. Of course there was good old Al Boggs, who over the years had referred most of his trusted clients to Walker's Financial Services and United Canvest. In addition, Walker successfully approached David Penhorwood, lawyer for Hyundai Auto Canada. Penhorwood accepted the invitation to the board purely out of allegiance to his father-in-law, Bob Staley.

When Penhorwood had married Bob and Betty Staley's daughter, Kim, in June 1985, Walker's daughter Sheena, then eight or nine years old, walked down the aisle as a flower girl as the entire Walker family looked on from the pews. The Walkers and the Staleys had stayed friends ever since Bob transferred out of

Ayr. In addition to their vacations in Scotland, the couples had frequently attended the symphony, opera and theatre in Toronto and had got together for home socials. Bob Staley had also played tennis and golf with Albert Walker and the two had gone skiing together. The Staleys had used Walker as a financial adviser and not only put money into United Canvest but bought bonds and other items as well. Through the Staleys, the Walkers met Betty Staley's brother, Bill Richardson, and his wife, Sheila.

In the late 1980s, Betty Staley and Bill Richardson were told by their ageing mother that she saw little reason to keep their inheritance — two plots of land in the Vandorf area north of Toronto — from them until her death. Better to sell the land so they could have the proceeds in their relative youth. The land was dear to Marjorie and her children; her great-great-grandfather, Capt. William Graham, had received it as part of a 3,000-acre grant when he retired from the military after serving for Britain in the War of 1812. When Bob and Betty mentioned Marjorie's wish to Albert Walker, he offered to be their real estate agent. The Staleys' plot, zoned for light industrial, was just south of the Toronto satellite city of Aurora, and the sale happened to coincide with a building surge that swept through the Toronto area in the late 1980s. Whether by luck, position or talent, Walker engineered a bidding war among land speculators. When it was all over, the Staleys had earned in the neighbourhood of $5.37 million. Upon hearing this, the Richardsons, too, jumped on Walker's bandwagon, and he sold their plot for $5.17 million. After taking his seller's fees, Walker turned the money over to the Staleys and the Richardsons, who were suddenly in a position to never have to worry about money again. The Staleys and the Richardsons didn't know much about money matters though, so Walker invested their windfall for them to not only keep the taxman's hands off it but earn them generous interest. They thought that was a great idea. After all, he was the financial wizard of Southern Ontario; after all, he was their trusted friend.

Laments David Penhorwood now, "I'd like to rewrite history and say I was suspicious of him and I didn't like him, but I really can't say that." Yes, he admits, Walker was a name dropper and he had a nervous laugh and in reality he was only a big fish in a little pond, but nothing about Walker would have led him to suspect anything sinister or illegal. Everything seemed cool between Albert and Barbara, and the children appeared well raised. Later, however, Penhorwood learned that the Walkers' marriage had been in trouble for some time but Barbara had kept the tension and stress from even her closest friends.

Penhorwood would listen with some discomfort when Walker would tell anyone within earshot that when he first met Barbara he knew immediately "she was the woman that I would marry" and "I asked her to marry me three weeks after I met her . . .

and she said yes!" Again and again Walker would tell this story.

Says Penhorwood, "I suppose you could colour that 'Isn't it terrific' and 'Isn't that true love,' but you could also colour it a sign of people — especially in his case — not being that well socially adjusted, and falling in love with people and pursuing people impulsively."

Penhorwood didn't ever have a friendship with Walker because their characters and interests were far apart, but he never thought ill of him. When Walker approached him about joining the board he was initially reluctant, until Walker turned on the charm. Said Walker, "I've come to know you and respect you, and you're a young lawyer and I'd like somebody like you on my board of directors."

After Walker's Capital Corporation went public, the board had little to do with Walker and his company. Penhorwood remembers a few conference calls and one luncheon in Woodstock in the summer of 1989, with a brief visit to the Riddell Street headquarters, otherwise the board had no contact with Walker. The board spent about one hour every six months discussing the affairs of Walker's Capital and made a business decision here and there; other than that it was mostly inactive.

Walker's bravado about Walker's Capital is evident in a 1990 prospectus, in which he boasts that revenues had grown by more than 85 per cent, while expenses had increased only 30 per cent.

"It's our goal next year to quadruple that profit and I look to everyone in the company, whether they be staff, client or shareholder, to help us achieve this goal," he wrote.

Twenty-one

LOVE FROM A STRANGER

CATHY NEWMAN SHARED ministerial duties at St. Paul's United Church with the head cleric, Rev. Mark Aitchison, and her husband, Rev. Phil Newman, but the bubbly thirtyish woman had a different kind of calling. She had a "clown" ministry — in which she entertained the kids with her wacky costumes, guitar playing and singing. If requested, Cathy would show up at birthday parties and various kiddie bashes. During her tenure at St. Paul's from 1986 to 1989, she was a big hit with the kids. And she was a big hit with Albert Walker. The two become close friends — perhaps too close considering their positions at St. Paul's and in life.

A taste of what was to come was seen at the Erie presbytery, a committee made up of representatives from area churches that discuss concerns and gives feedback to the United Church of Canada. Rev. Doug Willis and his wife, Joan, were appointed to the presbytery for their new church in Caledonia, where they served after leaving Knox United in 1981. Across the room from the Willises sat Albert Walker and Rev. Cathy Newman, representing St. Paul's. Rev. Doug would chuckle at some of the more boring presbytery meetings, bored, some members would yawn, some would even nod off in the middle of a presentation. It was during one of the more mind-numbing gatherings that Joan Willis suddenly nudged her husband and flicked her eyes towards Walker and Reverend Newman. The two were sitting close beside each other, very close, chatting away, giggling, sometimes touching hands, giving each other what Joan would later call "goo-goo eyes."

"Hey, what's up with them? You don't sit that close to me," Joan remarked to her startled husband.

The chemistry between the two was tangible. They were acting like adolescents, whispering together as the others were trying their best to deal with issues important to the United Church and its parishioners.

Reverend Willis couldn't believe his eyes. Walker was the man whose wedding he had officiated at twenty years earlier and who now had four children. And what was an ordained minister, herself married with two children, thinking by acting this way at an official function? Especially in front of everyone!

Joan Willis, practical as ever, was shocked that Cathy Newman seemed to be more attracted to Walker than to her husband, Phil, whom Joan considered a "very nice fellow, a very good-looking fellow and real, whereas to me, Al was as phoney as a three-dollar bill."

Phoney or not, Walker meant more to Cathy Newman than pocket change. Rumours started to surface — that they were spending a lot of time together at the church; that they had been seen together in coffee shops and restaurants; that Walker had bought her numerous gifts; that he offered to buy her a car and take her on a vacation to Florida. A congregation member close to the Newmans believes that Cathy's attraction to Walker was not so much physical as emotional, that while she was beautiful, intelligent and effervescent, she was also very needy. The clown ministry apparently gave her the attention and acceptance she craved. Phil Newman was a sweet man who tried his best to make sure his wife was happy, but it didn't seem he could ever do enough. Walker, too, was needy. To observers, when the two were together they looked made for each other. Although it is widely said the two had an affair, there is no proof. Documents filed in Ontario court do show that Cathy Newman accompanied Walker on a trip to Britain. Only Cathy Newman and Walker — perhaps even Phil Newman and Barbara Walker — know the full truth.

Whatever happened, the church transferred Cathy Newman to the Oakville area in June 1989, and subsequently her marriage to Phil broke apart. Later, Walker and Cathy were reportedly seen together in Woodstock. Cathy Newman later complained that she was driven out of Paris because she was a woman and the people around her, mostly men, couldn't handle the friendship. Now going under the name of Cathy

Seguin, she works at a London, Ontario church, to be near her children. Phil Newman also works in London. Neither Cathy nor Phil wish to talk about Walker or what happened.

It was some time in 1989 that raven-haired beauty Geneviéve Vlemmix became snared in Walker's increasingly complex web. Through family, Geneviéve was acquainted with Al Boggs, who one day invited her into Walker's office, where she asked him for a job. Geneviéve, recently separated from her husband and looking after her young boy, was twenty-five years old, slim, tall, dark haired, and from all accounts a strikingly good-looking woman. She knew how to dress, she knew how to walk and she knew how to talk — in several foreign languages. When she entered Walker's office that day she looked like a million bucks. Geneviéve had only limited experience as a medical secretary, and minor financial skills, yet within minutes of laying eyes on her, Walker hired her as his personal business secretary.

Throughout late 1989 and early 1990, Geneviéve accompanied Walker on trips to Switzerland, France and England. In keeping with Walker's desire for the best, he and Geneviéve flew first-class and stayed in the most lavish suites in the most opulent hotels. There were also trips across Canada, including one visit to the heady ski slopes above Banff. They always booked separate, but adjoined, rooms. Ostensibly the trips were for business, but mostly Walker had fun.

The costs of these exotic trips were written off as a business expenses to avoid paying further taxes. Walker had taken trips to Europe and Mexico with another young woman on staff, but he moved her out to a satellite office when Geneviéve came on the scene. With his beautiful new secretary at his side, and armed with information from the dozens of international business magazines he read, Walker approached some of Europe's biggest financiers, asking if he could meet them and perhaps interest them in investing in a company — his company — that would give them tremendous growth. With her startling looks and linguistic ability, Geneviéve reinforced the image Walker wanted to project of the I-have-it-all winner. None of these meetings, however, paid off for Walker. Throughout this time, Walker didn't take vacations with his own family.

Investors who read their annual reports from Walker's Capital Corporation were taken aback by how much their globetrotting frontman was spending. Walker's landlord, Larry Roddick, couldn't help but take a dig at Walker one day when he saw him getting into his car, "Things aren't going too bad, Al, but jeez, if you cut down your travel, your shareholders would make more money."

Walker gave him an indecipherable look, mumbled some comment and drove off.

In April 1990, Barbara Walker telephoned David Penhorwood and told him something strange was going on with her husband. She had found love letters in Al's coat pocket. But there was more: she had found garbage bags stuffed with receipts and copies of bank statements. Barbara smelled a rat and asked Penhorwood if he and the other directors of Walker's Capital had any inkling of what was happening. In their infrequent contacts, Penhorwood had sometimes chided Albert Walker about the lack of board meetings and the lack of information, but now the situation was serious; Barb's concerns seemed well founded. When Penhorwood canvassed the Staleys they were even more concerned than he was. After all, Walker had in excess of $5 million of their money in United Canvest and various bonds and loans. The Staleys pressed Penhorwood to find out the state of Walker's financial affairs. Penhorwood called Ken Rae and Rev. Mark Aitchison and explained that, from a legal perspective, if they didn't do anything they might be held liable if anything went wrong with Walker's business. Potential creditors would put the question: Had the board exercised due diligence? All three agreed they would have to act, and act quickly. With input from the other two, Penhorwood drafted a letter asking Walker to provide board members with regular information about the degree of financial control and the breakdown of financial dividends, and to give the board greater input on major decisions. The board asked Walker to consider the letter and then meet with them for discussions.

Walker called Penhorwood thanked him for the letter and asked if they could arrange lunch; he said he would answer any questions. Penhorwood, Rae and Aitchison met with Walker at the Holiday Inn in Guelph. To their surprise, the meeting went well. Walker listened to every concern, and at the end of the meeting, he was reassuring.

"I value you guys as outside directors and I understand what you're asking for. Give me about two or three weeks and let me speak to my accountants about this and figure out what I have to put into place to give you guys this kind of regular, internal financial information, maybe on a monthly basis or something." With that, Walker was on his way.

About ten days later, Penhorwood, Aitchison and Rae received an astonishing letter from Walker: "I'm shocked you three would challenge me in this way. I thought you understood you were just on the board in an honorary capacity . . . I am Walker's Financial and I alone will make all the decisions for this company." Walker then asked for their immediate resignations. This came as such a surprise after the hopeful harmony of the business lunch. Penhorwood was stunned. It wasn't as if the board's requests were unreasonable; they had sought only what any public board would.

Now the trio smelled a fish. After further talks among themselves, they told Walker in writing that if he wanted their resignations he would have to call a meeting of shareholders and enlist enough votes to get rid of them. Wrote Penhorwood: "We don't think our requests are unreasonable. Obviously, you are trying to sweep our requests under the rug, which just raises suspicions even more."

In preparation for the meeting Walker had arranged in the company's London offices, the rebellious board members asked for a list of shareholders so they could distribute copies of their April letter to Walker to ensure that their concerns would be understood. They reasoned that if the sharcholders knew of the board's concerns and still wanted to back Walker and get rid of them, so be it. At least the shareholders would have been warned and the directors would have upheld their fiduciary trust. But Walker flatly refused to reveal who owned stock in his company. At the meeting, Penhorwood was surprised to find that Walker and Barbara held more than 51 per cent of the shares of Walker's Capital Corporation, and that through a power of attorney Barbara had signed over all rights to her husband, making him the majority shareholder. In a preventive move, Walker had solicited proxy votes from other shareholders, even though he did not need more than 50 per cent to turf the rebels.

Walker was in a mean spirit at the meeting. He glared across the table at the men who had the audacity to question his authority. In a short, grim exchange, he decreed that the trio were gone.

"So the shareholders, not even to this day, didn't understand, and probably didn't hear of, the questions and the concerns we outside directors had," said Penhorwood.

Barbara Walker was noticeable by her absence. Walker, she said later, wouldn't let her into the meeting. Penhorwood met with Barbara later that day. She told him she believed that her husband was planning to vanish, and the board members represented her only hope. Penhorwood reluctantly told Barbara that because he, Rae and Aitcheson were off the board there wasn't much any of them could do.

Penhorwood briefed the Staleys and the Richardsons. They became nervous about the millions they had entrusted to Walker and called him, asking where the money was invested and when could they get it back. Walker responded with a series of statements that, in retrospect, were designed to put the Staleys and Richardsons off the scent for a while: he'd put details and money in the mail; he was going out of the country and he'd get back to them; "I'll call you back." Over the summer, the Staleys and Richardsons set up lunches with Walker, but at least twice he cancelled at the last moment because of "other commitments." The Staleys didn't want to push their friend too hard.

Barbara Walker later took the matter to the OPP in Brantford. But when she couldn't deliver any proof of a crime, only suspicion and speculation, the officers told her they could not act against her husband.

"If you have proof, we'll be right there," they assured her.

Barbara Walker must have wondered then, as she has since, why it was up to her to deliver proof.

Twenty-two ▬▬▬▬▬▬

SPARKING CYANIDE

WHILE LOVE MAY be blind, it appears hatred had set in, and Albert Walker had his eyes wide open in June 1990 when, some weeks after he cut the three board members, he took out a $90,000 mortgage with Walker's Financial Services on the farmhouse and the land, repayable over five years at an interest rate of 12 per cent. As long as the interest was paid, it didn't matter when the principal was paid off. In short, he had an indefinite line of credit, albeit an expensive one.

Only three days after Walker carved out the secret mortgage to himself, Barbara challenged him over his relationship with his business secretary, Geneviéve Vlemmix. Walker admitted that he had had an affair with a female co-worker while in Switzerland the previous month. Barbara, who had put up with years of marital turmoil and had even tried couple's counselling in an effort to save their marriage, exploded and told her unfaithful husband to move out of the house. But Walker had other ideas: Barbara would move out of the house and his girlfriend would move in and share the matrimonial home with him and the kids!

Walker would allege in legal documents that Barbara wanted a reconciliation after the confrontation. He claimed that on June 28, 1990, at Barbara's request, he transferred his lover employee to another company partially owned by WFS. Barbara, however, wasn't on Walker's reconciliatory wavelength.

It appears this straw — or was it more of a giant steel girder — had broken the back of whatever was left of their tattered marriage.

The next day, in a letter mailed to Walker at his 15 Riddell Street office, Barbara's lawyer, Robert Snyder of Gowling, Strathy & Henderson, wrote:

> Please be advised that we have been retained by your wife with respect to your outstanding marital difficulties.
>
> We understand that you have informed your wife of your existing and intended ongoing relationship with your paramour, Geneviéve Vlemieux [sic].
>
> We are prepared on your wife's behalf to negotiate a settlement between yourself and your wife which will settle all outstanding issues between yourselves, including custody, access, child support, spousal support, and division of property.
>
> Understandably, the strain to your wife arising from your revelation as to your paramour necessitates at this time a physical separation if mean-

ingful negotiations are going to be possible.

We would request on behalf of your wife that you make arrangements immediately to obtain alternative accommodation so that your wife and children may continue to occupy the matrimonial home on a temporary basis with minimal further disruption. We are advised that reasonable visitation with the children is quite acceptable to your wife. In the interim and pending our further negotiations, we will expect you to continue to maintain the mortgage and other shelter related costs of the wife and children in the home.

We would suggest that you refer this letter to your solicitor in order that fruitful negotiations might begin. We would wish to emphasize that your wife has instructed this writer to handle the negotiations on her behalf and wishes any negotiations to be directed accordingly.

We wish to further emphasize that before a settlement can be reached, it will be mandatory for both yourself and your wife to make full financial disclosure in accordance with the Rules of Civil Procedure and the Family Law Act. Your solicitor will assist you in this regard. Initially, we will require the following:

1. A sworn financial statement in accordance with the Rules of Civil Procedure.
2. A copy of your T1 General Return to Revenue Canada for the last three taxation years.
3. Copies of Financial Statements for 372629

Alberta Limited [a holding company for Walker's
Capital Corp.], or any other corporations in
which you own shares, for the past four years.

4. Full details of all investments, including RSPs,
Pensions, GICs, stocks, bonds, insurance
polices, etc. . . .

And with that letter, the Walkers were on the path to
a vicious legal battle that threatened to disrupt the
cosy double life Walker had enjoyed for more than a
decade and reveal the shortcomings and misappro-
priations in his business affairs.

In the middle of an impending marriage break-up
and a crisis at his company, on August 9, 1990, Walker
took Sheena, Duncan and Heather to Britain for a ten-
day vacation. Walker later would say he offered Barbara
a spot on the trip but she declined. Taking advantage of
his absence, Barbara Walker prepared a legal motion
that would give her custody of all four children, interim
child support, spousal support and exclusive possession
of their home until a trial could be held.

In an affidavit filed with the motion, Barbara Walker
stated:

My husband and I separated on or about August
9, 1990, as a result of his admitted ongoing relationship with another woman and his repeated
request for a separation.

We are still living in the matrimonial home,

but I concluded that the marriage was over on August 9, when the defendant left for an alleged two-week holiday to England with the children. I verily believe that he is using this trip in attempts to remove money from Ontario and out of my reach and the jurisdiction of this court.

My husband is already very angry with me. He seems to think that he can carry on with his girl-friend and has even suggested that I leave the home with the youngest children so that she and her child can move in.

My solicitor wrote to him earlier in the summer requesting that he provide a financial statement and other financial information in consultation with his lawyer and further suggesting that he arrange for alternate accommodation on a temporary basis.

He will be furious when he finds out that I have started legal proceedings. He has already threatened me that he will "blow me away" and that I will get nothing if I do not do what he tells me to do.

My husband is a successful entrepreneur and businessman. He is a chairman and CEO at Walker's Capital Corporation, a financial services company with various offices throughout Ontario. The stock of the said Walker's Capital Corporation is publicly traded and listed on the Alberta Stock Exchange.

I verily believe that my husband has an income

of approximately $120,000 per year. In addition to this salary, he derives further substantial benefits by way of use of a vehicle, vacations and entertainment, which are charged to the company.

My husband and I hold 51 percent of the issued common stock of Walker's Capital Corporation through a holding company being 372629 Alberta Limited which was set up by the defendant. This holding company is controlled totally by my husband. He has refused to provide me with any information concerning this company, which he is now able to use to effectively control Walker's Capital Corporation without any input from me and at the same time, tying up my shares in the public company.

I am a mother and housewife and am currently employed as a financial consultant with Brant Business Incentive Corporation and earning $30,000 per year. I have been obtaining credits on a part-time basis for prerequisites to enter a Masters of Business Administration program. It is my intention to complete the course prerequisites for the MBA program and commence my MBA studies in 1991 in attempts to obtain economic self-sufficiency.

Our children are 18, 15, 11 and 8 respectively. I believe that I should have custody of the children for the following reasons:

• I have been the primary caretaker of the children and my husband has historically been content to leave all matters affecting their care to me so that he could pursue his business undertakings.

- I have been more closely involved with the children than my husband has and there has been a close attachment between the children and myself which benefits the children.

- My husband has a hostile temper and does not have the patience necessary to provide a stable parenting environment.

- Duncan and Heather, ages 11 and 8 respectively, are particularly in need of a consistent and stable environment.

- My husband's behaviour in his relationship with me and now openly carrying on his relationship with his girlfriend is an inappropriate role model for our children.

Barbara demanded exclusive interim possession of the farmhouse because of the "intolerable" atmosphere:

My husband comes and goes as he pleases. His relationship with his girlfriend has been flaunted in front of me and as previously indicated, he has even suggested that I move out so that she could move in. I am finding it personally very difficult to cope with it. Obviously my anxiety with my husband is having a negative effect on my ability to parent the children . . . My husband's temper and threats "to blow me away" as previously indicated and his constant verbal abuse is both frightening and intimidating to me . . . It would be in the children's best interests if they could remain with me in the matrimonial home, close to their friends and schools so as to minimize the impact of the separation upon them.

She added that her husband could not only afford to keep her and the children in the house at the "comfortable lifestyle" they had enjoyed for years but could also assist her in upgrading her education. Anyway, she noted, Albert could get his wish and go live with Geneviéve.

On August 18, 1990, Walker returned from Britain with Sheena, Duncan and Heather. As Barbara had anticipated, he was furious. The very next day he rented a house at 139 Viscount Road in Brantford. Despite the seething anger between them, Albert and Barbara Walker lived in the same house for another week. Friends of the family recall hearing Walker trying to coerce both Sheena and Jill by telling them that they really didn't like living with their mom and saying, "You would be much better off with me." Once the two older girls promised they would move out with him. Walker tried for the next two weeks to manipulate his younger children to join them. But that was nothing new. From all accounts, Walker, whose travels and business functions had forced upon him the reality of being an absentee parent, had subtly manipulated the kids for years. Whereas Barbara was stoic and practical and in other ways firmly committed to her Presbyterian roots, Albert had created an image of himself as a do-it-all, have-it-all and take-it-all mover and shaker who enjoyed the awe of his kids. Jill's letters to the divorce court suggest that either she truly felt that her mother was restrictive or that her father had convinced her it was so. One thing is clear: Barbara Walker would never have given her teenage daughter wads of cash to go on shopping sprees, which Albert Walker had done on many occasions.

On August 19, Walker was sitting at the dinner table with Barbara and the younger children when, according to Barbara, he "asked Duncan and Heather to choose whether they were going to go with [him] and the two older children or stay with Mom. They were both undecided." Three days later, Walker said, in a legal affidavit, Heather told him she wanted to join him and a day after that Duncan also confirmed he wanted to be with his father.

Twenty-three ■■■■■■

BY THE
PRICKING
OF MY
THUMBS

EARLY ON THE morning of Friday, August 24, 1990, Albert Walker, dressed in one of his best business suits, told Barbara he was catching a flight to Calgary for a business meeting. Barbara roused the children from bed, and after helping them get breakfast she went off to work. The kids were on summer vacation, and Jill and Sheena were entrusted with looking after the younger two. At some point in the day, Barbara called home to check that everything was well. To her surprise, a recording announced that the number had been disconnected. She rang the number again, and again she got the message. Puzzled, she called her friend Davina Webber, who checked out the house and then phoned Barbara with amazing news: "Al is there!"

Frantic that something odd might be happening, Barbara contacted St. Paul's minister Mark Aitchison, told him of her concern for the kids and asked him to visit the house and see what was going on. As Barbara would tell it later, when Aitchison drove up to the old farmhouse he saw a moving truck parked in the driveway. And there was Albert Walker, in jeans and a T-shirt, and the kids standing around the truck. As Aitchison pulled into the driveway, Walker told the kids to scatter. Off they went, running to hide in the corn and behind the barn and the house. As he got out of the car, Aitchison saw eighteen-year-old Jill peeking from behind some cornstalks.

"Jill, come on out. What are you doing?" Aitchison called to the eldest daughter. When she didn't move, he walked over to the truck. Walker was sitting behind the wheel.

"Al, what are you doing?" Aitchison asked.

"We're moving," Walker stated, matter-of-fact.

"Have you told Barb?"

"That's none of her business," Walker responded, adding that it wasn't any of Aitchison's either. "Move your car out of my way. It's my property. Move it!"

With that dismissal, which Aitchison must have known was a valid, legal request, Albert Walker continued moving his children and possessions out of the house without any input from his wife of twenty-two years. He took not only the kids but any object of value, including the television, stereo and microwave oven. Barbara Walker was left with the dregs of the furniture.

In true Agatha Christie style, Aitchison followed the moving van to Brantford but lost it in traffic. Still, Walker didn't shake off the inquisitive minister.

Aitchison had jotted down the licence number and the moving company name and number. He visited the rental van company, and after telling them the situation, he appealed to the staff on humanitarian grounds to give him the address for where the van was bound. Aitchison then went to the new house himself and pleaded with Walker to let him in so they could talk, but Walker flatly refused.

When Barbara heard what had happened, she was terrified for the children. She tried to get a telephone number for the new address, but found it was unlisted. She drove to the Viscount Road house with Aitchison, but again Walker wouldn't have anything to do with it. He would not even let her visit the kids or pick them up at night for their soccer games. For days, Barbara Walker went through the heartbreak of not being able to see or talk with her children. There was no point in going to the police, because the children had chosen to go with their father; presumably the police would see this as a family dispute that would require a civil court remedy.

That same day, the children apparently wrote notes that Walker would later file with the courts as proof that they wanted to be with him. Wrote Duncan:

Dear Mom,

I have chosen to go with Heather, Jill, dad and Sheena and I hope to visit you a lot and maybe someday choose to live with you.

Love Duncan

In a note that was almost identical, Heather wrote:

> Dear Mom,
> I have decided to live with Duncan, Sheena, Jill and dad. I hope to visit you.
>
>   Love
>   Heather

That Sunday, Barbara Walker spoke with Jill and Sheena on the telephone. The girls told her they wanted to stay with their father and followed this up with handwritten notes to the court. In her note, Sheena's handwriting appears juvenile for a girl of fifteen.

> August, 28, 1990
>
>   Sheena Walker,
>   [born] July 28th, '73
>   Gr. 10
>   Paris D.H.S.

These are the reasons why I don't want to live with my mother
1) If I did live with my mother I wouldn't be allowed the freedom that I would get if I lived with my dad.
2) My mother and I often disagree on a lot of matters and often end up in a real fight.
3) I don't feel that the relationship between my mother and I contains enough love and affection for us to be together on a daily basis.

However, my father shows me a lot of affection on a regular basis and we are very close.

I feel that it would be better for everyone if I stayed with my father.

In an undated letter, Jill Walker trashed her mother:

> Jill Walker,
> b. Jan. 19, 1972
> Gr. 13
> Paris D.H.S

There are many reasons why I would rather live with my father than my mother

1. She shows very little love or affection towards me. The affection that she does show towards me is never at the right time. When I have a problem in which I would appreciate a hug she never realizes it and more than likely assumes that I am just being grumpy. Dad on the other hand usually realizes that I have a problem and comforts me no matter what it is.

2. She has very rarely shown any understanding to me and has never helped me work through any problem or situation, whereas my father has often offered to personally help me work a problem out.

3. She constantly is in an argumentative mood with me and had called me several names (ingrate, twit, bitch) in the course of these arguments.

4. She constantly bothers me to get a part-time job to earn extra cash. My father on the other hand has allowed me not to have a part time job so that I can concentrate on my studies as well as supplying me with extra cash for weekend dates etc.

5. She is an extremely messy person. A quality which I cannot stand. I spend an estimated 15 per cent of my time cleaning the house, making dinners, doing laundry etc. to make up for her sloppy and unorganized way of living. This quality leads also to her and the younger children's unsanitary condition. My mother herself showers only once a week. I recently have taken on the responsibility of seeing that the children shower at least four times a week. They also leave the house many mornings with their hair uncombed and without brushing their teeth. She also constantly complains about my need for a shower every day, even though I take sailor-style showers.

6. She doesn't allow me the freedoms as a teenager that I feel I need to be happy.

7. Very often she is late for scheduled appointments and pick-up times by more than half an hour.

I find this very frustrating.

These reasons are in no particular order of importance.

Five days after he moved the kids from the farm-house, Walker allowed Barbara to meet with them at a local restaurant, but he insisted on being at the table through the entire meal. Barbara would later say in court documents that the "younger children were clearly under tremendous pressure and his influence was apparent."

Walker also sought to exercise his influence in the courts. On the same day as the restaurant meeting he filed a cross-motion in which he gave a rambling, self-aggrandizing statement. At many junctures, he appeared to twist his wife's words until they somehow worked in his favour. He sought all the things Barbara had sought of him, but in addition asked for an order appointing the Official Guardian to represent the best interests of the children. Clearly, this was done in an effort to usurp what he knew would be the court's reluctance to separate the children from their mother.

In his affidavit, Walker explained that he and his wife had had "marital difficulties" for five years and had undertaken professional counselling with Pat Tummon of Kitchener for one and a half years. That had ended in August 1989. He acknowledged telling his wife about his affair and how, "in the heat" of their argument, his wife demanded he move out and he stated his desire to move his girlfriend in. He didn't want to leave the marital home, he said, but the ongoing arguments with his wife and her "constant screaming" created an "unpleasant atmosphere," and he had moved to Brantford purely for the well-being of the children. In the days before the move, he said, the kids had asked if they could go along with him. The two older girls, he said, believed their mother was "impossible to live with."

. "The plaintiff's suggestion," he stated, "that I encourage my 18 year old daughter to have sexual relations with her boyfriend is false. Unlike the plaintiff, I do not cross-examine her as to everything she and her boyfriend do when they are together." And he stated categorically: "It is totally false for the Plaintiff to suggest that I moved money out of the country during this vacation; I took £500 and credit cards with me to Europe."

Walker wrote:

It is my desire to return to reside in the matrimonial home with the four children as soon as possible. Although I and the four children have been sleeping overnight at Viscount Road, I return daily to the matrimonial home to look after the property and animals. I spend approximately one hour daily looking after six sheep, 12 chickens, and cats and dogs, the swimming pool and grounds and crops. The plaintiff has never been involved in looking after the animals or crops on the farm. I grow grain crops on 55 workable acres, which involves ploughing, discing etc. The five-bedroom matrimonial home is inappropriate for the plaintiff to reside in alone . . . Ultimately, I would hope to buy out the plaintiff's one-half interest therein. During the latter years of our cohabitation, the plaintiff was not the primary person responsible for housekeeping; this was in fact largely done by our eighteen-year-old daughter, whom I paid, as well as a cleaning lady I hired for one half day weekly.

If I and the four children are permitted to reside in the matrimonial home (where our family has lived for 12 years) the children will be able to remain close to their friends and attend the same schools. I estimate the matrimonial home has a current fair market value in the $350,000 range, with two outstanding mortgages totalling $150,000.

While it is true that I have been a successful businessman the plaintiff is employed full-time, earning a salary in the $30,000 range for the last year with the Brant Business Incentive Corporation and accordingly, is fully self-supporting. For 15 years earlier, the plaintiff was actively involved in my business.

Walker went on to say he had earned only $91,202 in 1989, $42,321 in 1988 and $23,122 in 1987. He estimated earnings for 1990 would be in the $50,000 range. On paper, Walker wasn't making much and so Barbara Walker wouldn't get much. He argued against a preservation order, declaring that Barbara had an equal share in everything.

He even drew up a proposed expenses and revenues budget for him and the kids living at the farmhouse. The expenses covered almost everything under the sun, including mortgage, property taxes, utilities, telephone, gardening and snow removal, toiletries, grooming, laundry, dry cleaning, groceries, outside meals, school milk, school photos, lunches, his clothing ($6,000 a year), kids' clothing, transportation, taxis, dental work, drugs, life insurance, tuition fees, books, entertainment, vacations, gifts, kids' activities, newspapers, booze and tobacco, charities, kids' camp, kids' soccer and bank payments. By the time his budget was finished, Walker had told the court that his monthly expenses would be $8,905 but his income only $4,583.

On the same day he filed this motion, Barbara Walker fired a reply salvo, claiming that it "contains many gross inaccuracies:"

I am deeply concerned that he has been manipulating and attempting to influence the children and in particular the youngest two children, Duncan and Heather, who are eleven and eight, respectively. I believe this was largely accomplished by him during the one week that he took the children to England on a holiday . . . The older children . . . have been influenced by their father and the freedom that living with him offers as opposed to the accountability and household rules which I expect them to abide by . . . I believe that the youngest two children should reside with me at this time in the matrimonial home. I further believe that Sheena will want to return to live with me in the near future as well, but I am prepared to respect her wishes in the interim. I verily believe that it is intended that Jill will continue to reside in the Brantford property as promised by her father in any event.

Barbara pointedly told the court that she had always been responsible for the "day-to-day care of the children," while Walker has been "totally pre-occupied with his corporate business dealings and has been out of the country on major excursions on numerous occasions over the past year."

With her affidavit, Barbara attached an affidavit from Davina Webber:

As a neighbour and friend of Barb Walker for over 10 years, I have observed that her involvement with all her children has always been one of love and concern.

Barb takes time and makes the effort to be with the children for their personal, school and sports activities, and regularly attends their games and competition functions.

Al, however, due to business or other commitments, rarely has the time to attend this type of activity. He does however, on occasion, take one or several of the children on holidays or trips.

As a working mother and student, Barb requires help with the home making activities of washing, cooking, yard maintenance and cleaning, particularly during the summer months when the children are home from school. The help and co-operation of all family members encourages responsibility and commitment.

Barb has displayed fairness in the moral upbringing of her family. She does request reasonable hours of return to the home following parties and outside functions. The health and well being of her family has always taken precedence.

As a wife and mother, Barb has always displayed honesty and fairness. During their recent marital dispute, she has not discussed or criticized her husband's activities nor asked the children to take sides.

On September 11, 1990, Ontario Court Judge J.A. Kent of Brantford ordered a psychological assessment of the three younger children, Sheena, Duncan and Heather. He also asked the Official Guardian to represent the children. In addition, he gave custody of Sheena and Jill to Albert, while Barbara got Duncan and Heather. He stipulated that both parties should have "reasonable access to the two children not in his or her custody." Barbara was accorded interim possession of the home and Walker was ordered to pay her $150 monthly for each of the two children and to pay for the upkeep of the home.

When lawyer Paul James met with Heather and Duncan in his capacity as the Official Guardian, Jill Walker, who had already chosen to live with her father, sat in on the meeting. On November 6, she delivered a letter to James that Duncan and Heather had penned jointly:

> Dear Mr. James,
> We would like to live with our Dad and sister Jill because it would be more of a family with them. Also when we live with our mom we are always late for everything and always going from baby sitter to baby sitter because our mom is always running around to meetings. So we would like you to tell the judge that we would like to live with our dad.
>
> Thank you,
> Yours truly,
> Duncan Walker
> Heather Walker

Within a couple of weeks, Walker filed a motion to overturn Judge Kent's order and give him sole custody of all the children and possession of the farmhouse. In an affidavit filed with the motion, Walker noted that he earned only $35,000 that year, or a net monthly income of $2,131, while Barbara was making $32,000. Since Kent's order of two months earlier, Walker said, he had "incurred significant debt." Each month, he said, he had expenses of $2,800 and an average deficit of $676. Meanwhile, he said, his wife had $2,400 in monthly income. In contrast, Barbara estimated her expenses as half this amount. Walker went on to warn:

My personal line of credit is now $300 over my $10,000 limit. As well, I have outstanding approximately $4,000 in bills to pay . . . my bankers are not prepared to advance me any further monies on my personal line of credit. On Tuesday Nov. 20, I will be attending a meeting with Mrs. Kaye Allard, a trustee in bankruptcy with Peat Marwick Thorne to start proceedings for personal bankruptcy."

Only a change in fortune would prevent this, he offered, saying that Barbara should pay him $450 a month in child support. That way, he said, his wages, Barbara's support payment and $100 in family allowance benefits would give him $2,681. Even paying support, he noted, Barbara would make $2,000 and could easily attend to her own rent, estimated at about $700. "If the above can be accomplished, both parties will survive financially. If it cannot be accomplished in the next two weeks, I will be bankrupt and in turn, Barbara Walker will be bankrupt because she is liable for all of the debts that we have."

Walker concluded his affidavit by asking his lawyers. "I do not care what the costs may be, please just get us back into court as soon as possible."

As with all matrimonial cases, it would be a long time until the war of the Walkers saw the inside of a courtroom, but the two continued to go at each other's throats. At one point, Albert assaulted Barbara in the farmhouse, but she chose not to pursue it with the police. But another time, during a November 1990 visit with the children, Walker burst into the Paris farmhouse against his wife's will and pushed her around. Feeling she had no choice in the matter, Barbara demanded that Brantford OPP lay charges against her estranged husband. He was charged with forcible entry and, in a routine police procedure, his fingerprints were taken.

The act of fingerprinting Albert Walker on a minor domestic-related charge meant little to anyone at that time, but these prints would come back to haunt Albert some six years later when Interpol would match them with the prints the Devon police had taken from the mysterious David Davis.

DESTINATION UNKNOWN

ON DECEMBER 4, 1990, Walker took his four children to a chic restaurant and told them he would be going to England and Switzerland the next day on a two-week business trip. There was nothing unusual in this, Walker had left at a moment's notice on business many times in the past. This time, however, there was a twist: Sheena, an aficionado of Scottish highland dancing, would go with him. On December 13, 1990, the day Walker's Financial staff were to gather for their annual Christmas party, Walker called John Moran at his Kitchener office and told him his plane home from England was delayed at the airport due to a storm; he would be unable to make the gathering and it should go on without him. Twelve days later, Barbara Walker celebrated Christmas with her family and all the children except Sheena, wondering what had happened to her wayward husband and why Sheena had not called or written. Nobody had heard from Sheena or Walker since they'd left — at least that's what Barbara believed. Everyone worried about Sheena — everyone except Jill. It struck Barbara as odd that Jill didn't seem in the slightest bit concerned about her absent sister.

It wasn't until January 10 that police received the first complaint, from John Moran of John Moran and Associates, that Albert Walker had disappeared with one of his daughters and might have taken investors' money with him. Moran told the RCMP that before his disappearance Walker had put some questionable charges on the company's American Express card — namely, $11,556 on November 16, 1990, for the purchase of a ring and earrings from Birks' Jewellers in Toronto, and $12,542 in first-class British Airways tickets from Elegant Tours of Toronto. The tickets had been bought November 28, 1990, seven days before Walker disappeared. Moran also wondered about almost $46,000 he had turned over to Walker on September 21 for the purchase of shares in Walker's Capital Corporation. Although he had given Walker a cheque, he noted, he hadn't received the shares. Later investigation showed that on September 25 Walker had put Moran's cheque not into stock but directly into his own bank account in Woodstock.

Woodstock Police Services detective Brian Crozier recalls that over the next few months numerous investors came to him with their stories. They included "little old ladies" who had put $20,000 and $30,000 into Walker investments, then learned upon going to Walker's Financial Services that the various certificates and documents and statements he had given them might be worthless. One elderly woman came into the police station in tears, having discovered she may have lost her life savings.

By February, two months since Walker had disappeared, all kinds of inconsistencies were showing up at Walker's Financial Services as one investor after another came in to cash certificates that didn't exist. And yet the company was still accepting business from new clients and covering up the fact that nobody had heard from or seen the boss.

John Slamon of Burford, Ontario had invested more than $67,000 in a Walker's Financial-backed GIC through its Brantford office on December 27, 1990, two weeks after Walker failed to show up for the Christmas party. Nobody told Slamon that Walker was missing in action, even though "Al was obviously lost." In fact, the saleswoman at the Brantford office told Slamon that Walker-backed investments were "a good thing" and "secure." She explained at length how Walker loaned money to doctors and dentists and restaurateurs to set up their businesses. Slamon learned later that Walker paid his salespeople 1 per cent of the total investment as an incentive.

"I trusted the girl," Slamon says. "She sold me the goodies. It was all on trust. We have to go on faith."

Joseph and Bev Jennings invested $66,000 in a one-year GIC in November and planned to use the money to finance the house they were building. Joseph had seen Walker's high interest rates posted in the Paris office when he stopped at traffic lights on Main Street during his drives home from his Hamilton workplace. As he sat there waiting for the lights to change, he'd mull over the higher returns that Walker gave out. Jennings got the same type of sales pitch Slamon later did. After looking at the literature for Walker's Financial, he felt it would be a safe and profitable investment.

"I guess I was a little bit greedy. I went in — they showed me the guarantee they had. I took it home, read it and thought about it for a day or so. We decided to go ahead. It sounded fine. I'm an ordinary guy. I questioned the woman about it and she said it was good. She likely feels bad about it now."

The Jennings had known the Walkers from St. Paul's United. They had seen the Walkers sitting in the front row of the balcony; Joseph had served with Walker as an elder and had joined him on several committees. The two were only acquaintances, but Joseph trusted Walker, despite his brashness. Through the grapevine, Joseph had heard that Walker was an educated person who gave lectures at universities and colleges. He had a good reputation in the church. As well, Bev's sister had babysat the Walker kids when they were younger. If they couldn't trust Walker, who could they trust?

As the news hit the media, the Alberta Stock Exchange suspended trading in Walker's Capital. Larry Roddick and others who had bought the junior shares for around 70 cents suddenly found their shares had dropped to 10 cents. With Walker out of the picture, Barbara Walker took over the helm of the company. She and other shareholders brought in various experts to help them sort out Walker's mess. At first, the experts reassured creditors that they would all be paid.

Among the worried people were Walker's "best friend," Bob Staley, his wife, Betty, and the Richardsons. The Staleys and Richardsons held more than $600,000 in promissory notes alone, but that was nowhere near their total loss, which was in the many millions. Arthur and Jean Traquair first invested $10,000 in United Canvest, Walker's Cayman Island scheme, in 1985. When the five-year certificate came due in June 1990, the Traquairs wanted to cash out, but when told by Walker that their investment had swollen to $15,500, they gave Walker another $10,000 to invest.

With the horror stories mounting and stretching far beyond Woodstock city boundaries, Crozier, his boss, Sgt. Ron Fraser, and police chief David MacKenzie asked for help from the Ontario Provincial Police anti-rackets section, which assigned Staff Sgt. Joe Milton to the case. Milton, a strapping man of six-foot-plus, had more than twenty years' experience under his belt. Because the Cayman Islands and other foreign countries might be involved, the pair were joined by RCMP forensic investigator Gus MacIntosh from Kitchener. They followed every lead; they tracked investors down one by one and interviewed them.

When the team of Crozier, Milton and Mac-Intosh was brought into the case it was to investigate allegations of fraud and the suspected flight of the perpetrator. At that time, fifteen-year-old Sheena Walker was considered only a missing person. Crozier recalls that when he first talked with Barbara Walker, she told them Albert had a "healthy" relationship with the kids. The detectives suggested to Barbara that there might be something odd in Sheena's relationship with her father to make her "just take off with him like that." Although Barbara didn't disagree, she didn't have any crazy notions about the potentially incestuous nature of a teenage girl running off with her dad. Whenever they thought about the Sheena issue and its implications in the case, Crozier, Milton and MacIntosh had to consciously shake themselves from the "horrid thoughts" they were having about the father-and-daughter flight. "Cops and their crazy minds. We see things and think things that the ordinary guy sees and thinks nothing about," said Crozier. Sheena's safety was always a concern, but Milton and Crozier reasoned that they must first track the money, because if they found the money, then they would find Walker and Sheena.

The pair's suspicions that something odd had gone on between Sheena and her father heightened when they interviewed the women Walker had been connected with in the few years before. In each case, noted Crozier, they were young and could only be considered "absolutely gorgeous." Crozier admired Barbara Walker for being positive, practical and upfront with her thoughts and for having such tremendous stamina, but Albert, it seems, had not appreciated her and instead was drawn by youthful sex appeal. In all cases, Crozier noted, the women in Walker's realm were going through messy divorces or were vulnerable in some other way. And they were all somewhat shy and certainly naive about the ways of men like Walker. Crozier learned that Walker's modus operandi was to hire the women, give them "protective, fatherly advice" and then move in for the kill, using romance as his weapon.

When Milton and Crozier interviewed Geneviéve Vlemmix, she related how she and her family had invested more than $200,000 in so-called Walker-guaranteed GICs and the Cayman scheme. She told them as well that Walker had hired her to both make and keep track of his appointments and business bookings. Yes, there had been trips all over Europe and across Canada. She recalled this trip and that trip, but she was vague about dates and places. There was a May 1990 trip, though, when she and Walker stayed three nights at the luxurious Hotel Drei Könige am Rhein and met with Swiss financier Felix Oeri in Basel. When police asked Geneviéve if she had an affair with Walker, she burst into tears and left the room.

"She was obviously embarrassed about the whole thing," says Crozier. "In retrospect it was a dumb question. We were just being nosy and thought she might know more than she was telling. She was totally upset. We just didn't realize how delicate it was."

Zeroing in on any Walker bank accounts they could find, Milton, Crozier and MacIntosh pored over years of bank and credit card records and cracked numerous safety deposit boxes. A clear picture emerged. As Barbara Walker had suspected, Albert had been moving money out of Canada in the summer of 1990. Walker had apparently hatched his plan as early as July 1990, when he opened a CIBC account in Toronto and began diverting funds into it from various accounts. He made four sizeable withdrawals in July and another half-dozen in August. On August 8, 1990, before leaving for England with Sheena for a vacation, Walker opened a Credit Suisse account in Toronto and moved $20,000 into it from a company account. This cash was transferred to a private account he opened in Switzerland. The next day he bought $23,161 in Swiss francs and transferred these to his Geneva account, took out the second mortgage on his home for $90,000. On August 10, he told Credit Suisse his new address would be in East Dulwich, London, England. And on August 21, 1990, he moved $90,000 from his TD account into the new CIBC account. Numerous transfers took place during the fall, and only two days before he left Canada, in excess of $700,000 in Swiss francs and English pounds sterling and gold was wired to Switzerland through Credit Suisse.

But while the Swiss bank's staff in Toronto were glad to share this information with the detectives, the cooperation ended there. No matter what the detectives tried, they could not legally access the receiving account in Switzerland and had no idea what had become of the money. It seemed that Walker had broken up his stolen investor cash into chunks and wired it at different times from different accounts to prevent his actions from arousing suspicion. In a final visit to his bank on December 4, Walker withdrew the remaining $45,000 from his several accounts, which, records show, had once carried the proceeds from the Staley and Richardson land deals. In a final dip into his stolen cash, on December 8, 1990, Walker wired $100,000 from his personal account in Toronto into his secret Geneva account. Over the years, Walker had not stolen from *all* of his clients' accounts — he bilked mainly through the Cayman Islands scheme and from a handful of investment accounts, and it seems the money from the two land deals had also proved too tempting. In both the Caymans scheme and the public offering of Walker's Capital in Alberta, Crozier said, Walker held his companies outside Ontario to keep them away from any scrutiny.

The detectives also discovered that Walker had tried to dump Walker's Financial Services as early as the fall of 1989. David Holden, a financier in Hamilton, Ontario explained to them how Walker had first offered to sell him WFS for $5 million but over the next year the price dropped steadily. On

December 3, 1990, he related — only two days before
Walker left Canada — he had met Walker at the
Riddell Street offices to discuss a purchase for only
$1 million. Amazingly, Walker offered him the busi-
ness for $500,000U.S. if he could close the deal
within twenty-four hours and pay cash. "I'm willing
to take a substantial loss so I can concentrate on my
other business activities," Walker told Holden. Walker
gave him the business card of Preben Warga, of Credit
Suisse in Switzerland, and assured him that if he
wired the cash to Mr. Warga before the close of business the next day then WFS would be his. Walker
said he and his lawyer would meet with Holden on
December 5 and transfer the shares. Holden was leery
of handing Walker cash and instead offered certified
bank drafts through Chase Manhattan. When Holden
called Walker on the morning of December 4 with
his offer, Walker expressed outrage but told Holden
he could still close the deal that afternoon. Holden
waited for the call, but it never came. He never heard
from Walker again.

Following their noses, Crozier and Milton sought
out the Walkers' eldest daughter, Jillian. They had
learned that Walker had picked up a sporty-looking
$10,000 Chevy Cavalier for Jill, had spent $2,000 on
her dental work, bought her all kinds of jewellery and
clothes and set her up in a North York apartment
while she attended university. Even before that,
detectives discovered, Walker had often taken Jill and

Sheena on lavish shopping trips and had even lent Jill his vintage Jaguar. One night, Jill borrowed the Jaguar and was involved in an accident in Toronto; she stuck her dad with the $10,000 repair bill. It didn't make sense to the investigators that Walker would stiff everybody else in his life but leave Jill in reasonable comfort. They decided to visit her in North York.

After her dad's disappearance, Jill had moved from the rented house on Viscount Road into a one-bedroom basement apartment at 22 Snowood Court and enrolled in courses at York University. The apartment was spacious, tidy and fairly bright, and had a private entrance. Homeowners Farita Shama and her husband, Pawan, remember Jill as a quiet, clean girl who had two cats and few visitors. Although she never worked, she always paid her rent in cash for the year she lived there. When Crozier and Milton saw Jill, she talked for three hours or so but told them very little. Jill, who was twenty-one years old, said she paid the rent from her babysitting money and with the help of a boyfriend. She was not happy discussing either her father or her personal situation.

"I don't have to talk to you." she told the detectives. "Please leave me alone. Go away!"

Crozier and Milton wondered why Walker had set Jill up so well just before he left the country. Was he trying to keep her silent about where he was? Or was he trying to hush up something that had happened that she knew about or involved her?

But Jill wasn't only playing coy with the detectives; she was also fooling her mother. In an affidavit written in June 1991, Barbara Walker noted that Jill had travelled to the United States in March and investigation "on my part revealed she was very circumspect in terms of her destination, and I therefore believe that she met with her father on that occasion."

Barbara would later find a letter in Jill's belongings that sent her reeling. It was dated April 19, 1991, and typed on the letterhead of the Centre for Cosmetic Surgery in Toronto and signed by Dr. Michael Bederman. It reassured patients that breast implants were safe.

In the same affidavit filed in the custody and support action, Barbara Walker stated: "I am convinced that my daughter Jill, has with the consent and the assistance of the Defendant, received a breast implant. Under no circumstances would I have agreed that a teenager should undergo such cosmetic surgery."

The letter did not indicate the type of surgery to be performed, wrote Barbara, but the total cost was $2,800, of which $500 had already been paid as a booking fee. Handwritten notes on the letter suggest the outstanding balance was $2,300.

Barbara Walker asked for interim custody of Sheena "in the event she can be found": "I realize that it would be difficult to control a fifteen year old, who does not wish to reside with me, nevertheless, an order for interim custody would at least provide me with the necessary control to proceed with an assessment and to make sure that the child is receiving proper care . . . I have also received information from our family physician, Dr. R. Hunter, of Kitchener, that our 15 year old daughter, was placed on birth control pills, shortly prior to her disappearance."

In a later divorce action, Barbara wrote that she had been in regular contact with Jill at 22 Snowood Court. She asked the court not to send copies of the divorce action to her daughter. "On occasion, there has been conversation with reference to her father, and on a number of occasions, I have left with her mail addressed to her father. In particular, documentation and correspondence from the lawyers representing Walker's Financial Services Incorporated has been delivered to Jill, and I verily believe that her father has received the same. Through this contact, I have been left with the impression that Jill is in contact with her father."

Barbara stressed that if the court served Jill with a copy of the action, she would send it to her father.

From the admissions of Walker to Isabel Rogers in the therapy office, it appears he was, in fact, in contact with his daughter Jill — not in *New* York, as he maintained, but in *North* York. Among items British detectives seized from the Little London Farmhouse in November 1996 was Sheena's calendar, which showed several neat and organized entries in the month of January 1991 for operas and plays. Interspersed were more personal reminders: "Dad facial" and "Call Jill 5 p.m." This suggested that in the two months after Walker disappeared with Sheena, Sheena was calling Jill at prearranged times. After Walker's arrest, police found evidence that for several years Walker had anonymously wired sums of money. Sheena, too, told British police and OPP Staff Sergeant Milton that she and her father had been in touch with Jill.

As the police officers did their work and investors scrambled to recoup their money, Barbara was doing her utmost to sell the house so she could buy out Walker's share and keep the place. A July 1991 court order decreed that the land be sold, with Barbara Walker getting first option of purchase. The 2,950-square-foot home was valued at $275,000. It would take Barbara Walker more than a year to have the property signed over to her name. Despite her apparent financial despair, she quit her job with the Brant Business Incentive Corporation and enrolled in the one-year master's of business administration program at Wilfrid Laurier University in nearby Waterloo. For the rest of that year she lived on $20,000 from her retirement savings, personal savings and student loans and grants. She wasn't a spendthrift like her husband.

Those investors who had been bilked, meanwhile, did not accept the restructuring plan of Ontario financier Chris Sides to keep Walker's Financial afloat, which would have given investors 35 to 40 cents on the dollar, and instead pushed the company into bankruptcy.

One of the prime movers for bankruptcy was Geneviéve Vlemmix. John Slamon recalled that throughout the various bankruptcy meetings of 1991, Geneviéve was very vocal and "wanted blood out of Walker." As far as Geneviéve was concerned, noted Slamon, "Anything with Al was going down the tubes. She had a vendetta." Geneviéve and other investors didn't like Sides's plan because they felt he was the culprit in their loss. Slamon, however, saw Sides as an opportunist, and together the investors and Sides had a vested interest in salvaging something. On the night that creditors finally pushed Walker's Financial into bankruptcy in 1992, Slamon stopped Geneviéve outside and told her, "We're going to regret this day." Investors received first 12 per cent and then a further 7 per cent of their initial investment.

Standing on the sidelines of all the meetings was the elderly and frail Al Boggs. Initially suspected of having helped Walker in his cheating, Boggs was later seen as the honest, caring man his reputation held him up to be. At one meeting, Slamon approached Boggs with a friendly hello and advised him to go home and forget about the messy business.

"This isn't your baby," he told Boggs.

But Boggs, despite a heart condition, wanted to see things through to the bitter end and help all he could. His friends and his trusted clients had been betrayed. Not long after, Al Boggs died.

"I'm not a medical doctor," said Slamon, "but logic tells me that it finished him off."

Many of those involved were changed forever. Bob Staley, says a friend, "damn near had a nervous breakdown." Because Walker had been Staley's trusted friend and through him he was introduced to the Richardsons and David Penhorwood, Staley apparently felt responsible for losing most of his wife and brother-in-law's inheritance. To this day, Bob Staley hurts deeply whenever he hears Walker's name and has been known to spontaneously cry whenever the topic of the missing money is raised. Those who have seen him note his gaunt face and his limited movement. From all accounts, Bob Staley is a very sick man, old long before his time. The Richardsons were equally devastated. And according to Joan Willis, a Woodstock farmer who lost almost everything he owned later hung himself because he couldn't face an uncertain future without his life savings.

It wasn't until April 2, 1993, that the police team of Milton, Crozier and MacIntosh announced they had laid charges against Albert Walker. In a statement to the media, Milton said Walker "may be in Canada or Europe — we don't know." He added that police did not mount a full-scale search for Walker until all the financial charges against him were laid because no further charges could be brought against him once an extradition order was issued.

The detectives believed Walker had taken up to $12 million from his clients, but they had proof of only $3.2 million missing as a result of criminal acts. Criminal case documents filed in Ontario Court,

General Division, allege that Walker milked a total of $2.6 million from the United Canvest Corporation (Cayman) Ltd. between 1982 and 1990. In addition, charges were laid for other alleged thefts from 1980 to 1990, including $165,000 from Bill and Sheila Richardson; $205,142 from Bob and Betty Staley; $10,000 from Odette Van der Wolf, Geneviéve's mother; $45,937 from financial consultant John Moran; $55,000 from the matriarch Marjorie Richardson and her daughter Betty Staley; and $41,564 from Amex Bank of Canada.

Police did not lay criminal charges relating to the roughly $10 million Walker took from the sale of the Richardson and Staley farmlands because Walker had breached no agreement with Bob Staley or Staley's family. That matter was something for the civil courts, noted Crozier. "Basically, they gave him their money and trusted him. They gave him the money willingly, so there is no crime. It is money owing, not money stolen. It's not misappropriated by deceit or default. It's not a fraud." That was the same reason British police did not charge Walker with the theft of £200,000 from Frank Johnson.

After laying criminal charges, Milton set about trying to get Walker's and Sheena's names and photographs onto Interpol's list, hoping to spark a tip to police. Getting a suspect on the Interpol top-ten list is no easy task. At every opportunity, Milton pushed his case, but Interpol officials told him the Walker case wasn't as dramatic or as potentially lethal as others they were given from around the world.

Barbara Walker, meanwhile, wasn't prepared to let the police do the chase alone. Apparently fed up that the police weren't more actively searching for Sheena, she hired a private investigator, Mike King of Toronto, who offered to work for her for costs and out-of-pocket expenses. Paris United Church held various fundraising events and barbecues to help pay the private eye's bills.

Two credible sightings of Walker and his daughter surfaced. In 1994, Northfield-Doon Racquets Club pro Gary Schneider was down at the South Carolina vacation island of Hilton Head attending tennis camp. One morning at a Shoney's Restaurant he believed he saw Walker and Sheena having breakfast. Sometime later, John Cook, owner of the Cook's Market Café in the upscale Buckhead area of Atlanta, spotted an older man and a young woman in his store who resembled a photograph of Walker and Sheena in a *New York Times* article. Neither tip, however, panned out.

Sheena would later tell police she and Walker never left Britain. It is quite conceivable, however, that Walker did leave the United Kingdom by himself, and that at some point, as Barbara Walker suspected, he met up with Jill.

In 1995, Joe Milton had a breakthrough: he successfully listed Walker and Sheena with Interpol. Their photographs would be distributed around the world. Still, Milton pushed and pushed to get Walker more notoriety. In 1996, Walker officially became Interpol's fourth Most-Wanted man in the world. Milton had put his suspect in with some lofty company: number one was a Spaniard sought for abduction, rape and murder; number two was a Croatian wanted for genocide; number three was an escaped convict wanted in the United States, Costa Rica and Spain. Lengthy articles also appeared in the *New York Times*, the *Washington Post* and *The European* as well as the *Toronto Star* and *Hamilton Spectator*.

But as time passed, Barbara Walker became embittered by the police investigation.

"It seems like it's my job to find my daughter," she told the *New York Times*. "I'm afraid at this point we don't know whether we even have a living person. The police are no longer actively looking."

For her commitment to her family and her never-ending tenacity, Barbara Walker drew Milton's and Crozier's respect. "She's a tough woman. Hard, intelligent. I should imagine she is very domineering," said Crozier. "Her only concern all along was Sheena and she never gave up. She is like the dog with the old shoe."

Others, too, were concerned about Sheena. "What has he done to that girl to brainwash her?" wondered Mike King in a 1996 *Toronto Star* article about Walker's likely control over Sheena. In the same article, Dr. Susan Bradley, head of psychiatry at the Hospital for Sick Children in Toronto, said that "a teenager in Sheena's position might have gone along with her father if he showered her with money or presents. Over time, she might have come to think the world was out to get them and they had to stick together."

At that time, nobody knew about Emily and Lily Platt.

Twenty-five

A DAUGHTER'S
A DAUGHTER

IN EARLY NOVEMBER 1996, almost six years after she accompanied her father in his flight from Canada, Sheena Walker was freed from custody on her own recognizance, having assured British police that she would testify for the prosecution, and was slowly emerging to a new reality after years of living a make-believe life as Noël Platt. In the days after the arrest, while Sheena was being interviewed by police, Marion and Ed Jones looked after Emily; social services workers had taken Lily to an authorized safe house. Marion and Ed accepted the mysteries surrounding the Platts and did their best to assist the young woman who still held herself out to them as Noël Platt. Marion, Ed and the others in Woodham Walter had not one inkling yet that Noël was in fact the purported Ron Platt's daughter.

Marion had reconciled herself to letting matters fall how they would. She felt it was her duty as a friend, a woman and a human being to help out Noël during this time of great distress. If Noël offered anything about her situation, then Marion would listen; if asked, she would give an opinion or advice; but otherwise she would keep her questions to herself. In the nights following the Hallowe'en showdown, Noël had called to speak with Emily. Noël never gave an explanation of what was happening. Her focus was always on how Emily was doing at Marion's.

The day after Noël was released she was reunited with her daughters. Later that night, Marion visited Noël and the kids, taking with her milk and some groceries. Noël seemed delighted at her arrival, more so than ever before. But at the same time she seemed overwhelmed. All alone, unable to drive and without much money, she was as housebound as ever with the children and had nowhere to turn. Noël had become thin and gaunt in the days since Ron Platt's arrest. Marion had so much compassion for this young woman. How must it feel to have your home invaded by police, your baby girl taken away by social services and your husband in jail facing a murder charge? Marion and Ed had never let on to Noël that they knew her husband had been arrested for murder and Noël had never volunteered anything. Yet knowing what they did, how could Ed and Marion offer comfort? It seemed so ridiculous to mouth the usual platitudes — "Oh, it'll be all right" and "Don't worry. Everything will work out fine."

Once, Marion accompanied Noël to Gepp and Sons law firm in Chelmsford. Emily and Lily tagged along. On the way, Noël told Marion of her worries for the future, saying she had no money for basic necessities. In the days after that, Marion helped Noël struggle through, bringing her food and helping her prepare meals for the kids. Marion encouraged her to organize herself, and meet her schedules and keep her appointments. On two occasions thereafter, she arranged for Noël to get to Exeter and then Bristol prisons to meet with her jailed husband.

"How's Ron?" she asked Noël upon her return from the second trip.

"Fine" was the one-word reply. And then nothing. It was situation normal.

Despite this blanket of silence and mystery, Marion continued to support Noël. At times, though, she couldn't help but be perplexed by the young woman. Within days of Ron's arrest Noël had walked with the children to Waggers cat shelter and paid an outstanding £80 bill for lodging the family cat whenever the Platts were away that summer of 1996. Even though her husband was in jail facing a murder charge, even though she was alone and penniless in a strange country with no job and with two youngsters to feed, Noël somehow rounded up enough cash to pay the cat sitter what she owed. Astounding, Marion mused, that Noël would think that way. Maybe she wasn't with it, or maybe, when left to make her own decisions, she was just a very honest person. The truly amazing thing was that after paying the bill, Noël gave the cat away!

• • •

Throughout November, Marion met with her struggling neighbour as much as her own busy work schedule would permit. One day Marion and Noël were grocery shopping when Noël casually said, "It's too bad, Marion, you just missed my mom. She's been over." They had met in Maldon, Noël said, and were meeting again later that day. Social services workers, Noël said, were taking her to and from appointments.

"Oh, lovely," Marion replied, trying to cut through Noël's superficial nonchalance and take the conversation to a more intimate level. "Your mom must have been thrilled to meet the girls."

"Yes," said Noël, adding that her mother had brought over notes from her brother and two sisters.

This was the first time Noël had ever talked about her mother. She smiled when she recounted to Marion that her mother had hugged her like a long-lost daughter at each of their two meetings and seemed genuinely accepting of her only grandchildren. Marion had many questions, but she was careful not to pry too deeply into private areas. Marion could see that Noël wasn't up to a rigorous cross-examination. She looked worse than she had ever looked.

On December 3, 1996, Marion was visiting at the Little London Farmhouse when Noël handed her a newspaper clipping from Canada. And there it was. Marion had the truth at last. Noël was not Noël Platt but Sheena Walker. And her husband was not Ron Platt but Sheena's father, Albert Walker, a fugitive from Canada, where he faced charges of theft and fraud.

"It is true," Noël quietly said Marion. "My name is really Sheena."

Sheena told Marion that Canadian police officers had followed in her mother's footsteps and sought to question her. She also warned Marion to expect a lot of media attention in Woodham Walter. She, however, would be taken away for a few days until the press interest died down.

The truth and its ramifications were mind-boggling to Marion. Yet in a way she had almost expected this — there had never been anything normal about the Platts. But the truth was too much, even sinister, with the children and all . . . Still, Marion stuck with Noël and the task at hand. She refused to focus on the bizarre facts that embroiled the young woman, and instead continued to help see to the two little girls.

"From now on, you must think about what you want," Marion ventured to Sheena. "The British police want you, the Canadian police want you . . . you're not your own person now. But you'll have to start thinking about yourself and making decisions for yourself. Can you stand back from it all and work forward for yourself?"

It all seemed too much for Sheena to understand. Instead of being practical or saying something profound, Sheena wondered aloud whether she would be permitted to stay in Britain. Marion held her thoughts, aware that that option was only a pipe dream.

That same day, Sheena Walker and the kids were whisked away to yet another social services safe house, and the day after that they were taken to London for appointments with Canadian police and Canadian consular officials.

On Sunday, December 8, Sheena Walker invited Marion and Ed to London, and they met her in Grosvenor Square that morning. She told them her mother had asked her to go home to Canada and she was going to go the very next day. She explained that Devon and Cornwall police detectives had cleared her of any wrongdoing in the Platt affair and had lifted her bail conditions. With that, British and Canadian officials had cleared the way for her and the children to return to Canada and the home of Barbara Walker. The Joneses and Sheena enjoyed their day in London. Sheena shopped for gifts for the family she had not seen for six years, buying little British mementoes such as shortbread and tea.

Sheena admitted to the Joneses that day that she had something on her mind other than the children and the quickly approaching family reunion: "I've been thinking about my father a lot . . . I'm concerned about him," she said, seemingly unfazed by her own incredible situation.

As the day drew to a close under the blanket of a dark-grey sky, Sheena stood beside a London taxi that was painted red in the style of a giant Rowntree's Kit Kat bar and that bore in large white letters the chocolate maker's decades-old slogan, Have a Break! Wearing

a checked jacket over a maroon turtleneck sweater
and her customary blue jeans, Sheena stood holding
the bundle of pink jumpsuit and tiny white socks that
was eleven-month-old Lily Platt. Standing behind
them, three-year-old Emily gave her best cheese grin
as Marion clicked a photograph. Emily's crunched-
up smile pushed out her chubby cheeks and her dim-
pled chin and accentuated the freckles on her nose.
Sheena's hair, losing a bit of its blondish red dye, was
neatly pulled back in an Alice band. She, too, allowed
a smile. Sheena in turn took pictures of the friends
who had given her everything yet had asked for nothing in return. After hugging Sheena goodbye, Marion
showered hugs and kisses on Emily and the baby. For
the first time in the three years since she had come
into their lives as Noël Platt, Sheena showed emotion. Tears streamed from her eyes as she said her
last goodbye and then shepherded the kids into the
waiting cab. As she rode off, waving through the moving Kit Kat bar's tiny windows, Ed and Marion realized that, apart from being brought to England for her
dad's trial, it was possible she would never return.

The next day, Monday, December 9, 1996, Albert
Walker appeared in a Torquay courtroom and for the
first time in six years answered to his own name. It
was read into the public record that Albert Johnson
Walker was accused of murdering Ronald Platt between
June and July off the coast of Devon. Wearing a dark
blue crew-neck sweater over an open-necked light-
coloured dress shirt and blue jeans, his grey hair

showing noticeably along the fringes and at the roots, since hair dye is not a commonplace item in Her Majesty's prisons, Walker peered over thin reading glasses for most of the fifteen-minute hearing, after which he was remanded in custody and told he would appear at a subsequent date. Standing in the crowd alongside reporters were OPP Sgt. Joe Milton and Ralph King of the Royal Canadian Mounted Police. The two had already spoken with Sheena Walker and now asked to speak with Walker. He immediately dismissed the request.

Sheena had told the pair the previous day at the Canadian Consulate that she and her father had stayed at the exclusive Ritz Hotel in London after leaving Canada on December 5, 1990. Records would later show that Walker and Sheena stayed at the Ritz under their own names from December 6 to 12. Walker paid the bill with an American Express card in a transaction he had no intention of honouring. From London, Sheena said, they flew to Geneva, where her father rented a car and drove to a downtown bank. She waited in the car while he went into the bank with a briefcase. When he came out with the same briefcase, they drove off. She admitted to the detectives that during their time in England her father went under the name of Ronald Platt and she went as Noël Davis. Dad, she explained, had told her all along that his money came from "investments in Canada." In all their time in England, she revealed, there was never any other source of income. Sheena also told the detectives that she and her father had never left England, which, if true, would dismiss the reported sightings at Hilton Head and Atlanta. Alerted to Sheena's sensitivity over the paternity issue, the detectives avoided the question.

Within hours of Walker's court showing, an exhausted Sheena walked with her two children through Terminal 3 at Toronto's Pearson International Airport and was smuggled out a back door, then whisked into hiding. It would be another forty-eight hours before Sheena and the children were secreted past reporters and photographers lined up outside the Walker family's Paris home. It had been almost two weeks since her mother, Barbara, had been summoned to Joe Milton's Downsview office and told that her daughter had been found and that she had two grandchildren. After flying to England and meeting Sheena and the kids in Maldon, Barbara had returned to Paris to relay the news to Sheena's siblings and prepare for their arrival. When Sheena came home on the night of Wednesday, December 11, Barbara Walker showed elation. In a rare interview she expressed happiness that Sheena was found and decreed "a new beginning" in their relationship.

It had been six years since Sheena had seen the home she had been raised in: "We want to celebrate this occasion . . . It's wonderful, but nobody wants to write about that," Barbara lamented. The reunion was a "wonderful, joyous occasion . . . It's so nice to see my four children together again."

In the days before Sheena's arrival, the weekly *Paris Star* published a short article based on a brief but exclusive interview Barbara Walker had given the friendly editor. Barbara told of her nervousness at the initial meeting with Sheena and how they became reacquainted in the subsequent days. She spoke of the happy reunion, but also of how Sheena hoped the media "badgering" would soon cease. A week before, the *Paris Star* had printed a letter from Barbara Walker under the headline "The Angels versus the Devil."

The story of our search for Sheena has twisted and turned for almost six years and throughout we have loved the angels who prayed for our side against the devil. The biggest devil in the story now resides in maximum security but it took a murder and a wide trail of fraud, theft and destruction to put him there.

The press are harassing my family because murder is a newsworthy event. Why does a man have to give up his life before the press can show some interest? Why is the story of a missing daughter and hopeful family reunion so uninteresting?

Why do police forces take years to compile evidence but never start an active search? Why did the RCMP ignore the phone calls made before the criminal left Canada? Why do police forces waste time and taxpayers money on wall plaques commending themselves for a fine job done in their Walker's Financial Services Inc. investigation while the case is far from closed? Why did an OPP officer tell me not to bother looking for Sheena because "She would not be the same kid anyway?"

This story will never get published because criticism is not appreciated in any profession. Attention has been hard to attract because stories involving just another impoverished single mother and a dead-beat dad are common, everyday occurrences. Why did I have to hire a private detective when I can barely make ends meet at home? I felt that I had no choice. My daughter was missing and there was no official search.

Nobody cared. Or nobody seemed to care.

Then the angels started to arrive. Friends organized a benefit dance which brought 500 people together and provided funds for a detective who took our case for expenses only. My brother used his influence unsuccessfully to get stories on CNN and local TV.

America's Most Wanted turned us down and *Unsolved Mysteries* lost interest without even an apology. At that point our story had no public appeal. Not enough blood and gore. Now the press are parking in our driveway, pestering my family even late at night.

Meanwhile the angels have gathered round to care for Sheena in England. Some are dressed as social workers and some work as detectives but they all understand the need to care for her as a victim not a criminal. The British officials have operated on a level that we Canadians can barely hope to achieve.

Thank you God for angels. In this world we will take all the angels you can send us.

The same day she wrote this letter, Barbara Walker lashed out at OPP Staff Sgt. Joe Milton, alleging he and others had ignored tips she gave in the years Sheena was missing. Milton, she told the *Kitchener-Waterloo Record*, as she had the *Paris Star*, tied up a fraud investigation in Canada while ignoring Sheena's plight.

Barbara's bald accusations hurt big Joe Milton. He felt he had done his best in the case. How could he chase anything when he didn't have any leads? How did he know that Walker had been living as David Wallis Davis and Ronald Platt? How could anybody know that Walker would end up being accused of murder and Sheena would end up with two children? Milton was sure that every lead Barbara and others gave him had been followed up. If it had not been for the Swiss bank privacy laws, Milton felt that he and Crozier and MacIntosh would have nabbed Walker in short order. Besides, he had worked miracles to get Walker on Interpol's list when his crime was nowhere near as heinous as those others listed with the agency. It was Milton's belief that the Interpol listing had generated quite a bit of media attention, which, he speculated, must have put stress on Walker and forced him into making mistakes. Still, Milton didn't feel he had to explain himself in public. When the *Toronto Sun* later reported that Sheena Walker had been writing letters to her sister Jill, possibly until at least 1994, Barbara demanded, and was given, an interview with the OPP top brass. Not long after that, Milton, who had reached retirement age, left the police and became an investigator with the Ontario Workers Compensation Board. It also bothered Milton that Barbara Walker had noted Jill's ongoing contact with her father in a divorce file yet had never mentioned it to Milton himself.

While Barbara Walker either put on a happy face or just plain refused to be interviewed, nobody was asking the hard questions that had to be answered: What did Sheena know about Ronald Platt and the switch of identities? Did she know about the alleged murder? Why hadn't she run away from Walker? And, of course, the question that was on everyone's lips: Was Walker so sick that he had had her pose as his wife and had twice impregnated his own daughter?

When a *Toronto Sun* reporter started to ask that very question in the days after Sheena's return, Barbara Walker replied, "I'm not comfortable answering that."

Around this same time, Barbara demanded that the media back off. She scolded reporters who were hanging around outside the house hoping for the interview she had implied was coming. As it is with almost any member of the public who gets caught up

in a major event without having any say in the matter, Barbara apparently failed to understand both the
intensity of news and its competitive nature. She also
failed to understand that she and Sheena were major
players in a major news story. After Walker's bilking
clients for millions of dollars, years of public searching for her daughter and her own stinging criticism
of the OPP, and amid the bizarre facts coming out
of England about the murder and the kids, it was
naive of Barbara Walker to expect that she could
wave her hand and have the media just vanish into
thin air.

At one point, Jill Walker complained her sister
"feels like she has been jailed in her own house, even
though she has been convicted of nothing."

"It's like we are the bad guys and he's the good
guy . . . She has done nothing wrong," said Jill, noting the five cars and the photographers and reporters
parked outside. "She doesn't want to talk to anybody,
and she is very serious about that.

"It's been hard. Half the time you are happy, and
half the time you are concerned . . . we are hoping
everybody will go away. Sheena hasn't even told her
own family much about the six years she was on the
run with her dad. So why would she tell the press?"

In a clear indication that the Walker family wanted
to pose the same questions as the reporters, Jill said,
"I kind of asked some questions a little bit last night
and she [Sheena] said, 'I don't want to talk about
it yet.'"

Leading up to Christmas, reporters were still hanging around outside the Walker home, and the family felt besieged. Early one Sunday, a neighbouring farmer used his tractor to pull three farm wagons onto the property to block the media's view of the side entrance. The same day, Barbara Walker wrote down the licence numbers of media cars. In bizarre contrast, later that day Duncan brought his easel and paints out onto the front porch and set about doing abstract art of the reporters. The cheerful Duncan even waved to the reporters when he gathered firewood in the afternoon. The reporters asked the disgusting question again.

"I don't think anyone knows for sure who is the father of the children, except Sheena," he offered.

That same day, too, Barbara Walker again wrote to the *Paris Star*:

"My Plea:

I look out of my window and watch you watching us. I leave for work and you set up the telephoto lens. You trail me and then harass my clients on the telephone. I come home and you block the way to my mailbox. You photograph my children returning from school. You trespass onto my property. You openly laugh at us. You find pleasure in our pain. You lurk around the church. You pretend to offer sympathy in return for a quote. You threaten to reveal my personal financial problems to the world. If I don't cooperate. You laugh again. You keep vigil far into the night, spying on us while we decorate our Christmas tree.

But this is your job. Your editor forces you to wait on a cold and lonely sideroad for days, as many as seven cars at a time. Your editor demands results. Your family won't survive if you come home empty handed. Your editor has no heart.

But you could take a stand. You could challenge the system. You could get off the side roads and make a difference. You have the power and the skill to perform miracles. You know how to make a story interesting. You could send that story anywhere in the world. You have a sixth sense for investigative journalism. You could put a family back together. You could feel good.

You wouldn't have to give up your pay cheque. A report once a week would be enough. You could get your readers involved. You could challenge them to phone in with information. Truckers have done this for years by watching for hitch hikers and circulating posters. These stories could be written in the warmth of your own home where you could enjoy time with your families.

I look out at your cars and expensive cameras and I see a huge waste of time and talent. There are lots of families who need to know. Even if the trail leads to a grave then at least there will be closure and start to the grieving.

I look out of my window and I watch you

watching us. I wish I could say, "Please return home and take good care of your own families. Never let anything happen to them. Please return home and let us be free."

Twenty Six ━━━━━━━━━━━━

THE MOVING FINGER

AS MARCH 1997 ARRIVED, Albert Walker prepared to test the prosecution's case in a committal hearing, the British equivalent of the Canadian preliminary hearing, which determines whether there is enough evidence to send an accused to trial. Whereas in Canada the prosecution determines which witnesses will appear at a preliminary hearing, in Britain it is the defence who elects which evidence it wishes to accept on paper and which it seeks to test in.

In the days leading up to the committal hearing, Walker's lawyers had indicated that they wanted to test the evidence of Barbara and Sheena Walker and OPP Staff Sgt. Joe Milton, perhaps even David Davis, should the British authorities call them. But when British police booked their flights and gave every impression that Barbara, Sheena and Milton would be making the transatlantic trip, the defence accepted instead their "papers" or written testimony, about Walker being a fugitive from Canada and acting as both David Davis and Ronald Platt while on the run.

On March 24 in a tiny courtroom in the coastal resort town of Teignmouth, about six miles north of Torquay, Albert Walker pleaded not guilty to the charge that he murdered Ronald Platt. After three days of evidence, his lawyer, barrister Gordon Pringle, argued the Crown could not prove that Platt was murdered; that he was ever attached to the anchor; that he was aboard the *Lady Jane* on July 20, 1996; or that the *Lady Jane* was ever in the vicinity of where Platt's body was found.

"You can say that Mr. Walker had the opportunity. Well, all the South Coast had the opportunity," he said. "You have a yacht, but you can't prove he was on it."

But the magistrate noted that the Crown's case was circumstantial and had to be assembled like a jigsaw puzzle. A reasonable jury, properly directed by a judge, could conclude that Walker murdered Platt, he said, and he remanded Walker in custody until a full trial could be arranged. Outside court, Pringle said he wouldn't advise Walker to file an alibi.

"Whenever the deceased was murdered, we weren't there," he said on Walker's behalf. "It's not my client's intention to account for every twenty-four hours of each day for a month."

In short, the prosecution would have to prove its case against Albert Walker. He wasn't going down without a fight.

On each day of his three-day hearing, Walker put a coat over his head to avoid photographers. One

spunky British freelance photographer asked if
Walker would remove the coat so he could get a "nice
picture." Walker was heard to say from behind the
locked truck door, "If you give me £2,000!"

By this time, Canadian police had figured out how
Albert Walker had been able to masquerade as David
Wallis Davis. Davis had told detectives how, back in
1981, he had borrowed $35,000 through Al Walker
in his efforts to keep his business going. Walker had
asked for his birth certificate as part of the collateral
for the loan.

"Al had to have some kind of identification," Davis
recalled. "I gave him my birth certificate. And I had
no idea that my stuff was missing until October of
1996, when I needed my birth certificate to apply
for Canada Pension and I couldn't find it. So I con-
sequently never thought anything of it and I got other
documents to justify who I am."

Davis indicated that Walker had done all his bookkeeping in the 1980s, so he would have been privy to
his Canadian social insurance number and other
details, not to mention his exact signature.

During one interview, Cpl. Ralph King of the
RCMP's commercial crimes unit, noted the similarity
in appearance between Davis and Walker: Davis was
six foot three, with brown hair and brown eyes; Walker
six foot one, with brown hair and brown eyes. Their
ages were similar too: Walker was born August 9, 1945;
Davis on February 17, 1944. It wasn't lost on King
either that the dead Englishman, Ronald Platt, was

born in 1944, about five foot ten, with brown hair and brown eyes. Both men, it appeared, were hand-picked by Walker in the earliest days of their friendship.

Davis now recalls Walker talking with him one day and suddenly giving him a funny look.

"Ya know, David, we could pass as brothers."

Davis also revealed that in 1991 he had received an income tax slip from a London, Ontario, bank that stated he had earned $122.49 in interest. Knowing he had never done business with the bank, Davis phoned and was told that an account had been opened that year in his name and with his social insurance number. The bank gave him photocopies of all the transactions written on the account, but it didn't help Davis figure out what had happened.

"I knew something was up, something was weird. Someone could have my name, but how could someone have my social insurance number?" The tax statement was sent to David Davis, in care of Palmer Reid Capital Ltd., at an address in downtown Toronto. Davis had never heard of the company. Nor had he any knowledge of another bank account that he purportedly held in Brantford.

Was it just coincidence, King wondered, that the real David Wallis Davis last saw Albert Walker on December 1, 1990, only four days before Walker fled? At that time, Walker handed over another $35,000 to Davis, enough to pay off a $10,000 debt and start up a used car business. Davis, who was then still using Walker as his bookkeeper, was to pay back only 12 per cent in interest annually and pay nothing off the principal. Walker told him they would work out the repayment of the principal later. Knowing Walker as the sharp card he was, detectives wondered whether he had orchestrated the December 1 meeting with Davis in order to tie up loose ends in his plan to escape.

In any event, Davis appears to have been the perfect man for Walker to copy. Having been born in England, Davis was a British national and thus eligible to return there. Walker could also use Davis's birth certificate to obtain other identification in Davis's name. Once Walker had entered Britain as himself, it would have been easy for him to switch identities. Just as he later did for Platt's identity, Walker could, through the fact of Davis's birthplace, explain how he ended up in the United States and why he had returned to Britain. It was also a convenient cover to explain his "American" accent.

A few weeks after the committal hearing, a colourful greeting card appeared at the *Toronto Sun*. It was dated March 25, two days after Walker appeared in court and two days after the *Sun* ran a four-page special on Walker's case. The card was in response to separate requests of Barbara, Sheena and Jill to give interviews.

Dear Mr. Cairns,
Thank you for your letter, and I'm sorry that I haven't had time to reply sooner. Unfortunately I

am unable to help you with your book but I feel
that it would be improper of me considering the
fact that I am a witness for the Crown Prosecution
Service.

Sincerely,
Sheena Walker

Barbara, meanwhile, was doing some writing of her
own. While Albert Walker was seeking money for his
photograph in Britain, Barbara was asking Canadian
publishers if they would print her book and wanted
to know how much they would pay. Barbara asserted
in her letters that she was the only one who could tell
this very personal story.

As Albert Walker spent the rest of 1997 in Exeter
Prison and his defence lawyer, Roger Bryce, scrambled to get him the best possible criminal lawyer,
police in Britain and Canada assisted each other with
their respective cases. British police were firmly
focused on the murder case, while their Canadian
counterparts zeroed in on finances. Under Canadian
bankruptcy law, RCMP Cpl. Ralph King's investigation was not only limited to the criminal side of the
case but also had to probe Walker's assets and report
to the trustee.

Hoping to recoup some of their enormous losses
at Walker's hands, investors and their bankruptcy
trustee, KPMG of London, Ontario, forced Walker
into bankruptcy in Britain in the same way they had

taken Walker's Financial into bankruptcy in 1992. If
Walker had cash and assets, they argued, then they
were bought with stolen money from Canada. In mul-
tiple visits to the Devon and Cornwall Constabulary
at Paignton, Milton and King had examined hundreds
of items seized upon the arrest of Walker. These
items, KPMG argued, must be turned over to the
estate for ultimate sharing among the fleeced
investors.

Among Walker's assets was $29,000 in cash seized
at the Little London Farmhouse and in storage units,
as well as seventeen gold bars. In addition, the trustee
wanted to seize the *Lady Jane* and Victorian art works.
King ascertained that on June 5, 1991, Walker, posing as David Davis, had paid the Royal Academy of
Arts, in London's Piccadilly, £2,275 for *Sunset
Llanddwyn* by Kyffin Williams and £3,000 for *Ever-
lastings* by Olwyn Bowey. Only nine days later, Walker,
again posing as Davis, had appeared at Christie's auctioneers and bought three Victorian-era paintings,
paying £7,000 for *The Very Image* by Joseph Clark,
£2,400 for *A Rest by the Gate* by William Bromley,
and £3,500 for W. Powell Firth's *Portrait of Nora
Creina*.

Attempts to track down £10,000 worth of furniture that the bogus Davis bought at Harrods in
Knightsbridge had failed. Walker had purchased the
furniture September 20, 1991, and February 19,
1992. If Walker did take the furniture from Yorkshire
to Devon, and on to Essex, then it was likely among

the goods that his lawyer had removed from the Little London Farmhouse after his arrest.

Through the remainder of 1997 and early 1998, King pressed various foreign authorities for access to the dozen or so English bank accounts and the nine accounts in Switzerland, Italy and France, as well as the Canvest account in the Caymans. In the weeks leading up to the June 22, 1998, start of Walker's murder trial at the Exeter Crown Court, King tracked down $500,000 in various English accounts but still hadn't gained access to all the European accounts. King and officials with KPMG wondered whether the pot of gold they felt still existed had been expertly hidden by Walker. Surely, there had to be more than $500,000. Frank Johnson alone had given him that much back in 1995.

As the trustees attempted to piece together the puzzle, Elaine Boyes did her best to help fill in the blanks and dispel any beliefs that she and Platt had been in cahoots with Walker. If there was any blackmail or payoff involved, Boyes suggested, it hadn't started while she and Platt were together.

"Giving David Davis [Walker] his driving licence and birth certificate would have been crazy, as Ron would have needed them in Canada," Boyes wrote in an April 21, 1998, letter to KPMG. "If Davis had wanted them, Ron would have wondered why."

Boyes wished the trustees every success in their quest to get money for the creditors: "These people have been conned of their money and their trust. This is atrocious and unforgivable. I have been conned of my trust of a man I thought was a friend and my life as I knew it before is no longer. This man has left me mentally and emotionally scarred, probably for life. I feel dreadful.

"Sadly, Ron . . . was conned not only of his trust, but also of his life. It is so sad that his life has ended in this tragic way. Ron would have never hurt anyone. He was a very caring, sensitive soul . . . Ron and I believed this man to be an honest, honourable, kind, decent, caring human being. Sadly, we now know the reverse is true."

Boyes wrote that she believes in "total honesty. That's most likely what Mr. Davis found attractive in me. I have always believed that honesty is the best policy and have been brought up to believe this and to also trust people. Unfortunately, being this way can lead to being used and manipulated by others. I find it extremely hard to understand this man and to accept what has happened, as he appeared to be such a gentleman."

Among Canadians looking for some kind of pay-back was Eric Winter, whose wife, Myrtle, had shown so much faith in Walker when she invested almost every penny she had with him back in the mid-1980s. Myrtle Winter died of a heart attack on July 15, 1995. Eric says his wife's premature death came on because of the stress of losing her life's work to Walker. After having two legs amputated this past decade because of poor circulation, seventy-five-year-old Winter found himself renting the house he and Myrtle had once owned and lived in for forty years. He now subsists on a meagre pension. Still, despite his own loss, Winter feels sorry for Sheena Walker, who, he believes, "was just an innocent victim."

Twenty-seven

MURDER IS EASY

AS WALKER'S CROWN Court trial approached, his solicitor, Roger Bryce, sent out a defence brief to renowned London barrister Richard Ferguson, a Queen's Counsel and a rugged veteran of high-profile and dramatic trials who had polished his brilliant oratorical skills in Parliament as a Unionist member for South Antrim in Northern Ireland. The grandson of a lay preacher, the son of a cop and the product of a staunchly Methodist family, the sixty-three year-old Ferguson is a perfectionist who for decades has demanded nothing short of perfection from the caretakers of Britain's legal system. The presumption of innocence, the right to a fair trial and full answer in defence are principles sacred to Ferguson. The Crown has the power to lay charges; the accused can plead guilty or not guilty. If all unfolds as it should, then justice will be served. Acting for an accused does not depend on whether Ferguson feels a person is innocent or guilty. If an accused maintains his or her innocence, then he accepts it.

Ferguson's strength is his ability to eloquently poke holes in a prosecution case in a way that even the simplest men and women can understand. If there is a reasonable doubt, then he is sure to find it and exploit it vigorously. Ferguson couldn't resist taking the intriguing Walker file, and in the months before had planned a strategy with Roger Bryce and fellow barrister Gordon Pringle, the lawyer who had stood by Walker at the committal hearing.

How fitting, Ferguson mused when poring over the Walker file, that he, a self-admitted fanatic of the London-based Arsenal, should be defending a man alleged to have told people his cousin was David Platt, the famous Arsenal footballer. Ferguson, however, doesn't rely on any football analogies when he talks about a court case. Rather, it is a game of rugby: You play your hardest, and rely on the referee.

Ferguson and his team were up against a police and prosecution squad led by Bristol barrister Charles Barton, himself a Queen's Counsel with an impressive résumé of convictions for the Crown Prosecution Service (CPS) and some noteworthy successes as a defence lawyer. Barton, too, is highly regarded in British legal circles. A huge, plump man of about three hundred pounds, Barton is the antithesis of Albert Walker. His round, bespectacled face always sports a five-o'clock shadow, like the cartoon character Fred Flintstone. But there is nothing cartoon-like about Barton's intelligence and legal acumen. He questions an accused the way a seasoned heavyweight boxing champion deals with a rambunctious young upstart; he innocently jabs at his opponent while scheming to set him up and deliver a devastating knock-out punch. His loud voice has the same tenor as Horace Rumpole of the Bailey, but Barton's great asset is that he is believable. Helping him on the prosecution bench was barrister James Townshend, who had conducted the Teignmouth committal hearing for the CPS. Assisting the legal team were Det. Insp. Phil Sincock, Det. Sgt. Bill MacDonald and exhibits officer Det. John Carlyon.

The referee, as Ferguson would put it in rugby terms, was Justice Neil Butterfield, a former Queen's Counsel and a veteran ex-trial lawyer who once practised in Exeter. Butterfield has a reputation as a gentleman and man of fine humour. In the words of one Essex Crown Court staffer, "He is one of the best."

How ironic that the Exeter Crown Court would host the trial of a man who purported to love history, tradition and antiques and who had dreamed of retiring quietly to Scotland by age fifty. The two-storey courthouse and its expansive courtyard are reached by climbing a sharply sloping, narrow cobblestone street that passes the eleventh-century red stone Rougemont Castle tower of the Normans. On the castle wall a plaque commemorates the "Devon witches," four of whom were tried and hanged in Exeter in the 1680s for practising witchcraft, the last witches to be executed in England. The court itself goes back to 1536.

The piercing morning sun painted the courthouse and cobblestone courtyard white at 8:30 on Monday, June 22, 1998, as a Reliance Security van carrying Walker squeezed through the narrow castle gate, past a throng of photographers and camera crews. Forbidden by police to take cameras beyond the front gate, eager lensmen tried to get a shot of Walker heading into court. They were thwarted when the van parked parallel to the courthouse so Walker could enter out of camera sights, through the receiving door.

Despite handcuffs and a security escort, Walker still managed to look distinguished as he stepped from the van. His hair and close-cropped beard had turned from grey to near white, making his face, especially the big brown eyes, even more prim, proper, noble. Comfortable in his black suit, pressed shirt, familiar old-school-style tie and shining leather shoes, Walker slowly walked inside. There was no need to run, no need to cover his head with the now crumpled raincoat draped over his arm. In the courtyard, a white Churchfield's rental van also pulled up, and plainclothes detectives began unloading cardboard document boxes with FARRIER slashed across the sides in black crayon.

At 10:15 a.m., right on time, Judge Butterfield and his entourage arrived in a chauffeur-driven Daimler. They were welcomed outside the courthouse with a four-part-harmony salute by Royal Marine trumpeters, splendid in their white pith hats and royal-blue uniforms. "Make way for the judge. Don't turn your back on the judge," a concerned court staffer barked at Canadian journalists, who had failed to comprehend that this regal holdout is part of the deep respect accorded the British judiciary. Clutching the traditional cluster of posies given to visiting judges, which have symbolized protection since the days of the Black Death, Butterfield strode through the court foyer with his lady, his cleric and other members of his staff.

As Judge Butterfield prepared for the trial in his chambers, Courtroom 2 began to fill up. It is a roomy, box-shaped hall with a high ceiling. Dark wood panelling that reaches halfway up the high walls, rows of dark wooden pews and desks from which business is done and a giant oil painting that hangs behind the public gallery and overlooks the scene give the room a richness. Wood plaques on the walls remember the famous lawyers and judges who have served there — the knights, the viscounts, lords and barons, and, most notable of all, a prime minister named William Pitt.

A score of journalists sat in the press seats. In front of them was the prisoner's dock, from which Walker would view his trial. A few yards beyond stood the prosecution and defence tables. Across from them were the law clerks' seats, and directly in front and above, the judge's bench stretched from wall to wall. The police team lined a table on one side left of the courtroom, while the twelve seats of the jury stand were on the other. Behind the jury seats, a pair of crinkled olive-green curtains covered the entrance to the jury's room.

On the dot of 10:40, a court clerk opened the

door behind the judge's bench and called, "order." As everyone stood Butterfield entered court. To the irreverent eye, the judge and the barristers looked ridiculous in their traditional blond half-wigs with curls on the sides and top, and wispy tail; from any perspective but the front, the wigs leave natural hair in view.

Having waited below in the basement lock-up for almost two hours, Walker made his first trip up the thirteen stairs and into the prisoner's box. He stood at attention as the clerk dished out the usual protocol and read the murder charge against him.

"Are you Albert Johnson Walker?" asked the clerk.

"I am," Walker answered in his deep, nasal voice. They were his first public words since he had pleaded not guilty more than a year before.

Barton dramatically advised that thirty-six witnesses in all would be called and the trial would likely last four weeks, and Butterfield gave the green light to start. In short order the jury was picked: eight women and four men from all walks of Devon life, ranging in age from their twenties to their sixties. Then Barton rose to give the Crown's opening statement, a road map of the evidence. Leaning his corpulent body over the lectern, he barely looked at his notes as he spoke to the jury.

"This case depends upon detail," started Barton, reassuring the jury that if they could grasp the specifics and put them into place the full picture would present itself in the end. After giving a quick chronology of the evidence against Walker, Barton paused briefly, turned from the jury and announced, "The first witness I'm going to call is Sheena Walker."

A disbelieving murmur arose from journalists and the public gallery. Until that point it had been unclear whether the prosecution would call her at all. If people *had* expected Sheena to testify, they hadn't expected it to be so soon in the trial. It took a few moments for Sheena to arrive from the back room courthouse staff had squirrelled her into shortly after her surprise arrival. Wearing a brown tweed jacket (the kind her father loved to wear) over a beige blouse and a pair of black dress pants, Sheena walked in with the help of a large-sized woman in a large-sized yellow dress. It was later revealed that Sheena's helper was a victim services worker.

Sheena's gait was fast and she almost fell when climbing the steps to the witness box. Taking the Bible in her right hand, she stumbled over her words as she began to say she would tell the truth and nothing but the truth. Then, at a whisper from the clerk, Sheena picked a candy out of her mouth and put it into a napkin. She hastily gulped down some water. Walker's eyes were glued to her from the moment the courtroom door opened. He continued to stare at her in the witness box. Sheena pushed back at her neatly chopped shoulder-length red hair, then tugged at her bangs. Her eyes moved right towards the prisoner's box and for a moment fixed on her father. Although her smile was nervous, she showed no fear.

"Look over here, Miss Walker, please," Barton bellowed. Sheena immediately jerked her head back and looked straight ahead. "That's the best plan. Keep looking in that direction," he said, pointing towards the jury. "Will you do that?"

"Sure," said Sheena.

"Your full name is Sheena Elizabeth Walker?" the probing Rumpole voice began.

"Correct," said Sheena.

"And you were born in Canada?"

"Correct."

She replied quickly, in a strong voice. Despite all that had happened, she seemed quite self-assured. She certainly didn't come across as the wallflower people had painted her as. Responding to Barton's questioning, she acknowledged that she had lived in Paris, Ontario, and her father had done tax returns, again answering with a formal "Correct" instead of just a plain and simple "Yes."

"And at age ten to twelve, could you please describe your childhood," Barton said.

"It was nice," Sheena offered.

"And how was the relationship with your parents at that age?"

"Fairly normal," said Sheena, although appearing somewhat unconvinced.

"Did it continue that way?"

"No, it didn't."

"In your own words, when did the signs of problems show up?"

"I guess I was about twelve years old," Sheena lamented, a hint of despair in her voice.

"As time went on, did things get better or worse?"

"Things worsened." The court held its breath: What exactly did she mean? But the elaboration didn't come. Barton turned Sheena's attention to her father's business.

In a firm yet detached voice, Sheena recalled that her father's company had appeared profitable and that money in her family was "relatively plentiful." In 1990, the year her parents split, she came to England on vacation with her father and two siblings. Upon returning to Canada, she went to live with her father.

"When you came to England with your father [again] . . . was it your choice to accompany him?" asked Barton.

"Yes," she said, exploding the long-held public suspicion that Walker had coerced her into leaving.

Sheena explained how her father used the name David Davis after arriving in England, and she used Noël Davis, a name, she said, chosen by her father.

"Who made the decision — why was it necessary to change names?" quizzed Barton.

"'Coz my mother was going after custody of my siblings and after my father for financial support, which he thought was a great deal of money, and he wanted to make it difficult for her to accomplish."

At Barton's prompting, Sheena recalled her father

meeting Boyes. But she had no clue how Cavendish Corporation was set up or who had been named directors. It wasn't until after Boyes and Platt went to Canada that she became aware her father had Platt's driver's licence and birth certificate. By late 1993, when she and her father had moved to the Tiverton area and he was using Ron Platt's name, she still had no idea that Elaine Boyes had returned to Britain.

"And what name were you using?" asked Barton.

"Noël Platt."

"Were you holding yourself out to be his daughter Noël?"

"My father suggested that with a small child along . . . that we should sort of present ourselves as a couple."

"As husband and wife?" asked Barton.

"Yes."

"Were there other names?"

"Because of complications with my mother, my father suggested I use Elaine Boyes's name for medical purposes."

In November 1994, Sheena recalled, they moved to Woodham Walter as "the Platts." She glanced sideways at her father, but then quickly turned back. She seemed frightened. While they lived at Woodham Walter, she said, the real Ronald Platt returned.

"What did Ronald Platt call your father? What did they call each other when they were together?" asked Barton, hoping to present to the jury evidence that in 1995 Platt still believed Walker to be David Davis.

"He'd call him David."

"You were still Noël?"

"Yes."

"Was your father known as Ronald?"

"Yes . . ."

Barton never asked Sheena what kind of cover story Platt got about the birth of her two children, Emily in Tiverton and Lily in Maldon. Sheena said she didn't really keep up with Platt's comings and goings because she was "busy" then, meaning she was at home with the two children playing house-wife and mother and cutting the grass. She didn't know much about any arrangements between the two men, she said, as any business dealings were "between themselves." She last saw Platt at Christmas 1995. In June 1996, her father told her he had left for France.

"Can you recall the precise words for what your father said happened?"

"That he had given up . . . and had travelled across to France . . . I think to the Bordeaux region."

Remembering her stay at the Potter's Loft flat in Dittisham, starting July 12, 1996, Sheena said her father made no mention of Platt that week, and at that time she still understood him to be in France. On July 19, 1996, she recalled, she, Walker and the kids moved to another Dittisham flat, the Old Brewhouse. The next morning, July 20, 1996, the suspected day of Ronald Platt's alleged murder, her dad went out sailing by himself and didn't return until approximately 10 p.m. They talked briefly about his sailing and the weather, but that was about it. No, her dad hadn't told her about any injury. The next morning, they went down to the boat at Galmpton moorings and tidied it up.

A month or so after that, she said, a police officer called her father and told him Platt's body was found. "He was shocked at first. He said it probably wasn't Ron," said Sheena. Seconds later she ventured, "Maybe he said that to reassure me . . ."

"What happened immediately after the phone call?" asked Barton.

"We were hoping to move to the Birmingham area. My father wanted to get out of the therapy partnership . . . and go out on his own. He didn't think it was wise to do it in the same area."

"Were there any preparatory steps taken?"

"I went up with him to that area to have a look around, to see what would be a good place to move to."

"Where?"

"Leamington Spa."

"Did you assist your father in any furniture removal?"

"We only had three bedrooms and four people and it just was not working out. The situation we had was no good. We were trying to tidy up boxes from the move of a year ago. We did move boxes into a storage container to help get our house sorted out."

Sheena said most of her father's furniture from

"his" bedroom was taken to a Northampton storage unit, but she didn't recall him storing the GPS system. After that, she said, they rented a cottage for a month in a village near Leamington Spa. When asked by Barton what they had told the neighbours about this trip, Sheena recalled saying they were going to "the States." Apparently she had forgotten the bogus death of her own father and her teary heartbreak in front of Isabel Rogers and Neil.

Two months after she returned to Canada in December, her father called. "He had asked me to change my testimony . . . He asked me to say I knew that Ron was down in Devon during the vacation in the July period of the year before and to tell them that I just forgot," Sheena stammered. "And that I was supposed to know that Ron had been on the boat as well . . . he was supposed to have told me all of this . . ."

Again Sheena took a quick look at her dad but then swung her head back towards Barton. A few more questions and her role for the Crown was fulfilled. Tomorrow she would be thrown to the defence lawyer. Sheena almost fell out of the witness box and stumbled as the victim's services worker whisked her out of sight. Walker's eyes followed her every move, down to the court doors and into the lobby. Moments later she was driven away to a secret police hideaway in a van with tinted windows, her face hidden behind a tabloid newspaper.

So the prosecution plan was obvious: stay completely away from any peripheral questions about Sheena's life with her father and the lingering question of the paternity of her two children; stick only to the facts of the murder case. Her testimony might lack drama and pathos, but the direct evidence alone would work for the prosecution. It was a difficult case as it was, they realized, so better simplify it. The lack of information could not help but confuse the jury, however. They were clearly puzzled about the real relationship between the bogus Mr. and Mrs. Platt, and about which Platt, if either, had fathered the children.

As the day drew to a close, Walker put away the pen he had used to make copious notes on a pad of paper. He stuffed the notepad into a manilla envelope and was escorted down to the basement holding cell.

When Sheena took the witness box the next day for cross-examination by Ferguson, she appeared more comfortable than previously. Either this odd woman's nerves and stomach were made of steel or else she didn't feel. Some people ventured she had been through so much trauma, that by contrast a simple court appearance was nothing. She glanced at her father, then stared straight ahead. Unlike the previous day, Walker didn't even bother to look at his daughter. Maybe Ferguson had told him the jury wouldn't like it, or maybe he realized that Sheena had reconciled to do what she must do and he was powerless to stop her. Whatever it was, the woman who had once lived as her father's child and then his wife was now just a pawn in a legal match.

Ferguson began his questioning. "When you came to England, that was at your request, was it not?"

"Yes, it was," Sheena answered unashamedly.

"You wanted to go."

"Yes, I did."

"After you arrived here, was it you who chose to go by the name Noël Davis?"

Sheena paused and confusion came over her face, as if she hadn't expected the question. "No . . . I really didn't wish to change my name . . ."

She hadn't wished to change her name to Noël Platt, either. And she disagreed with Ferguson that she was the one who wanted to move away from Harrogate, out of fear that Elaine Boyes might discover she had become pregnant and was using Boyes' name.

Ferguson led Sheena along a line of questioning designed to bolster Walker's claim that Platt had, in fact moved to France and Walker had nothing to do with the death. Yes, her father had talked of Platt's depression after he lost his job in December 1995; yes, Platt hated living in Britain; yes, Platt had problems with Britishers; and yes, there was mention of Platt going to France and in the spring of 1996 he did go and brought her back some leaflets from some fashion magazines.

Then Ferguson went on the offensive, claiming that her father had told her Platt was in Chelmsford and was going to help take the boat to Devon.

"No, that was never suggested to me."

"That was never said to you?"

"No, it wasn't," she shot back defiantly. "Ronald wasn't . . . he wasn't partial to water."

She recalled that in early July, her father went to Devon to "look at the boat," but there was no mention of the real Ronald Platt being there and no mention of Platt helping him move the boat to Essex.

Moving to the police phone call about Platt's body being found, Ferguson suggested that Sheena believed then he had committed suicide.

"That was my immediate thought."

"That's what you told police!"

"I hadn't had time to think about it."

"You told the police: 'We thought that Ron had committed suicide'!"

"A lot of people thought that . . . A lot of the information I gave police was based on information my father had given me."

When Ferguson suggested that in the last of five telephone calls her father made to her Paris, Ontario, home after his arrest, he didn't tell her to lie but actually said she should change her statement because she in fact knew Platt was in Devon and they went sailing together, Sheena spat out another "No!"

"He didn't say you're going to have to change your statement?"

"Not in those words."

With that, Ferguson sat down. Barton had no

further questions. Sheena appeared relieved. Her ordeal on the stand was over.

Judge Butterfield asked Sheena what she meant when she said Platt wasn't partial to water. "Are you saying he didn't like water?"

"No, he did not. He didn't swim. He didn't like getting on a boat, even a large boat."

Then, eyebrows creased, Butterfield addressed both lawyers. "It is obvious that there were matters raised that were not explored in detail. Are you absolutely comfortable that all the matters relevant to the jury's case have been heard?"

Each agreed that no further questions were necessary.

And with that Sheena was gone. And so it was over. The strategies had been accomplished. In a most extraordinary way, both the prosecution and the defence had avoided getting into Sheena's relationship with her father and the paternity of the children. The reasons for her apparent devotion and total subservience for all those years on the run would not be explored in the courtroom. The dirty laundry, as it were, would not be washed in public. The question on the jury's lips, as stark, rude and intrusive as it might be, was not to be answered, at least not by Sheena.

The jury then heard from Brixham fisherman John Copik, decked out, as Judge Butterfield humorously put it, in his "weddings and funerals" suit. One after another the Crown's witnesses came forward.

When Dr. Gyan Fernando took the stand, he testified that in the first post-mortem he'd missed the bruise marks on the hip and therefore missed their significance. After the anchor was recovered and placed next to Platt's corpse according to the police theory of Platt's demise, he noted that the bruises matched with the ends of the anchor. In cross-examination by Ferguson, Fernando agreed the marks could have been caused in many ways and there was nothing inconsistent between Platt's death and suicide.

Ferguson then tried to trip up Detective Sergeant Redman's memory of what Walker had told him in August 1996 about the last time he had seen Platt. Redman didn't budge, though, recalling that Walker told him it was in June of 1996.

When Ferguson, in his Irish brogue, challenged Det. Const. Ian Clenahan on his memory and the integrity and accuracy of his notes and tried to attack Redman's recollection of events through him, Clenahan's Liverpudlian accent was in full bloom.

Ferguson: "Is it possible that Sergeant Redman might have told you that Mr. Davis said the last time he saw Mr. Platt was 'a couple of months earlier,' the 'end of June, the beginning of July'?"

"When I spoke with Detective Sergeant Redman he said the last time he had spoken with him was in June of that year. Mr. Davis said the same thing. If he had told me July, I'd have written it down. I am very curious indeed of the time . . . I am trying to put it down to small times."

"So he didn't say that?"

"That is 100 per cent reported very accurately."

"Are you sure. There appears to be some confusion . . ."

"There is certainly no confusion. What more can I say?"

At this, Butterfield intervened and asked if Redman could possibly have said the end of June, or early July.

"I am 110 per cent sure what he actually said is written down on that paper, My Lord," said Clenahan.

After a flurry of questions around the telephone calls, Ferguson again posed the Redman question to Clenahan. This time, in frustration, Clenahan answered directly to Judge Butterfield. "That is not correct, My Lord," he said.

Then it was Elaine Boyes's turn. She had been so nervous before her day in court.

"No need to worry, just be Elaine and tell the truth," a friendly Devon officer advised her in the week leading up to the trial.

She couldn't help but be nervous, she replied, what with the nation's media focused on her.

She was so nervous that when she walked into the courtroom she didn't dare lay eyes on the man in the prisoner's dock. The man she had known as David Davis, the man accused of manipulating her and her boyfriend into going to Canada, the man who allegedly killed her boyfriend two years earlier. Barton started his questioning and soon got to showing her the Rolex watch found on Platt's body. There were tears in her eye as she identified the watch as his "pride and joy." Afterwards, Boyes said that she almost asked the judge if she could hold on to the watch during her testimony so that she could "touch something close to Ron" and have enough strength to get through her traumatic appearance on the stand. In addition to drawing details from Boyes about Walker's tricks, Barton skilfully used her testimony to put both a face and an identity on the victim. Naturally, by way of her own testimony, Boyes showed her goodness and her sincerity. In the jury's eyes, she was a totally believable witness.

Now Ferguson took over. Furthering his notion of suicide, he tried to use Boyes to show that Platt was a beaten man in his final months of life. In her sincerity, Boyes recounted how her former lover had once called from Canada "in tears," begging her to return.

"Ron came back from Canada depressed," he offered.

"Yes," said Boyes, "suicidal to a point." She noted that he had a prescription for antidepressants.

Was he a drinker?

Yes, she said, Ron would have a drink and a cigarette in the evening while watching the late-night news, but he would control his drinking.

Near the end of his routine, Ferguson deftly slipped in the question of whether Platt gave his driver's licence to the so-called Davis.

"He didn't give him his driver's licence at all!" she asserted forcefully.

"Or credit cards?" asked Ferguson.

"No!" said Boyes.

Her testimony finished, Boyes sat down in the public gallery alongside two of her friends who had taken notes since the first day of the trial to help with Boyes's book. Although she told all the reporters she would not speak to them, throughout the next week she spoke to just about everyone. Such was her friendly nature.

Twenty-eight ▬▬▬▬▬▬▬

NEMESIS

LEAVING THE SO-CALLED Ronald Platt in the lurch at Solutions in Therapy hadn't hurt Isabel Rogers. Her dream of joining a therapy practice now became a dream of starting up a therapy office of her own. In 1997 she opened Horizons, in Brentwood, ironically is in the same building Platt and the partners ran Solutions in Therapy. The building was, after all, well located.

Failing to heed the phoney Platt's advice, Isabel not only kept on dating her policeman friend, Neil, after Walker's arrest, but went on to marry him in September 1997. While these parts of her life were in order, Isabel still wouldn't be able to purge herself of the Walker virus until she both testified at his trial and witnessed his prosecution through to its conclusion. As a therapist, now a fully qualified one, Isabel puts great faith in understanding. Through it comes a cleansing and a healing. But appreciate this as she might, when Isabel boarded the train for Exeter at Chelmsford station the night of Wednesday, June 24, 1998, she took along her mother for support. She had known the accused murderer for almost a year and a half. She had told her innermost thoughts and secrets when he conducted the three therapy sessions. She had been to his house. Her husband had held Sheena's baby! It all seemed like an awful dream, but it had been her own reality.

On Thursday morning, Isabel went into the courtroom to find herself part of what the prosecution team referred to as the Woodham Walter witnesses. Sitting in the foyer were Audrey Mossman and Frank Johnson and Ed and Marion Jones.

It was Marion's turn first. She stood in the witness box rather than sat. Marion could have told the court all kinds of stories, but the prosecution most needed her to tell of Walker's money and how he had hurt himself on the boat. Questioned by James Townshend, she recounted how Walker had introduced himself as Ron Platt and given her and Ed the story of having been a banker in Geneva. She also described how he'd once shown off his taste and wealth by bringing down pieces of art and a gold bar from the Little London Farmhouse loft. Marion also recalled that shortly after the "Platts" returned from their Devon vacation in 1996, they had supper together, and "Ron said he hurt himself while tying up the boat. He didn't get into any more details."

Looking a little older and more frail than when Det. Sgt. Peter Redman knocked on her door back in October 1996, Audrey Mossman clasped her hands together in the witness box as she tried to find her

voice. At first she struggled to squeeze the words out.
Audrey recalled Platt's talk of being an American and
having a degree from the University of Edinburgh and
of his experience in stocks and shares and of Sheena's
attending Chelsea Art College and his meeting her
there. Audrey said when the "Platts" returned from
the sailing holiday in Devon and she asked Ron if he'd
had a good time, he said he had hurt his shoulder and
the kids had colds. Audrey also recounted how the
bogus Noël's bogus father had died.

After their short appearances, Marion and
Audrey sat in the public gallery with their partners
and awaited the appearance of Isabel Rogers.
Although none of them had ever met her, they'd all
heard of Isabel through "Platt." They were all eager
to hear how Walker had conducted himself at the
therapy business.

When her name was called Isabel, looking sharp
in a double-breasted black blazer and a grey business
skirt, walked briskly into the courtroom and settled
into the witness box. Anger swept through her as she
looked over to the prisoner's dock. She felt so vulnerable that "Ron Platt" had seen her before she laid
eyes on him. Walker gave her a smirk, as if to say, "I'm
okay." She turned away.

Isabel's value to the prosecution lay in her
knowledge of the calls from his "cousin" David and
the desperate telephone call on July 21, 1996 — the
day after he allegedly murdered the real Ronald Platt.
From her, Townshend first drew out Walker's claims

about his background, but then he quickly turned to Isabel's memories of "Cousin David."

"He told me he had a cousin David and also a brother called David," she said, matter-of-fact. "He made out that David Platt the footballer was his cousin."

With these words Isabel had the jury in an uproar. The dark-haired young man in the front row was laughing so hard he had to look down at the floor. Most of the eight women laughed. Even the court clerks chuckled. At the height of the World Cup fever sweeping England, this one comment from Isabel had put all Walker's lies into perspective. This was something the everyday people on the jury could understand. Isabel had touched a common root. She had delivered a strong blow to Walker's credibility. She'd known that of all the things she could say, his line about David Platt would be the most damning. The eyes of the jury were on Walker now. Isabel interpreted these amused gazes to be saying to Walker, "You're pathetic." Anxious to escape the jury's stare, Walker peered down at his knees. As the chuckles subsided, Isabel looked at Walker. His brown eyes showed hurt.

"Would the phone calls always be for Ron?" Townshend continued.

"Most of the time," said Isabel. "But sometimes we'd get calls for David, and he would say they were for him. He would explain it was his cousin. He gave me the impression that occasionally he dealt with his cousin's business and it was easier sometimes to be dealt with as David."

Then she recalled the telephone call Platt made to her the morning of Sunday, July 21, 1996, the day before a scheduled workshop together.

"I was still in bed. It was eight to nine o'clock. He said he'd had a bad accident on the boat and that he couldn't come back. I said, 'You sound in a bad way.' He was breathing quite badly. He said he had hurt his head and his chest and he'd hurt himself pulling heavy things off the boat."

After a few brief questions from Ferguson, Isabel's testimony was finished.

Before she left the stand, however, Judge Butterfield said he had a question about David Platt the footballer.

"Was that before or after he was at Juventus?" asked Butterfield in his regal voice.

The court burst into laughter. Such humour from the stand was unusual.

"I haven't got a clue, Your Honour," said Isabel.

No doubt if Butterfield had asked Ferguson, the Arsenal fanatic, his question would have been answered.

Isabel caught the train home that night, but sensing that Walker would take the stand later the next week, she vowed to come down and be there. As a therapist, she couldn't resist seeing how he would act and hearing what he would say. She ventured privately that Walker would try to dominate the courtroom — just as he had tried to dominate all situations in his life — with his conviction that he could persuade the jury he was not a killer. Isabel did not relish the prospect. She had first-hand knowledge of this bizarre man and worried that all he had to do was give some fascinating story and convince one of the jurors he wasn't guilty beyond a reasonable doubt and he would get off.

"I suspect he has worked his own case," Isabel told a journalist after her testimony. "Even a good lawyer like Ferguson would not be able to keep Walker in the back seat."

The rest of the week, instead of calling witnesses from Canada, the prosecution read in "admitted facts" that had been agreed to by the defence. Among these was a short statement outlining how Walker had once run a financial company in Canada and was now sought by Canadian authorities for a $4-million fraud. The jury would not hear the fine details of how Walker ruthlessly bilked friends, clients and business partners. They would not hear about Walker's various infidelities, or his treatment of Barbara Walker on the eve of his flight. They would hold their focus on Walker's activities in Britain. He was not on trial for actions in Canada.

Barton took over as testimony was given or statements were read from the owners of the Steam Packet and the Seven Stars in Totnes, Potter's Loft and the Old Brewhouse in Dittisham and the Anchorage in Dartmouth. Simon Baker, John Foale and others involved with Platt through the *Lady Jane* also chipped in their information.

The prosecution's case would conclude with testimony of the forensics specialists from the Forensic Sciences Centre in Chepstow. The jury heard that despite its dull appearance, the 10-pound plough anchor recovered from John Copik's net via the car boot sale was quite new. The sea's salt water, it was explained, had quickly tarnished the galvanized steel. The most striking evidence, however, was that flashing had remained on the anchor's chain eyelet, meaning the anchor had never been used for its intended purpose. In addition, the kink in the belt on Platt's body contained zinc that may have come from galvanized steel. If Platt threaded his belt to the left, that galvanized mark on the belt would directly line up the anchor with the bruises on his leg. In addition, the shank of the plough anchor had traces of fibrous material consistent with leather.

The jury also heard that DNA in the three head hairs found on a pillow in the *Lady Jane* and was identical to Platt's. The chance of a match, the jury heard, was three million to one. Platt's fingerprint was also found on a bag in a locker on the boat. From this evidence the jury knew Platt had been on board the *Lady Jane*.

The jury then heard that a fully wound Rolex would tick for forty to forty-five hours if kept stationary — important information in the Crown's assertion that Platt met his end July 20. And of course they heard of how the GPS system was recovered and tested and how it showed that at 8:59 p.m. on the asserted murder day of July 20 the *Lady Jane* was at sea off Hope's Nose, only 3.78 nautical miles from where Platt's body was pulled out of the sea.

The evidence seemed overwhelming to most, but some journalists wrote that it didn't show proof beyond a reasonable doubt.

When Barton wrapped up the Crown's case on Tuesday June 30, everyone involved in the proceedings drew a deep breath and waited to see if the defence would have Walker take the stand.

Twenty-nine ▬▬▬▬▬▬▬▬

ORDEAL BY INNOCENCE

Peering over his half-moon reading glasses, Richard Ferguson stood up behind his lectern and addressed the jury. Only a few yards from them, he was closer than Barton had been. Part of his job was to reach out and touch them. Move their minds away from the week's worth of mountainous Crown evidence and get them focused on his opening remarks. Now it was the defence's turn to offer evidence.

"But even if you stop now and hear no further evidence in this case, you still have to pause, and pause for a long time, before you can be satisifed by the version of events as purported by the prosecution," Ferguson said in his delightful lilt. "The fact Mr. Barton very eloquently sets out a theory is not evidence — it's a theory! Whether the evidence lines up with the theory is up to you to decide.

"The Crown's case is theory-driven. What they've done is come up with a theory of how Mr. Platt met his death and have worked backwards. They fit the evidence into the theory. You will determine whether they are fitting the evidence into the theory or whether they are squeezing it in!"

A classic example of squeezing, he suggested, was Dr. Fernando failing to find the leg bruises in the first post-mortem but then finding them four months later when police handed him an anchor and theorized it had been tucked into the dead man's belt.

"Good theory, but what about the facts?" asked Ferguson. "Is the anchor the same one purchased at Sport Nautique? Is the anchor the same one dragged from the sea? Was the anchor from the *Lady Jane*? Was the anchor in a locker on the *Lady Jane*? Was the anchor stolen? I suggest the anchor evidence may be pushed upon you to deal with the point made — that the body wouldn't have moved from the sea bed!"

Ferguson nosed around the evidence of the head injury, the kink and zinc on the belt and other items he said just didn't add up: "There are many maybes in this case . . . Some things can't be explained. There are, maybe, mysteries, where we don't know what happened. It may be the death of Ronald Platt is such a mystery . . . What you need are facts, concrete evidence, not maybes!"

With that, Ferguson called his client to the stand.

Walker stood up in the prisoner's box, pulled the lapels of his black suit jacket together and walked slowly, lightly, almost effeminately, into the witness box. Whether by design or accident, he didn't come across as the tall, erect man people had known in Canada. Visually at least, the jury couldn't possibily perceive this man as a cold-hearted killer. In the witness box Walker smiled at the jury, took the Bible into his hand and began to repeat the words spoken by the clerk.

"I swear by almi-mighty God . . ." Right off the bat Walker stumbled. But he quickly recovered. "To tell the truth, the whole truth, and nothing but the truth."

At this point, the jury didn't know of how, a decade earlier, he had shattered his relationship with God at St. Paul's United Church. They didn't know he had broken nine of the sacred Ten Commandments and society's recognition of a tenth breach lay in their hands. They didn't know Walker had ripped off some of those same parishioners who had prayed and sung their faith alongside him on Sunday mornings. If the past could predict the future, Walker's first perjury came when he'd taken the oath. He chose to sit, crossing his right leg over his left thigh. He played his left hand under his chin; then, as if realizing he had overdramatized the situation, he put his hands together on top of his right knee. His left hand went up to his chin again. A finger extended up his left cheek and rubbed across the top of his silver beard. His body language showed his nerves.

His first words to Ferguson were his name: "It's Albert Johnson Walker," he said in a deep, bass voice;

his slight lisp made him sound like Sean Connery with a sinus problem. He did a series of blinks as Ferguson continued. It took only a few preliminaries before Ferguson turned matters to Sheena, and how she came with him to England.

"I didn't want her to come, but she wanted to come and pleaded with me. She didn't want to go back to the farm."

Such a caring father. He didn't want to leave his teenage daughter behind because he cared so much for her feelings . . . Of course, the jury didn't know he had helped get Sheena the birth control pill, while he planned and plotted to transfer clients' money to Switzerland and leave a trail of despair behind him. What about the three kids he loved so much he left them all behind?

Without much prompting from Ferguson, Walker set out his version of events after leaving Canada in December 1990. He told of staying at the Ritz on an Amex card, although he failed to elaborate that he never paid the bill. He was vague about how much he stole from Canada, but he said that after picking up the cash in Geneva he stashed it in three safety deposit boxes in Knightsbridge, Belgravia and Golders Green.

"I kept the money separate. It was a good idea. These places are occasionally robbed," he said.

They were living in Chelsea at the time. He wasn't in good shape and "wanted to get fit," so he and Sheena joined the exclusive Hogarth Club in Chiswick. After the workouts, he spent his afternoons reading, as he enjoyed "reading novels and literature." In the evenings he would watch TV or go out to a movie.

He gave his goofy laugh and told how the land-lady at his Chelsea flat once put it to him that he must be a secret agent from North America. The jury sat poker-faced, not seeing his humour. Clearly, their first impression of Albert Walker wasn't a good one.

With over twenty years of trial practice under his belt, Ferguson tried to lead Walker to his time in Harrogate, yet Walker jumped in, telling his lawyer they had to "back up a little." At the Hogarth Club, he offered, a fellow told him how nice it was in Harrogate. Well, Walker had been to York once, and how he had loved York. It was by chance in Harrogate, he said, that he saw a Dranbinsky painting in the win-dow of Harry Spencer autioneers. "similar to what I'd had in my office in Canada." And it was there that he met Elaine Boyes.

His hands moving all over the place as he talked, Walker then went off on a tangent. He talked of how thieves broke into the flat and stole an $800 ring that belonged to Sheena.

"It had diamonds in it — it was quite nice," he lamented, but then chuckled that the crooks missed £15,000 stored in a briefcase.

Ferguson stood speechless as Walker babbled on. It was as if Walker's ego wouldn't allow anyone else, no matter how talented and experienced, to control his fate. This was his trial, his story. Walker still wore a thin smile as he admitted he had taken funds from Canada and intended to return to Canada and face those charges. He had needed someone to launder the money in Britain. His strategy was clear. He would admit to the jury that he was a thief, and he would try to convince them that he wasn't a killer.

Again, Ferguson tried to draw Walker back to Harrogate, and again Walker asked him to back up. He chatted away that he needed to organize his financial affairs so that he "didn't have to pay cash all the time." He had experience in setting up businesses, he offered, "moving funds around the world — clients' funds, my funds." He sat back and stroked his beard. The jury was blind to the allegations that about $12 million was missing in Canada. They were also unaware that the only money he had moved around the world was stolen money.

Walker said he took to Boyes immediately. She was a "lovely girl," and trustworthy enough that he could use her for his money laundering. He recalled his first meeting with the real Ron Platt in an Italian restaurant and seemed gleeful to tell the jury that Ron Platt and David Davis had similar stories to his; both had emigrated to Canada when they were ten years old.

Changing his stolen money took time because each country's currency changers had to report any denominations larger than 10,000 units to authorities. Not wishing to raise suspicion, Walker paid the expense of sending Boyes to Europe to cash smaller amounts of money. For example, 10,000 Swiss francs brought him about £6,000, but it cost him several thousand pounds just to have Boyes fly to Switzerland. In the end, he said, it was best that she take out a Swiss bank account in her name. This way, he could get bank cards.

Soon he opened Cavendish Corporation and bought a house in Harrogate. "It was quite nice, with a south-facing garden," he recalled. Oh, he loved Harrogate. He was working out at a fitness club; he was taking oil-painting lessons; he was attending church; he was going to Christie's and Sotheby's and buying antiques and drinking French wine. Elaine, he noted, had been looking at properties in France, where house prices were one-third of those in England. The weather was better, too!

The jury members were getting visibly bored with Walker's apparent nonchalance over spending other people's money. Diamond rings, houses, Italian restaurants, south-facing gardens, lovely neighbours. You could see the resistance in the eyes of these common folk from Exeter, who, unlike Walker, had put their blood, sweat and tears into work for the pennies they had received. One or two jurors started looking into their hands or into space. One middle-aged gent's eyes began to close and his head began to droop. Soon he nodded off.

Brimming with confidence, Walker kept on talking and talking. He couldn't stop himself. Recalling that Ron served with the army in Germany and often spoke of being on the front line and how daunting it was to have all the Russian missiles facing him, Walker related that he always "teased him a bit" and "ha, ha . . . I said, 'Ron, I think they'd have gone over you!' Ha, ha, ha." It was a poignant moment. Realizing he was the only one laughing in the courtroom, Walker quickly cut off his laughter.

Up in the public gallery, Ed Jones whispered to Marion that he thought Walker had gotten off to a pretty good start. Obviously, butter wasn't going to melt in his mouth. But his confidence had seemed to be overtaken by the ego and arrogance that had been plainly visible in Woodham Walter. Marion, too, noticed that Walker had begun embellishing almost everything. There was so much unnecessary chatter, nervous talk, that didn't have any substance.

At Christmas 1992, Walker said, he decided to help Platt and Boyes emigrate to Canada, partially so Ron realize his dream but also to cut, in a "humane way," the tie with Boyes, who had outlived her usefulness to him as an "employee" and was costing him £12,000 a year.

"Ron was on cloud nine," he chuckled. "It was the best thing that ever happened to him!"

Over the next two months, Walker said, he asked Platt for his driver's license because he wanted to go driving in the beautiful Harrogate countryside. In yet another abysmal attempt to ingratiate himself with the jury, Walker added, "It's not like London, where you can never find a place to park . . ha, ha, ha."

Platt not only turned over his licence but also

offered him his birth certificate. And then Platt opened a personal bank account and obtained a cheque book and a cash card. Walker said Platt then wrote away to everyone saying he had lost his ID. Walker kept the copies and Platt the originals. And it was after that, said Walker, that he realized he could go further underground by becoming Ron Platt.

Walker acknowledged he was upset when Boyes returned to England in 1993, leaving Platt behind. Ferguson asked how it had affected him.

"It saddened me . . . I myself had gone through . . ." He trailed off and there was a long pause. First with his fingers, then with a napkin, he wiped tears from his eyes. "I had gone through a marriage break-up and I know what it is like . . . it is a hard decision not to go back, and she was feeling the strain of it."

After Elaine returned, he said, he and Sheena, living as Ronald and Noël Platt, moved to Devon, mainly because Sheena "was pregnant, with the baby due in a month or so . . . She was embarrassed that she was a single girl and wanted to have that aspect — that she wasn't single."

Within a year he had taken the therapist course at the Iron Mill Centre, joined Solutions in Therapy and moved to Woodham Walter.

Meanwhile, the real Platt was still in Canada. Boyes, Walker said in a judgemental and accusatory tone, "would only contact me if she needed money. She'd always spend more than she earned! If her back was to the wall, she'd call me and I'd bail her out!"

Upon Platt's return, he said he stayed close to the man because of their close friendship. And what were friends, he said, if they couldn't help each other out? Platt worked for about six months, but after he lost his job in December 1995, Walker said he rented a van and helped move him to Beardsley Drive in Chelmsford. There, Walker hoped, Platt could find a cheap premises and open a TV repair business. It was because of friendship that he helped Platt financially with his lodgings and his food.

Ed Jones winced at those words. It was comical, he whispered to Marion, that Walker saw so much of a friend in Ronald Platt when he had no time at all for the "55 million other brilliant people on this island!" Ed suggested that Walker had indeed deluded himself into thinking he was a nice guy and the jury would really buy all this loving and caring stuff.

The entire this time, Walker went on, Platt was fully aware he was using his driver's licence as identity. At no point, though, did Walker tell Platt that he was wanted by Interpol. As far as Platt knew, Walker wanted to stay underground to keep his wife off the trail. After a Christmas dinner in 1995, Walker offered, he was driving Platt home when he was pulled over at a police checkpoint and asked to take a breathalyzer. Walker said he told the police officer he was Ronald Platt, and when they drove off the real Platt had a good laugh.

Shortly after Christmas, Platt became very depressed. His dream of a life in Canada had been shattered. And he hated England, what with the football hooligans and the lager louts! Walker suggested counselling and Boyes suggested counselling, but to no avail. On the topic of counselling, Walker said that when employed in Brentwood under Platt's name he had worked hard as a therapy teacher, tutoring nurses, police officers, probation officers and psychiatric workers. While on a seminar, Walker discussed his cousin's unemployment dilemma with a colleague, who noted the answer was simple: "Send him to France!"

So off Platt went to France. And he liked it.

"There is a strong French presence in Canada." Walker smiled. "Ron told me that Calgary had a fair size French population and he was able to practise his French."

As he said this, a guffaw went up from the Canadian journalists in the crowd. French in Calgary? Walker didn't flinch. He told the jury that Platt used to talk with a francophone at a gas bar and "he was able to practise his French. He'd be very good at keeping along. I was quite surprised that he had this gift." As Walker gave details of Platt's movements in France, he waved his hands all over the place.

Following the move to Essex in 1994, Walker said, he wanted for two years to bring the *Lady Jane* up from Devon. He came up with an "adventurous" trip along the south coast of England; in 1995 such a trip with an experienced boat captain came to a grinding halt when the boat's engine mountings collapsed. Not to be deterred, Walker wanted to try it again in 1996. And he asked the real Ron Platt, the man who hated boats and could barely swim a stroke, to help him. Together they would go to Devon in July. After that, Walker and Sheena and the kids would have their own vacation.

"I assured him we wouldn't go out to sea for the first couple of days. We'd just go up and down the River Dart. There was no pressure on my part . . . I didn't want anyone with me who would panic at sea."

He explained that on July 6, 1996, he picked up Ron at the Tanunda Hotel and drove to the Steam Packet Inn. They would cruise the river a bit, see if Ron liked it. Sheena knew Ron was there. They went out on July 7, down the river and barely into the sea. But they were short on time because of the tides. He went off on a tangent again, talking about how the "seagulls are terrible, especially on my boat, it seems. Ha, ha, ha." His joke didn't cause a flicker of amusement on the jurors' faces. By this time the middle-aged man's head had slumped fully onto his chest. The next day, Walker said, the boat's propeller snagged on the mooring lines and he went into Dartmouth to buy a short knife. On that same day, of course, he bought a 10-pound Sewester plough anchor for the *Lady Jane*. It seemed his anchors always went missing. One had gone missing only the day before. And he always needed that second anchor. In a current, he could use the main anchor off the front to keep the boat still and throw another anchor off the back to keep it steady. When they returned to the boat, he put the Sewester anchor in an unlocked locker.

They spent the nights in a Totnes pub, where, he said, he was surprised to see how much Ron was drinking.

"I said, 'Ron, where do you put it all?' "

Walker laughed, but the jury were stone-faced.

"When we got up to the room he opened a bottle of sherry as well."

Then, on July 9, Walker asked Ron if he was ready.

"He said, 'Sure, let's give it a go.' "

Walker recalled that they set out after calling the coast guard with their plan to sail from the River Dart to Portland Bill. All was well at first, but by the time they got to Lyme Bay, Ron became seasick. Walker decided to turn around and go back to the River Dart. On the return trip, Walker said the GPS system showed the *Lady Jane* was moving along at nine knots, and it was "the best sailing I'd ever had." When they hit a wave, however, Ron went flying against a window in the cockpit and banged his shoulder on some instruments. There was blood on his nose. Within seconds he vomited over the back of the boat. That afternoon they tied to a floating dock at Galmpton Creek. The boat was stuck on the bottom of the river. That's the night they ended up at the Royal Seven Stars.

The next morning, he told Platt it wasn't a good idea to go sailing again. It was time for Platt to go to

France. Platt asked Walker, who was paying the bill, if he could stick around in Devon for a week, at the Steam Packet; he said he hadn't decided whether to take a plane or the ferry to France.

"We had kept his luggage at the Little London Farmhouse. He had intended to take it with him, but he said he'd coped well enough in the last three or four days with what he had and he thought he'd do okay over there . . . He said, 'Put it into storage with the furniture, and when it's time to ship the furniture we'll ship it as well.'"

Walker said he had planned to drive through Exeter on the way home and Platt opted to ride there with him. He turned and pointed to beyond the courtroom, towards the city centre.

"I dropped him off just out the back of here," he said, recalling that his memory was jogged when prison authorities transferred him from Bristol to Exeter Prison. "He said, 'Have a nice vacation.' That was the last time I saw him, there."

Walker said it was July 13 when he and Sheena and the kids rented a dinghy and boarded the *Lady Jane* to "clean up." This evidence was in stark contrast to Sheena's evidence, who recalled the tidy-up day as July 21.

Then he got to July 20, 1996, the day the prosecution asserted that he murdered Ronald Platt. He recalled sailing by himself on that "pleasant enough day. The sun was shining." But while out at sea he heard some trouble at the stern, tripped on a lip around the boat's cockpit and went flying into a locker. He hit his ribcage and "knocked the wind out of myself." After catching his breath, he couldn't start the engine in neutral or forward gear, but it would work in reverse. He said he tried the VHF radio, but there was no response and he didn't have a cell phone. So he sailed the *Lady Jane* backwards. Finally he made the River Dart and a helpful boater towed him to a dock downriver from Dittisham.

"It wasn't very late," he said. "I could still see where I was going."

What about the GPS and the position it showed? at 9 p.m. on that night? asked Ferguson.

"Oh, no, I'd be in the Dart by then," said Walker, matter-of-fact.

He then said he wasn't a good navigator and didn't know enough about the GPS, what it can and can't do.

"I'm sorry, but I do know at that time I was going up the Dart backwards. I got home at ten o'clock or thereabouts."

Contrary to what Sheena testified, Walker said that the next morning he told her the boat was running backwards and he hurt himself and she could help him clean up. And contrary to what she recalls of that day, he said the family rode the *Lady Jane* backwards up the River Dart, from the downriver marina to Galmpton. Two days later, he said, they cut their vacation short. A week after that he put Platt's suitcases into the Chelmsford Storage unit as they had planned.

Walker upheld his conviction, voiced by Ferguson, that when Redman told him they had a body and they thought it was Platt, that he last saw him at the end of June or early July. At that point, he said, police still were not certain it was indeed Platt. Still, when told of the find, he said he went into shock, "a state of disbelief." He tried to help Clenahan, too, but the next thing he knew he was on his way to pick up a new car when he was arrested at gunpoint.

"It was a total shock. Anybody with a gun pointed right at their head couldn't help but be shocked. I couldn't believe it was happening. It was unreal."

This elaboration was an absolute contradiction of police evidence, which showed that a gun was not drawn during the arrest.

"I had cooperated with these people and tried to help them. To be arrested at gunpoint in some ways broke a contract between two individuals trying to make something happen."

The irony of Albert Walker talking about the ethics of business deals wasn't lost on some people in the courtroom.

Ferguson asked him how he regarded Platt. He swallowed before he started into his spiel.

"As a friend. Somebody I had a responsibility to take care of."

"Do you have a bad temper?"

"No!" With this, Walker took off his reading glasses. "I've never hit anyone in my life. Nor have I ever been hit in my life. I'm a pacifist, actually. I will never go to war. Some people would hold that against me, but I do not believe in violence."

Walker cried as he spoke. But the tears, the few there were, seemed fake. He was clearly acting. Jurors didn't even watch him. They looked down at their hands, their knees, their notepads.

"Did you kill Ronald Platt?"

"No, I didn't. But I feel . . . if I'd not asked him to help me like that, that he might still be alive . . . I'm sorry."

There was another gush of teary reflection.

"Ronald Platt was a very nice person and I had no reason in the world to kill him or harm him, 'coz I always helped him and he helped me, and he went and sailed on that boat, even though he was frightened."

Walker dabbed his eyes. But the jury didn't see it. There was no pity in their eyes for Albert Walker.

As they left the public gallery, Ed and Marion were of the same mind: Walker had so over-acted his performance that in itself it was almost an admission of guilt.

Thirty

THE HOUND OF DEATH

PROSECUTOR CHARLES BARTON'S assertive voice and swaggering style dominated the courtroom the next day, July 1, 1998. Unlike the day before, when the jury had to put up with Walker and his egotistical storytelling, this day it was all Barton's show. Perhaps Walker had sized up Barton from his ample girth and judged that he could outwit him; perhaps Walker was so cocky he believed he could triumph over anyone. Well, whatever he believed, he would be no match for Barton. In the public gallery, Isabel Rogers and her husband, Neil, turned up to see the resumption of the show. Sitting close by them, Ed and Marion Jones also wanted to see him in action again. From time to time, Walker looked up at them. Isabel always held his stare: no way would she be the first to look away. The defiance was partly her way of dealing with the past. It was her statement to Walker that he hadn't taken anything away from her.

With Walker only yards off to his left, Barton

hardly looked at his notes and faced away from Walker as he asked his questions. But when Walker gave his answers, Barton strained an ear to catch every word. If Walker said one word out of place, Barton would pick up on it and throw a spontaneous question at him. Using this technique, Barton immediately tore apart Walker's story that on July 9 he and Platt tried to sail to Essex. Did he call the coast guard? "Yes." Did he know the distance from Dartmouth to Portland Bill? "I don't know." Give us a clue. "I haven't the faintest idea." How long would it take? "I don't know."

Then he turned to Walker's version of how the suitcases with Platt's most personal possessions ended up at Chelmsford Storage July 31 while Platt was supposedly in France?

"If you knew Platt was going to France from Devon, why didn't you take his suitcases with you?"

Walker replied that Platt was to pick up the cases before his trip but he opted to leave them.

"The lies are tumbling out, aren't they, Mr. Walker?" chided Barton, speaking to Judge Butterfield rather than Walker.

"There's no lies . . . there's no lies," Walker said unconvincingly.

"How could Platt exist in France without his clothes?" asked Barton in bewilderment.

"He was emigrating!"

With Walker apparently intimidated by his style of questioning, Barton moved to the real Platt's stay at the Steam Packet between July 10 and 17 and at the Anchorage bed-and-breakfast, July 18 and 19. Reminding Walker that he and Sheena were in Dittisham, he asked how the jury could believe that Walker didn't see Platt during that time despite the fact Walker had paid for Platt's Steam Packet stay, Platt was going to France on a business venture financed by Walker, Walker still had his suitcases and Platt was Walker's best friend.

"And you don't hear a single word from him?"

"No," offered Walker. "I didn't expect to hear from him."

Referring to Sheena's testimony, Barton asked him about the shock he felt when police told him of Platt's death.

"The shock was, it could probably be Ron and I was using Ron's name," said Walker.

This was precisely the point Barton wanted to make to the jury — motive!

Barton: "So your cover is blown and everything you worked for in the last six years is in jeopardy and all the money you have acquired is put at risk!"

Walker: "That is correct."

Barton: "The fact is, money was your main concern, wasn't it?"

Walker: "No, my freedom!"

Barton: "So if anything happened to Ron, it had to be in such a way that it couldn't be traced. That was central! Otherwise the risks were enormous."

Walker: "I hadn't thought of it that way . . ."

Barton: "Never, until I mentioned it?"

Walker: "No, I envisaged a car accident or a heart attack."

After the morning break, Barton came furiously at Walker on the falsities he'd told his neighbours and business colleagues.

"Can I just ask you, what are your qualifications? Your academic qualifications?"

"I don't have any academic qualifications," Walker answered ruefully.

"Do you have a degree from the University of Edinburgh?"

"No, I don't."

"Are you a Bachelor of Arts?"

"No."

"Do you have any professional qualifications?" asked Barton, with Rumpole-like emphasis.

"No, I don't."

"Was your wife ever a doctor?"

"No."

When Barton turned to Walker's flight with his fifteen-year-old daughter, Sheena, Walker said Sheena believed they were changing their names to hide from his wife, but later he told her he had taken funds from the company and was in trouble in Canada. At one point during Barton's cross-examination, it came up that Walker had maintained contact with his daughter Jillian by telephone and letter until 1992.

When Barton turned his sights to David Wallis Davis, Walker claimed he didn't get Davis's birth certificate until December 1990. Davis, he said, lent him the birth certificate after Walker told him he wanted to open a bank account because he was divorcing his wife and needed a place to hide the money.

Walker: "He had been in a divorce and he understood . . ."

Barton: "You're lying, aren't you?"

Walker: "No, I'm not."

Barton: "You took the birth certificate for an entirely different purpose!"

Walker: "No, I didn't."

Walker also denied Barton's assertion that he had intended to take over Platt's identity before he sent Platt and Boyes packing to Canada.

"How many birth certificates have you been offered?" he asked Walker, who skirted what was more of a statement than a question.

"Was the assumption of the name Platt permanent?" asked Barton.

Walker hesitated, as if trying to figure out where Barton was going. Walker was clearly taken aback at the tenacity of Barton's pugnacious attack, and rocked back on his heels. "Yes," he finally answered.

"You sound hesitant," Barton jabbed. "Do you need time to think about that?"

"Some things aren't permanent . . ." Walker offered.

"Surnames often are!" said Barton.

The gallery and some jury members chuckled as the right hook connected.

Barton produced a letter that Walker and Sheena had written while trying to get information to fraudulently obtain a birth certificate for a woman named Elaine Clair Boyes, born in 1973; Walker had reckoned that Sheena was too young to pass as their Elaine Clare Boyes, who was born in 1958. The letter was found in the Northampton storage unit. The letter began, "Dear Boyes family: My name is Elaine Boyes and I am interested in tracing my family roots." The writer went on to say she was born in the Humberside area and wanted to get in touch with all the Boyes families there in the hope "you will help me in my search." In return for their cooperation, Boyes families would get a "free copy of the Boyes family history as soon as it is complete."

Then Barton turned his attention to the real Elaine Boyes, Walker's so-called friend. He read from an August 22, 1993, letter, written by the phoney David Davis shortly before Walker and Sheena moved to the Tiverton-area cottage.

" 'Well,' " Barton quoted, " 'we're off to France. It's really a lovely boat and I have my own bedroom. Ian's wife is an excellent cook.' " He stopped. "Does Ian's wife exist?"

Walker looked glum as he responded, "No, it's just a fictitious name to explain why we're going."

"But this is a friend," said Barton, "who came back depressed! She appears to be emotionally dependent on you. Why do you write her a pack of lies?"

"I did not want her coming with me."

Barton continued reading. " 'The sun, the sailing, the lake water, the wine. What more could one ask for of life?' What's this? Are you trying to brighten her up or send her into the depths of despair? . . . 'I hope you are well and succeed getting a place in France or Italy as an au pair.' You didn't want her in the country, did you?"

Walker said he didn't want Boyes with him, period.

Barton turned to another letter to Boyes, dated September 10, 1993. After telling Boyes that it was good to hear from her four times in two weeks and of the £500 cheque he had enclosed, Walker talked of how the rain had delayed the sailing, but tomorrow, "weather permitting and God willing," they will set out for France.

"Total lies?" asked Barton.

"Yes," acknowledged Walker.

The letter also said that Noël and he would return to Paris, Ontario, after some shopping and were spending Christmas with his daughter Jillian and her new boyfriend.

"Is there a word of truth in that?" grilled Barton.

"No," replied Walker.

Barton read Walker's account of some rough sailing and how it had made him ill. "Are you somebody who lies just for the sake of it?"

"No," said Walker. "Just to confirm that she's at a distance and can't come to visit us."

"They're all lies!" shouted Barton. "They're just rolling off your pen. Lie after lie after lie. You just can't stop! Forgive me for a moment, but what's happened to the community-conscious man and his principles? You simply couldn't care less when you wrote this letter!"

On November 24, 1995, Barton revealed, Walker asked Elaine to no longer write to his London postal box under his name of David Davis. She must use Cavendish Corporation, he said, because a postal box costs more under an individual name than a company name.

"Well, it's rubbish, isn't it?" challenged Barton. "You were Mr. Platt and she was writing to you as David Davis, wasn't she!"

Walker signed one postcard to Boyes "Love Ron," instead of his usual nom de plume, David.

Barton: "You simply had forgotten who you were, hadn't you?"

Walker: "Yes, I signed Ron."

Barton: "It was genuine friendship with Elaine, wasn't it?"

Walker: "Yes."

The day had been a disaster for Walker. By now, the jury hated him. As Walker dolefully walked down the thirteen stairs to the basement holding cell, Isabel remembered the old maxim, Better to keep your foot in your mouth and appear a fool than to take it out and remove all doubt! What the hell was he thinking when he took the stand?

Walker's second day in cross-examination didn't go any better. And the look on his face throughout the entire day of questioning showed that he knew it. Barton had him on the ropes and was jabbing relentlessly at him, all the while awaiting that opening for the big knock-out punch. And more was to come.

When Mr. Platt visited the Little London Farmhouse, asked Barton, what did Walker call Sheena?

"Noël," he answered.

"And what was she calling you?"

" 'Daddy.' "

"But not in front of other people?" Barton asked, incredulous.

"Yes."

"That must have raised an eyebrow or two! I thought you were pretending to be her husband!"

Fatigue seemed to sweep over Walker when he answered, "Emily called me Daddy and Sheena called me Daddy. Actually, she called me Ron. But when Ron was there she called me Daddy or Ron."

The real Platt's move to Chelmsford must have made it all "a bit local," said Barton, on the attack again. Two Platts in the same town? Walker said he wasn't known as Platt in Chelmsford, where the real Platt was living.

Barton pounced, reminding Walker that he passed himself off all over Britain, to nurses and doctors and police officers and Barking college students, as "Ron Platt, therapist." Seeing another opportunity to make Walker look silly, the quick-thinking Barton lifted Walker's Solutions in Therapy business card to the jury.

Barton: "Where does the BA come from? What is the purpose of that lie?"

Walker: "Credibility."

Barton: "It has nothing to do with being wanted in Canada or being sought by your wife, does it?"

Walker: "No."

Barton: "It's just another gratuitous lie!"

Walker: "Yes."

There was a lie to Sheena, too, in the weeks leading up to Platt's death, said Barton, when Walker told her that Platt had gone to France when in fact they had been together in Devon and Platt was still in Devon and only miles from their boarding house. Walker maintained that Sheena knew Platt was there all along.

Barton asserted to Walker that, initially, he had planned to murder Platt after they set sail on the bogus voyage from Devon to Exeter on July 9, the day after he bought the anchor, but something happened.

"That was your plan, wasn't it?" Barton said.

"No," said Walker.

At the afternoon break, the jury put three questions to Judge Neil Butterfield. The judge refused to read out the first of the three questions in court but noted to the lawyers that "the jury is starting to speculate about sexual innuendo." Almost certainly, the jury were curious to know who had fathered the two children born to Sheena Walker. Butterfield read out two minor questions and then brought the jury back into the court.

"I am not prepared to read the first question," Butterfield told the jury. "It has no relevance in this case whatsoever. You may recall, at the end of the first witness's evidence, I expressly asked both counsel if there was anything further either of them wanted to ask her. I have to say, I had in mind the topic you have in mind, but they concurred. No questions were relevant. It has nothing to do with this case."

After the break, Barton returned to July 9, 1996, throwing back at Walker his assertion that he and Platt told the coast guard of their planned trip that day. Pressed by Barton, Walker couldn't recall the conversation.

"There was no such phone call, was there?" Barton barked out.

Walker paused. "Yes . . . there was a call."

"The log at the coast guard station . . . Didn't you think to have it checked to establish that you were sailing off on that day?"

Walker barely squeezed out an answer as Barton kept on hitting him.

"There never was a phone call on the eighth, ninth, tenth for the *Lady Jane* about this voyage!"

Walker said he remembered the call, from the Steam Packet.

"What did you do when the trip was aborted?" asked Barton.

"I neglected to call," said Walker, downhearted.

As he had done under questioning by Ferguson, Walker again pleaded ignorance when Barton asked if he accepted as accurate the GPS system.

Why, asked Barton, did he not tell Elaine Boyes of Platt's death when she called in September 1996? Walker said he didn't want to upset her while she was in such depression, at least not on the telephone, and in any event he thought the job should be done by police.

"So it was out of consideration for her feelings?" asked Barton.

Noting all the pieces of David Davis identification Walker carried the day of his arrest, Barton said it was obvious his plan was to "bluff it out" as Davis in a meeting with police later that day.

Suddenly, Barton murmured "Right" and grabbed his notes in front of him. "Do you not acknowledge that you had a motive to get rid of Ronald Platt, the real Ronald Platt?" he asked.

"What motive?" Walker shot back, much to Barton's chagrin.

"Did you not realize that Ronald Platt was a potential threat to you for the rest of your life?"

"No, I did not!"

"Did you not foresee the risk to you of him being in this country?"

"No!" Walker spat out.

"That he would jeopardize your money and your liberty?"

"No!"

Barton suggested that Walker smacked Platt unconscious. "The planning took rather long, but only the work of a moment to consign him to the deep," he charged.

"I did not murder Ronald Platt!" stated Walker.

"The only thing you missed was the Rolex, wasn't it?"

"I did not murder Ronald Platt!"

"That anchor was bought for an express purpose, wasn't it?"

"No," said Walker. "To have on my boat."

Barton's pummelling petered out with an inaudible comment. He was like a heavyweight boxer who had thrown so many punches he was just tuckered out. Still, Walker looked beaten as the jury filed out. As he walked towards the stairs leading down to the basement, his eyes searched the floor.

Thirty-one

THE VERDICT

BARTON'S PUNCHES RESUMED the next day, Friday, July 3, 1998, when in submissions to the jury he accused Walker of being a liar before his arrest and a liar while giving testimony under oath.

"His account . . . was designed to meet each and every aspect of the prosecution's case. It was tailored to do just that, contrived to do just that, and concocted over a period of eighteen months to do just that . . . He practised a certain expertise he had practised successfully in this country for over six years."

"Despite his success in charming everybody . . . he didn't succeed in charming you," said Barton, in deadly accurate gauge of the jury's feeling. When taking into account the deceit and the lies, the "overwhelming" motive and the forensic evidence, is there any doubt that Platt was murdered? Barton asked the jury.

Barton honed in on the forensic evidence — the plough anchor, the zinc on the belt, the bruises on the body — then Sheena's appearance at the trial. "What a job for a daughter! To come over here from

Canada, facing what she knew would be a barrage. To come over to nail the fundamental lie. It is not easy for a daughter to do this to her father." The lie, he said, was Walker's deceit to her that Platt was in France when in fact he had gone with him to Devon. The lie continued with Walker's phone call to Canada asking Sheena to change her testimony.

"We will never know what Ron was told. What did he believe? Whatever it was, it was sufficient for him to get into the boat. There's a probability he thought he was going to a new life ahead of him.

"I have branded [the accused] in your eyes, as a liar. In that matter, there is no argument. He's absolutely blatant, isn't he! Be very careful how you treat that. He had a multiplicity of motives for telling lies, didn't he . . . But he not only told lies, he told them for the purpose of avoiding the murder of Ronald Platt . . . It's not our fault that this case is riddled with lies. But the fact is, you have to find your way through his web of deceit."

Barton brought up the lie he caught Walker in on the stand, the lie of the telephone call to the coast guard. "It's a lie designed just for you, to mislead you into thinking it was a planned trip, July 9, 1996, moving the boat from Devon."

Then he brought up the possibility of chance, or was it fate, that the killer forgot the Rolex, that fisherman John Copik dragged up the body and the anchor, that Peter Redman knocked on the wrong door, that Elaine Boyes called Walker out of the blue and he didn't tell her about Platt's death, that the anchor wasn't sold at a car boot sale, that the GPS system was found with such precise details of the *Lady Jane*'s movements. In other words, Barton was suggesting to the jury that some power from above was watching over the misdeeds of Albert Walker.

Next it was Ferguson's turn. In his softer Irish voice, he urged the jury to ignore the "good theatre" that Barton used during cross-examination to reveal Walker's lies to Elaine Boyes.

"But you must remember that Mr. Walker, or David Davis, as he was known to her, was a man on the run. A fugitive from Canada. And he was on the run from his wife and his domestic responsibilities. He had programmed himself to lie."

While Walker admits that he used Boyes and showed her a lack of affection, he wouldn't be the first man to "trifle with a woman's affections," said Ferguson. It was an insult to the jury's intelligence. "He's not on trial for causing emotional damage to Elaine Boyes, nor is he on trial for telling lies, nor for lying to other people who've been before you.

"This case is unique. The defendant's existence in this country was a lie. Put it aside. Put Elaine Boyes aside. Let's get to the real point of this case. We're not here to decide what you think of Albert Walker as a person . . . what you have to decide is what conclusions you can safely, *safely* — I underline that word — you can safely reach on the Crown's evidence."

Ferguson stressed to the jury that the burden of proof on the Crown is of a "very high standard indeed." Guilt is not sealed by a likelihood or a probability but by "beyond a reasonable doubt."

Stating there were many, many gaps in the case, Ferguson first turned the jury's attention to the Rolex watch. Did it move while on Platt's wrist on the sea bed? Is there any certainty that Platt kept the day correct? Is the 11:35 in the morning or at night?

And there were so many more issues: how did the prosecution prove that Platt met his death aboard the *Lady Jane* on July 20, 1996, when there was no evidence he was on board; doctors couldn't say if the blow to the head was inflicted before or after death; how could any faith be put in the bruises on the leg and hip; it was unclear that the coordinates on the GPS in fact represented the last position of the *Lady Jane*; was the anchor in the net the same anchor bought at Sport Nautique; how could they be sure the zinc on the belt didn't come from another source?

Ferguson didn't finish his submissions on Friday, but the following Monday, July 6, 1998, two years to the day that the bogus Ronald Platt picked up the real Ronald Platt at the Tenunda Hotel and took him on a Devon vacation that ended in his death, Ferguson addressed the biggest mark against his client — motive.

"There's not a shred of evidence that Ronald Platt was anything but complicit in allowing Albert

Walker to use his identification. They were booking hotel rooms together and Mr. Walker was using Ronald Platt's name as he stood there. The Crown case would be so much stronger if they had evidence Ronald Platt was becoming unhappy his friend was using his I. D. If Mr. Platt were to go to another country, then the problem would be gone. France would remove that danger as surely as Canada would."

And with that, the prosecution and defence cases were closed. The rugby ball was now in Judge Neil Butterfield's capable hands, and he in turn would toss it to the eight women and four men of the jury.

In his charming, well-heeled way, Butterfield noted that the prosecution relied solely on circumstantial evidence. While circumstantial evidence can be powerful, he pointed out the prosecution submission was "overwhelming" against Walker. "But is it realistic," he asked, "and does it prove guilt?" After reviewing the forensic evidence in detail, Butterfield put a stake through Walker's heart when he told the jury to "consider all these factors, not in isolation but in combination."

There were an abundance of lies, started Butterfield, suggesting that Walker had perhaps uttered a falsity every day of his life. Many of his lies were plainly told to protect himself and Sheena and there were many gratuitous lies, Butterfield said, but none of these would be used to judge guilt. Using the lies to support the validity of other lies, however, was allowable. The lie to Sheena that Platt had left for

France when he was in Devon, and the lie to Elaine Boyes that Platt had gone to France when in fact Walker had been told he was dead, as well as the lies to Clenahan, were for consideration.

"Did he lie? Does it matter? If you are sure he did lie, why? You may choose to find what he said on the stand is sanctimonious humbug and rank hypocrisy, but that does not make him a murderer."

Butterfield concluded by saying the defence contends there are too many gaps and the evidence is too tenuous to convict Walker, whereas the Crown asserts that Walker murdered Platt, and if he didn't do it, who did?

After asking the jury for a unanimous verdict, Butterfield advised the jurors that they should take their notebooks and pencils into the jury room with them, "but, above all, take with you your common sense and your knowledge of the world." He dismissed the court at 1:05 p.m. Noting that it was lunchtime, he said he didn't want a verdict prior to 2:30 p.m. The jury disappeared behind the olive green curtain and, over lunch, began their scrum.

It was only minutes before three when the red light above the curtain went on to signal the jury wanted to speak with a clerk. Seconds after she disappeared behind the curtain, the clerk returned and whispered "Verdict" to the other clerks. As the lawyers, the judge and the police officers were called back into Courtroom 2, Albert Walker walked from his basement holding cell and waited at the bottom of the thirteen steps for the call that would take him to judgement. His face was pale; he looked worried. A quick verdict could mean only one thing — guilty. If the jury had deliberated for hours or overnight, then his chances of an acquittal would have been good.

The court came to order as Judge Butterfield took his seat. Walker took deliberate steps as he made his way up each of the stairs. He tottered as he took his seat. Up in the public gallery, Isabel, who had stayed in Devon while Neil returned to work, thought how pathetic Walker looked at this moment. The jury filed in and sat. Walker was ordered to rise. He tried to get up, but his legs failed him. He managed to stand when a security guard motioned him up.

The clerk asked the jury if they had chosen a foreman and would that person rise. The large man with the curly black hair in the front row stood bolt upright.

"How did you find the defendant, Albert Johnson Walker, guilty or not guilty?"

"Guilty!" he said, with not a bit of hesitation.

With that word, tens of thousands of words of Albert Walker's bullshit were wiped away.

In the police ranks, Det. Insp. Phil Sincock looked at his junior officer with heartfelt thanks. His face turned red and tears welled in his eyes. After almost two years it was finally over. The rest of the Devon detectives, too, were quietly celebrating, giving a nod here, a smile there and a quick wink if they could give it discreetly. Up in the public gallery, the anxiety Isabel Rogers had felt throughout the trial was replaced by relief. The healing could begin now. Back in Woodham Walter, Ed and Marion Jones heard the news of Walker's conviction on the radio.

Judge Butterfield ordered Walker to sit. Walker brought his familiar notepad out of his manilla envelope. As far as he was concerned, it wasn't over yet. Obviously, from his actions, there would be an appeal. After confirming that the prosecution would seek its costs from Walker's assets, Butterfield turned to Walker and asked him to stand. Walker, still stunned, put his pen and paper down and got up slowly.

"You are convicted of murder. It was in my judgement a callous, premeditated killing designed to have eliminated a man you used for your own selfish means until, first, he became an inconvenience and then a threat to your continued freedom. He was expendable and a danger to you and he had to die. The killing was carefully planned and cunningly executed with chilling efficiency. You covered your tracks so effectively that only the merest chance led to any suspicion falling upon you.

"You are plausible, intelligent and ruthless, posing a considerable threat to anyone who stands in your way."

Butterfield told Walker the mandatory sentence for murder was life in prison and he would forward to the Home Secretary his suggestions for parole ineligibility. Under British law, Butterfield's remarks are made in confidence.

"You may go down."

With that permission Walker put his notepad into his manilla envelope, turned on his heels and was led back to the holding cell. From there, he was returned to Exeter Prison. He would be shipped out to one of Britain's life centre prisons — "lifers" — when space became available. Lifer centres focus on retraining prisoners for their eventual release many years in the future. From a lifer centre, Walker would have to work his way down the various security categories before he was eligible for parole. The Canadian warrant for his arrest on the fraud charges is still filed in Bow Street Magistrate's Court. It is unclear as yet whether Canadian authorities will seek his early extradition to Canada to face the fraud charges against him. Given that the average lifer in Britain spends about twenty years in custody, Walker, only one month away from his fifty-third birthday at the time of his conviction, could be seventy-three upon his release. Even if Walker serves only six to ten years in a British prison, his Canadian victims will still be older and some may have died.

After serving some time in Britain, Walker could certainly ask the Canadian government for voluntary extradition so he can serve the rest of his sentence in Canada. Canada's federal prisons offer superior comfort and their inmates are more benevolent than their British counterparts. Knowing Walker, once his appeal is concluded he will no doubt try to better himself in this way.

Even for Albert Walker, life, as they say, goes on.

Thirty-two

THE BURDEN

Even if it is not commonly used this way in everyday speech, there is a single word that applies to people like Albert Walker: *psychopath*. In his book *Without Conscience*, Dr. Robert Hare of the University of British Columbia, the world's foremost expert on psychopaths, describes this curious breed of people as "social predators who charm, manipulate and ruthlessly plough their way through life, leaving a broad trail of broken hearts, shattered expectations and empty wallets. Completely lacking in conscience . . . they selfishly take what they want and do as they please, violating social norms and expectations without the slightest sense of guilt or regret . . . Typically they attempt to appear familiar with sociology, psychiatry, medicine, psychology, philosophy, poetry, literature, art or law." One psychopath he studied claimed to have "advanced degrees in sociology and psychology, when in fact he did not even complete high school. Lying, deceiving and manipulation are natural talents of psychopaths. The capacity to con friend and foe alike makes it simple for psychopaths to defraud, embezzle, impersonate, sell phoney stocks and worthless properties and carry out swindles of all sizes," says Dr. Hare. "They display a general lack of empathy. They are indifferent to the rights and suffering of family members and strangers alike. If they do maintain ties with their spouses or children, it is only because they see their family members as possessions, much like their stereos and automobiles."

Not all of them are killers, however. Some even forge through life without incurring a criminal record.

Is there any doubt, as prosecutor Barton would put the question, that Walker is a psychopath? Clearly, when comparing what we know about Walker with Dr. Hare's criteria the word *psychopath* and *Albert Walker* are synonymous.

Isabel Rogers had a close-up view of Walker for almost eighteen months. In the tiny office at Solutions in Therapy, Isabel first revealed herself to her phoney therapist boss, but in the end it was Walker who confided all his secrets in Isabel. In an ironic twist, Isabel unwittingly became Walker's therapist. He had to get his tangled emotions off his chest and Isabel was all he had. She saw his total meltdown with her own eyes. Isabel is fully aware that Walker fits most of the criteria for a psychopath.

The psychopathy she ventures, developed early in his life. From what he told her, his relationship with his father was terrible, if there was any relationship at all. He painted his mother, on the other hand, as someone who could be hard on him, but at times she would be gentle to the extreme. As an adult, Isabel believes, Walker sought out those gentle women who reminded him of his mother. As in adulthood, there must have been two sides to Walker when he was a child: one that was in open conflict with his family surroundings, the other that would hide his frustrations until he could contain them no more and they erupted as anger. In healthy families it is acceptable to express feelings, but Isabel suspects that in Walker's family some unhappy consequence forbade him from being a real person. This unhealthy dichotomy set him off on a life of expressing in two different ways. To exist, he had to be a good liar, not only to others but also, and most important, to himself. He disassociated himself from all the unhappy feelings to the point where he changed into one someone for whom only the good things existed. In appearance, he was, in Isabel's words, when she knew him at first as Ronald Platt, "the typical American apple pie man," who had all good things in life: meaningful work, the respect of others, children, a beautiful young wife, the lifestyle he always wanted. But inside he carried his unhappy past. During his years in Paris, Ontario, of course, Walker shrugged off that unhappiness by saying his family had problems but he had moved beyond them. Yet during this time he defrauded and conned friend and foe alike. While acting as a church elder, choir singer, lay preacher, father of four children and a respected investor in Ontario, he was bilking friends, doctors, farmers and pensioners out of their savings and chasing young women. Years later in England, this inability to reconcile the outer and inner person would take on a greater and ultimately more sinister significance. While acting as a professional therapist in Brentwood and teaching moral and ethical codes to nurses, doctors and police officers, he was pretending to be his daughter's husband, taking old Frank Johnson for £200,000 and plotting the murder of the man whose name he'd taken.

Isabel suspects there must also have been a strong religious regimen in Walker's household. To have "completely trashed" his religion in the United Church of Canada in the way he did, with his inappropriate conduct with a female minister and his affairs and greed and trickery. Walker must have wanted to sully the values that had been forced on him in earlier years. The pain he brought to the St. Paul's United Church congregation and to the best friends of his wife, Bob and Betty Staley and their families, suggests, as well, that he was striking out at the "happy" shackles he had put himself in to gain the favour of his wife, Barbara, and the McDonald clan.

Like all psychopaths Walker was always on the prowl for what would benefit him. Isabel believes that he didn't just fall into his job as officer manager of Solutions in Therapy. More plausibly, he saw that all three partners had full-time jobs and he had envisioned a position of instant respect and credibility. With three professional therapists at his side, who could possibly question his integrity or his motives? Isabel was likely part of the camouflage scheme. With her looks and brains and Walker's fake degrees, any door would open for him.

Was this any different from all those years ago in the 1970s, when Walker and his new wife, Barbara, set up their bookkeeping business in Barbara's hometown of Ayr? No doubt he used the McDonalds to get what he wanted, just as he used Mark Aitcheson and David Penhorwood and the various financiers who joined his operation throughout its tremendous growth. Did he use Cathy Newman and Geneviéve Vlemmix in the same way he used Elaine Boyes and tried to use Isabel Rogers?

It is astounding to think that the blueprint for his business life in Britain — setting up a chain of one-stop therapy outlets — was no different from the blueprint for his business life in Ontario — setting up a chain of one-stop financial outlets.

But the similarities between his life in Canada and his life in Britain go further. Consider this: in Paris, Ontario he and Barbara lived in a century-old farmhouse. Each day he would drive a half-hour or so to work. Wasn't he trying to duplicate this setup in England, when he had the venerable Little London Farmhouse and drove thirty minutes to work? He and Barbara had four children, and according to what Walker told Audrey and Mossman, Frank Johnson and Isabel Rogers, Noël wanted — and he would be happy to give her — four children.

Was this duplication purely coincidental? Hardly. Chances are that as he had done in Canada, he wanted to keep his business life away from the dysfunctional life he forced upon his family, and at the same time wanted to keep his family isolated, dependent on him for money, companionship and transportation. Again, he had two distinct worlds: work, where he could represent himself as the successful businessman, and the part-time home, where he could take the happiness whenever he wanted and ignore responsibility, duty and, inevitably, the humdrum.

Isabel notes striking parallels in his various relationships with the women in his life. Each relationship kicked off at break-neck speed, with money, romance, laughter and music. This, she says, is fairly standard among people with a poor ability to relate. Typically, they need to have sex very quickly in order to form an uncomplicated bond. Walker, it appears, did not have the maturity and the skills to keep up fully functioning relationships with adult women and could satisfy himself only by finding vulnerable, perhaps needy, women who didn't, or couldn't, ask too much of him. Barbara's fate with Walker, was sealed in three weeks. His attempt to use Geneviéve Vlemmix started within seconds of her walking into his Woodstock office. Although his relationship with Elaine Boyes did not begin in a romantic vein, he had her wrapped around his finger in short order. In his first meetings with Isabel, Walker had her in an uneven therapist–patient setting and he probably mistook her for a vulnerable woman.

So is it any surprise that Walker became close to his own teenage daughters, who, to him, must have been the most vulnerable females on the planet? Isabel says his treatment of Jill and Sheena — what is known publicly — while he was still in Paris, Ontario, showed terrible disrespect, possibly even hatred, for women. Approving breast implants for Jill at age eighteen and allowing Sheena to go on the pill before she turned fifteen are "sexually significant acts" because they showed that Walker obviously identified with the sexual aspect of both daughters. And why, she asks, if Walker supported the girls' choices simply as a parent, didn't he consult his wife and their mother, Barbara Walker? Isabel says Walker was "a most inappropriate source" for approving such adult choices for such young girls.

Walker was incapable of having any close friendships, Isabel concludes. His friends were fair-weather, pretend friends. The only value they had to him were for external, clinical pleasures, such as money and sex. Did he have any real friends in Canada? Probably not. Did he have any real friends in England? No. Certainly not Elaine Boyes and Ronald Platt! There was only Sheena, if that can be considered a friendship. Domestically, his relationship with Sheena was a one-way street. She looked after the kids, she ironed his shirts, she kept house, she cut the lawn. Sheena, too, had no friends in England, with the exception, perhaps, of Marion Jones. Did Sheena choose not to have friends or did Walker order her not to have any? Interestingly, there has never been any mention of any man but her father in Sheena's life in England. Isabel ventures that Walker wouldn't allow any man access to Sheena, whom he undoubtedly viewed as his possession.

Isabel believes that Sheena Walker was brainwashed from her earliest days. And it was clear to Isabel from Walker's treatment of Emily that he placed too many boundaries on her, boundaries that stunt growth and development and prevent children from asserting themselves and making their own choices. She imagines Walker put the same boundaries on Sheena and the other three children he raised with Barbara. Ultimately, such boundaries are so restrictive that the children grow up to depend on them.

Perhaps Sheena accepted Walker's dominance over her because she didn't know any different life. Maybe it was Walker's form of brainwashing that led all four children to want to live with him instead of their mother when the marriage broke up. Isabel suggests that the reason Sheena was able to put on, and still continues to put on, a strong public face is that she is still unable to understand her role in what transpired. The reality, Isabel suggests, is that Sheena stayed with her father because she needed the financial security and the physical comfort he offered. Certainly, she notes, Sheena was not held a physical captive: if she had been truly unhappy she could have run away, taken refuge with the neighbours, told the babysitter, written to sister Jill, called the police or simply picked up the ever-present telephone and said, "Mother, it's Sheena." Sheena was there because in her own mind she wanted to be. There was probably gross confusion in her mind. But perhaps Walker had conditioned her to believe that life with him would be much better than life with her mother. Still, says Isabel, from the various accounts of Marion Jones and British social services workers, Sheena was, and is to this day, an excellent mother to her two children. There must be, then, a capacity to love.

Jill, too, must have felt her father's absolute dominance. How else could she secretly be in telephone and letter contact with him and accept financial assistance — aware that her mother was on the edge of bankrupcty and that he was sought by police for massive frauds? At the time of their last contact in 1992, Walker's criminality was well known. Why did the contact stop? Was it at Jill's doing? Was it at Walker's initiative?

Isabel believes that if indeed Sheena's children were fathered by Walker, he likely justified it in his own mind, assuring himself that he was "doing something positive for his daughter" and that he was not damaging anybody. If you think back to his statement to Isabel about pedophiles, that's exactly what he said. That would be part and parcel of Walker's personality. Despite all the transgressions against what

most people uphold as a moral code, Walker deluded
himself into thinking that everything he was doing
was acceptable. His philosophy, recalls Isabel, was "I
can do what I want and if they disagree, well, that's
okay. It's my right to do it!"

Ironically, in the end it was the vulnerable women
— Sheena, Elaine and herself — who delivered the
information that would hurt him the most. "It must
have been so belittling to him," she ventures.

As for violence and murder? Isabel doesn't think
they were part of Walker's original script. He could
quite well be the pacifist he'd touted himself as on
the witness stand. Until, that is, his comfortable existence was threatened. Then he would have indeed
taken up arms. It's obvious that Walker had woven
such a tangled web that when Platt returned from
Canada the life he had created for himself was in
danger of disintegrating. Isabel recalls that his breakdown began in May 1996, two whole months before
he eventually murdered Platt. His move from fraud-
ster to killer sprang from a collection of fears: the
fear of losing all his money; the fear of being
ridiculed when all his criminal deceptions were
revealed publicly; the fear, perhaps, of being labelled,
accurately or not, the father of his daughter's children. Ultimately, any sense of shame at committing
the murder and any fear of the consequences would
be nothing compared with the shame and fear that
would be his if his bogus life was revealed. When
Platt returned to England, Walker's decisions became

more and more limited. In his mind there could be no going back. He could either surface as Ronald Platt or go back to being David Davis or Albert Walker. He could have beaten the impulse to kill only if he'd been able to search inside himself and connect to his true feelings, says Isabel, but he was incapable of doing that because it was too frightening for him to risk.

As a last thought, Isabel wonders why, after police told him they had recovered Platt's body, Walker tried to go on the run while giving the excuse to Isabel and others that Noël's father had a heart attack and then died in the United States. Looking at it classically, says Isabel, he was creating another situation where he would do away with his old identity. But maybe, she ventures, he created the story from primal emotional need. Maybe he needed a catharsis to mourn the death of the real Ron Platt, and the passing of his act as Ron Platt.

"It is pure speculation," says Isabel, "but there probably could have been a part of him that really liked the real Ronald Platt and some part of him had to mourn."

Or maybe there's another answer. Perhaps, in Walker's own mind, he had become not only Ronald Platt in name but also Ronald Platt in mind and body. Perhaps he truly believed that he had the power within himself to create whatever he wanted to create and be whoever he wanted to be. He had created Ron Platt therapist, Ron Platt and his beautiful young wife, Noël Platt. He had created, if not in blood then in name, Emily and Lillian Platt. When he murdered Ron Platt in July 1996, maybe he deluded himself into thinking that his own "old identity" — including that as Sheena's father — was dead. The speculation no doubt will continue for years.

It is fascinating to compare what we know about Albert Walker with the vision he had of himself. Documents from his classes as a student at the Iron Mill Centre reveal how he deluded himself at even the earliest stages of his new life in Britain. In a question-and-answer sheet titled "The Professional Me," the so-called Ronald Platt responded this way:

> Things I like about myself: "My self-confidence."
> Things others like about me: "My self-confidence."
> Things I do very well: "Motivate people."
> A recent problem I've handled very well: "Helping someone sell their property or business."
> When I'm at my best I: "Am creative."
> When I'm glad, I am: "Imaginative/creative/mature."
> Those who know me are glad that I: "Feel free to express my feelings."
> A compliment that has been paid to me recently is: "That I have a good mind."
> A value that I try hard to practise is: "To be fair to all people."
> An example of my caring about others is: "To

refer them to someone else, even though I could use the fee."

And it went on.

In a paper titled "Who are you?" Walker wrote: "I am a person who has many gifts — artist, finance, etc. — who enjoys helping people and it is this enjoyment of helping people that has led me into the field of counselling. It is my desire to complete the diploma course. I am confident I can offer counselling to the public without the fear of doing damage to someone."

*And in a textbook found at the Little London Farmhouse after Sheena's arrest, someone had apparently paid specific attention to a section on psychopaths, underlining the various definitions and the symptoms of the psychopathic personality in stark blue ink. Was it Walker trying to define himself? Was it Sheena trying to figure out her father? Or had the marks been left by someone else's pen at some other time?

Within days of Walker's guilty verdict, Barbara Walker dropped off a press release to her favourite journalists at the *Paris Star*. Barbara, who during the trial was warned by police to calm down following an incident in which her car brushed past a television cameraman, said she was relieved the trial was over and that she had tried to stop Walker's "reign of terror" years ago; she claimed to have told investors back in 1983 that they should not invest money with her husband. This claim is an odd one, given that Barbara was still married to Walker in mid-1990, and appears not to have warned the Staleys and the Richardsons of her husband's intentions as of 1987. A week after the verdict, Barbara appeared on a Kitchener radio station with a host she called "a friend of the family." In that interview, Barbara said it was time for news organizations to forget the past and leave Sheena alone.

From the outside, Barbara Walker's life, for all of those years with Albert Walker, must have been a nightmare. Isabel suggests that Barbara must have constantly shut down emotionally. Barbara Walker suffered greatly when her villainous husband left her in the summer of 1990 and took all four kids with him, but it was nothing compared to the chaos to come that December when he fled with Sheena and left Barbara's financial and personal life in tatters. What transpired six years later must have been doubly devastating. Most of us cannot imagine what the Walker family grapples with now on a day-to-day basis. In the best-case scenario, Barbara Walker's psychopathic ex-husband is a convicted killer with whom she begat four children; one of those still-dependent children is a twenty-two-year-old single mom with two children of her own. The worst-case scenario has six of Walker's children living at her home. If the latter case is reality, both Barbara and Sheena Walker must have a heart of steel and faith of cast iron just to continue living each day.